· Cindy · 情境式must考

TOEIC
多益單字
滿分筆記

User's Guide 使用說明

全書以超有感的情境式方法學習單字，帶你朝多益滿分邁進！

01 情境插圖緊扣主題單字，達到聯想記憶效果

全書 60 個主題皆導入圖像輔助學習，每一主題特別繪製相關插圖並將必考單字整合、緊扣情境，讓單字學習融會貫通，記得更快、更牢。

02 特別設計單字交叉學習方式，達不斷複習目的

每一單元主題皆為多益考試必出現之重點；單字不會只出現在單一主題裡，利用不同單字或章節的例句做補強複習，在繼續往下學習的同時，還能溫故知新，不斷加強記憶。

04 repair
[rɪ`pɛr]
(v) 修理

- I found a defect in the item, and I'll have it repaired / replaced.
  我在這個東西上發現瑕疵，我會請人修理它／替換它。

10 mechanic
[mə`kænɪk]
(n) 技師

- A mechanic would probably know how to repair it.
  技師可能會知道該如何修理它。

03 生活化例句及測驗題設計，
讓多益實際應用在日常裡

本書單字例句及小測驗更以簡單好記、生活化、幽默風趣的方式編寫，助有效直取多益高分，連日常的口說、閱讀能力亦能同時大躍進。

schedule
[`skɛdʒʊl]
(n) (v)
行程；安排行程

- I have a tight sched
  我的行程很滿。
- Let's schedule a meetin
  我們來安排一個會議。

11 agenda
[ə`dʒɛndə]
(n) 議程

- There are s
  今天的
- Let

測驗

▶ 是非題
1. Orientation can refer to a person
2. Clerical is similar to clinical.
3. A reception desk is usually where
4. You can write a brief essay by add
5. To boost means to increase or to
6. You can measure the pressure
   ambience of surroundings.
7. A team tends to have bette
8. If something is being
   methods or rule

faster th
10. An agend

▶ 填空題
1. Mike prefers not to disc
2. Ever since the CEO anno
   in the office

(adj)
的、
comment (v) (n) 評論

他說她

補充說明

remark VS comment VS observation
這三個字都有「評論」的意思，但是卻是不同的

remark 是簡短且快速、未經過深思熟慮的評論。

comment 是評語、建議，帶有一點想法或是批評

ex: The teacher's comments on my essay helped
老師給我的評語對我幫助很大。

observation 是經過仔細觀察之後做出的評論。

ex: May I make an observation about the me
我可以對會議做一些評論嗎？

04 單字學習最清楚完整，
說明淺顯易懂不混淆

有效解決學習者最頭痛的「一字多義」以及意思相近的單字不知道該如何區分的問題，特別針對這些疑點補充說明，並且適時提供一些記憶小撇步，學習更清晰有系統。

05 單字＋例句，專業外師唸給你聽

每一主題皆有 QR Code，隨手一掃，外師逐字逐句將單字與例句唸給你聽！看字並搭配聲音練習說出來，不僅有效增強記憶，更能同步提升英文口語能力！

★ 因各家手機系統不同，若無直接掃描，仍可以電腦連結搜尋 https://tinyurl.com/y2yxocy8 連結下載全書音檔。

請與參加
plication and Participation

Track
001

Preface 作者序

　　Hello 大家，我是 Cindy！真的好開心可以在這邊跟您見面！不知道您是如何得知這本書的呢？如果您是 Cindy Sung YouTube 頻道的觀眾，那我真的要好好跟您說聲謝謝！因為有您的支持，這本書才有可能出版；如果您是在眾多多益單字書中剛好挑中這一本，那也很感謝您的青睞。

　　單字是學習語言的基礎，然而背單字卻也是許多學習者的罩門。身為一位英文老師，我常常在想要怎麼讓同學們更輕鬆地把單字記住？雖然老師總是要求同學們要經常複習並且大量閱讀，但是學生要學習的科目很多，還沒有時間複習昨天學到的內容，今天新的知識就又出現了！上班族就更不用說，下班後陪伴家人的時間都不夠了，哪有時間大量閱讀？

　　所以我一直在想要如何設計一本讓同學們可以**只要看這本就達到「不斷複習」的效果**的單字書。這本書是依照**多益考試情境**設計的，但是每一章節的單字不會只出現在該章節，而是會出現在不同章節的例句當中，讓讀者在閱讀的同時就能達到複習的效果。同學們讀完一個章節之後，不需要擔心很快就會忘記該章節的單字，因為只要繼續往下學習，之前學過的單字會再次出現！除此之外，每個章節都有提供測驗題，同學們可以在學習單字過後，利用小測驗檢視自己的學習成效，同時也達到複習的效果！另外，我也想幫同學們解決英文「一字多義」以及意思相近的單字不知道該如何區分的問題。所以書中對這些常見疑點會補充說明，並且適時提供一些記憶小撇步。

　　本書的例句和測驗題是另一個特色：它們都是我精心挑選和撰寫的！我認為在學習單字的時候，應該要用生活化或是幽默風趣的句子幫助記憶，而這些句子必須簡單好記！所以書中的例句不是給大家參考看看而已，是希望同學們可以把他們記起來，甚至未來有機會將它們使用在生活當中。

　　身為一個在臺灣長大的英文學習愛好者及多益滿分英文老師，我將自己學習單字的心得都在本書中分享給大家了！希望各位在閱讀本書過後，不僅能將書中的單字都記住，還能發現學習英文的樂趣！跟我一起開心地學英文吧！

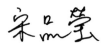

Contents 目錄

使用說明／004
作者序／006

Unit 01 申請與參加 Application and Participation ⋯⋯⋯ 010

Unit 02 申請相關資訊 Application Information ⋯⋯⋯ 016

Unit 03 商業一 Business 1 ⋯⋯⋯ 022

Unit 04 商業二 Business 2 ⋯⋯⋯ 028

Unit 05 商業三 Business 3 ⋯⋯⋯ 034

Unit 06 升遷 Promotion ⋯⋯⋯ 040

Unit 07 人才招募 Recruiting ⋯⋯⋯ 046

Unit 08 履歷準備 Résumé ⋯⋯⋯ 052

Unit 09 面試必備人格特質 Personality ⋯⋯⋯ 058

Unit 10 面試預約 Appointment ⋯⋯⋯ 065

Unit 11 工作面試一 Job Interview 1 ⋯⋯⋯ 072

Unit 12 工作面試二 Job Interview 2 ⋯⋯⋯ 078

Unit 13 新工作 Getting a new job ⋯⋯⋯ 084

Unit 14 公司環境一 Workplace 1 ⋯⋯⋯ 089

Unit 15 公司環境二 Workplace 2 ⋯⋯⋯ 094

Unit 16 公司環境三 Workplace 3 ⋯⋯⋯ 099

Unit 17 電話英文 On the Phone ⋯⋯⋯ 104

Unit 18 簽合約 Sign a Contract ⋯⋯⋯ 109

Unit 19 撰寫合約 Write a Contract 114

Unit 20 合約 Contract 120

Unit 21 協商 Negotiation 126

Unit 22 法律相關 Law 131

Unit 23 商業書信一 Business Email 1 136

Unit 24 商業書信二 Business Email 2 140

Unit 25 購買與付款 Purchasing and Payment 146

Unit 26 貨品運送 Shipping 152

Unit 27 採購 Purchasing 157

Unit 28 稽核 Assessment 162

Unit 29 工作表現一 Job performance 1 168

Unit 30 工作表現二 Job performance 2 173

Unit 31 優良員工特質 Good Workers 178

Unit 32 會議與簡報一 Presentation 1 184

Unit 33 會議與簡報二 Presentation 2 190

Unit 34 公關 PR 195

Unit 35 國際會議 Internation Conference 200

Unit 36 出差 Business Trip 205

Unit 37 機場 Airport 210

Unit 38 海關 Customs 215

Unit 39 飛機上 On the Plane 220

Unit **40** 機場與新冠肺炎 Airport & Coronavirus ⋯⋯⋯⋯⋯ 225

Unit **41** 商品通關 Moving Goods Through Customs ⋯⋯⋯ 230

Unit **42** 醫療衛生一 Medicine & Hygiene 1 ⋯⋯⋯⋯⋯⋯⋯ 236

Unit **43** 醫療衛生二 Medicine & Hygiene 2 ⋯⋯⋯⋯⋯⋯⋯ 242

Unit **44** 重要／不重要；大／小 Significant / insignificant ⋯ 247

Unit **45** 銀行業務 Banking ⋯⋯⋯⋯⋯⋯⋯⋯⋯⋯⋯⋯⋯⋯ 252

Unit **46** 投資 Investment ⋯⋯⋯⋯⋯⋯⋯⋯⋯⋯⋯⋯⋯⋯⋯ 257

Unit **47** 公司併購 Merger ⋯⋯⋯⋯⋯⋯⋯⋯⋯⋯⋯⋯⋯⋯⋯ 262

Unit **48** 製造業 Manufacturing ⋯⋯⋯⋯⋯⋯⋯⋯⋯⋯⋯⋯ 267

Unit **49** 旅遊 Travel ⋯⋯⋯⋯⋯⋯⋯⋯⋯⋯⋯⋯⋯⋯⋯⋯⋯ 272

Unit **50** 住宿 Accomodation, Housing ⋯⋯⋯⋯⋯⋯⋯⋯⋯ 277

Unit **51** 購物 Shopping ⋯⋯⋯⋯⋯⋯⋯⋯⋯⋯⋯⋯⋯⋯⋯⋯ 282

Unit **52** 餐廳用餐 Dining at a Restaurant ⋯⋯⋯⋯⋯⋯⋯ 287

Unit **53** 交通 Transportation ⋯⋯⋯⋯⋯⋯⋯⋯⋯⋯⋯⋯⋯ 294

Unit **54** 娛樂 Entertainment ⋯⋯⋯⋯⋯⋯⋯⋯⋯⋯⋯⋯⋯ 299

Unit **55** 政治 Politics ⋯⋯⋯⋯⋯⋯⋯⋯⋯⋯⋯⋯⋯⋯⋯⋯ 304

Unit **56** 政治延伸 Related to Politics ⋯⋯⋯⋯⋯⋯⋯⋯⋯ 309

Unit **57** 教育 Education ⋯⋯⋯⋯⋯⋯⋯⋯⋯⋯⋯⋯⋯⋯⋯⋯ 314

Unit **58** 閱讀 Reading ⋯⋯⋯⋯⋯⋯⋯⋯⋯⋯⋯⋯⋯⋯⋯⋯ 319

Unit **59** 全球經濟 Global Economy ⋯⋯⋯⋯⋯⋯⋯⋯⋯⋯ 324

Unit **60** 2020 2020 ⋯⋯⋯⋯⋯⋯⋯⋯⋯⋯⋯⋯⋯⋯⋯⋯⋯ 329

申請與參加
Application and Participation

Track
001

participate	participant
depart	departure
cooperate	cooperation
collaborate	due
expire	expiration
deadline	submit
application	apply
applicant	

01 participate

[par`tɪsə,pet]

(v) 參加

相似詞

take part in 參加、
join (in) 參加；加入、
participate in 參加；
參與

- If you want to <u>participate in</u> this game, you must follow the rules.
  如果你想要參加這個遊戲，你就必須遵守規定。

- I'm glad that you've decided to <u>participate in</u> this course.
  很高興你決定參加這個課程。

02 participant

[par`tɪsəpənt]

(n) 參加者

- To solve the mystery, every participant should do his or her part.
  每位參加者都要完成自己的部分才能解開這個謎。

補充說明

字根：part

(n) 部分

- (n) Let's move on to part 2. 接下來看第二部分。
- (n) department store （由很多部分組成的店 → 百貨公司）

(v) 分開

- (v) I don't want to part from you. 我不想跟你分開。
- (v) Her lips parted when she fell asleep. 她睡著時嘴唇分開了（嘴巴張開）。

03 depart

[dɪ`part]

(v) 離開

用法

leave / depart for + 地
點 = 去某地

- She'll <u>depart for</u> New York tomorrow.
  她明天要去紐約。

04 departure

[dɪ`partʃɚ]

(n) 離開

- I'll meet you at the departure gate.
  我在離境閘門等你。

05 cooperate

[ko`ɑpəˌret]

(v) 合作;配合

相似詞
collaborate 合作

- Participants should cooperate with each other to solve the problems.
  參加者應互相幫助以解決問題。

06 cooperation

[koˌɑpə`reʃən]

(n) 合作;配合

- Thank you for your cooperation.
  感謝您的配合。

07 collaborate

[kə`læbəˌret]

(v) 合作

相關詞
collaboration 合作

- The professor wanted us to work in pairs and collaborate closely with one another.
  教授希望我們兩人一組並且跟對方緊密合作。

補充說明

cooperate 跟 collaborate 都有「合作」的意思,但 cooperate 比較貼近「配合」例如 cooperate with the police 配合警方;而 collaborate 是雙方有意願合作,很常見的是 YouTubers 之間的 "collab"(也就是 collaborate 的縮寫),表示雙方都想合作。

另外有個跟他們長得很像的字是 coordinate 意思是協調、相配。

ex: We need someone to coordinate the event. 我們需要有人來統籌規劃這個活動。

a coordinator 協調員、統籌者

08 due

[dju]

(adj) 截止

用法
- **due date** 到期日
- **due to** 由於
（due to: because of
因為；由於）

- This bill is due next week.
  這份帳單下週到期。

- When is the due date?
  到期日是什麼時候？

- Due to safety reasons, the wedding is postponed.
  由於安全問題，婚禮延期了。

09 expire

[ɪk`spaɪr]

(v) 到期；結束

- The verification code will expire in 30 seconds.
  認證碼將在 30 秒後失效。

- The milk has expired.
  牛奶已經過期了。

10 expiration

[ˌɛkspə`reʃən]

(n) 到期；結束

- The expiration date is printed on the package.
  有效期限印在包裝上。

- What's the expiration date for this bottle of milk?
  這瓶牛奶的有效期限是幾月幾號？

11 deadline

[`dɛd͵laɪn]

(n) 截止日

用法
meet + deadline

- Applicants should submit their application form before the deadline.
  申請人須在截止日前繳交申請資料。

- Our leader requests all the workers to meet the deadline.
  我們的長官要求工作人員要準時。

12 submit

[səb`mɪt]

(v) 繳交

- Please submit your group project before the due date.
  請在截止日前繳交小組報告。

13 application [ˌæpləˈkeʃən] (n) 申請	• application requirements 申請必備資料 • The application deadline is this Friday. 申請截止日是這星期五。
14 apply [əˈplaɪ] (v) 申請；適用於； 應用 用法 **apply + for / to** 申請 **apply + to** 適用於	• Apply this <u>ointment / lotion</u> to your skin. 將這個藥膏／乳液塗抹到皮膚上。 • This method only <u>applies to</u> certain conditions. 這個方法只適用於某些情況。 • I would like to <u>apply for</u> the teaching position. 我想要申請這個教職。 • We should apply a different approach. 我們應該使用其他方法。 延伸學習 apply for a position 申請職位 apply to a company / school 申請公司／學校（機構）
15 applicant [ˈæpləkənt] (n) 申請人	• All eligible applicants should hear back from us within two to three weeks of applying. 所有合格的申請者將在二至三週後收到回音。

 測驗

▶ 是非題

_____ 1. To participate means to join.

_____ 2. A participant is someone who is sick.

_____ 3. Departing for means to leave a place and go to another place.

_____ 4. To cooperate means to work together.

_____ 5. Collaborate is a synonym（同義詞）for cooperate.

_____ 6. Due has a similar meaning to finish.

_____ 7. A rock can expire some day.

_____ 8. Deadline is another word for due date.

_____ 9. To submit means to take part in.

_____ 10. You can apply for a position or apply to a school.

▶ 填空題

1. The plane is about to _____. Let's hurry to gate D9!

2. This is an emergency. We'll need you to fully _____ with the police.

3. Let's _____ on this project!

4. The _____ seemed eager to _____ in the game.

5. I have to _____ my report before the _____.

6. The milk tastes sour. I think it has _____.

7. Her baby is _____ next week. She's about to become a mom!

8. I _____ for the position last week but I haven't received any reply yet.

Answer

是非題：

1. O   2. X   3. O   4. O   5. O   6. O   7. X   8. O   9. X   10. O

填空題：

1. depart   2. cooperate   3. collaborate   4. participants / participate

5. submit / deadline   6. expired   7. due   8. applied

填空題翻譯：

1. 飛機即將離開。我們趕快去第九閘門！

2. 這是緊急狀況。我們需要大家跟警方配合。

3. 我們合作做這個專案吧！

4. 參加者似乎很積極想參加遊戲。

5. 我要在截止日期前交報告。

6. 牛奶味道是酸的，我想它過期了。

7. 他的寶寶下禮拜出生，他要當媽媽了。

8. 我上週申請這個職位，但我還沒有收到任何回覆。

申請相關資訊
Application Information

applicant	require
requirement	request
acquire	inquire
inquiry	questionnaire
requisite	prerequisite
necessary	leader
lead	chief

01 applicant

[`æpləkənt]
(n) 申請人

- There are several applicants applying for this position.
  有幾位申請人申請了這個職位。

- Please include the applicant's name with the fee waiver.
  請在費用減免證明中附上申請人的姓名。

02 require

[rɪ`kwaɪr]
(v) 要求；需要

相似詞
demand (n) 要求、
necessary (adj) 必需的

- Applicants are required to submit a personal statement.
  申請人必須繳交自傳。

- Do you require any assistance?
  你有要求任何幫助嗎？

- Bachelor's degree required; Master's degree preferred.
  學士以上；碩士尤佳。

03 requirement

[rɪ`kwaɪrmənt]
(n) 要求的條件

- You can find the application requirements on our website.
  你可以在網站上找到我們的申請資料。

延伸學習 minimum requirement 最低要求

04 request

[rɪ`kwɛst]
(v) 要求；請求

相似詞
ask for

- You can request a fee waiver directly through the application.
  你可以在申請時直接要求學費減免。

延伸學習 to request help, to request information
請求幫助、請求給予資訊

05 acquire

[ə`kwaɪr]
(v) 得到

相似詞
get (v) 獲得、
gain (v) 得到

- She has acquired a good reputation throughout the years.
  幾年下來她得到了很好的名聲。

延伸學習 to acquire knowledge 獲得知識

字根介紹：que

question 是我們都熟悉的單字，它的字根 que 就是詢問、探究的意思，所以 require, request 意思都有一點相關。

---

06 inquire

[ɪnˋkwaɪr]

(v) 詢問

用法

inquire about + 事情

- You can <u>inquire about</u> the prices at the front desk.
  您可以在前臺詢問價錢。

延伸學習 inquire 是比 ask 更正式的說法

inquire + about + something → ask

---

07 inquiry

[ɪnˋkwaɪrɪ]

(n) 問題；調查

- If you have any inquiries, feel free to contact me.
  如果你有任何問題，歡迎跟我聯絡。

- The World Health Organization agreed to begin an inquiry into the global response to the pandemic.
  世界衛生組織同意開始調查全球對抗疫情的情況。

---

08 questionnaire

[ˌkwɛstʃənˋɛr]

(n) 問卷

- We would like your permission to fill out a questionnaire.
  我們需要您同意填寫這份問卷。

---

09 requisite

[ˋrɛkwəzɪt]

(n) (adj) 需要

- A driver's license is a requisite for the job.
  駕照是這份工作的必備之物。

- Driving is a requisite skill for the job.
  駕駛是這份工作必備的技能。

---

10 prerequisite

[ˌpriˋrɛkwəzɪt]

(n) (adj) 先決條件

- A bachelor's degree is a prerequisite for the job interview.
  學士學歷是參加面試的先決條件。

11 necessary

[ˋnɛsəˌsɛrɪ]

(adj) 必要的

- It's necessary to review what you've learned.
  學習之後必須要複習。

延伸學習 preferred, but not <u>necessary / required / mandatory</u>
（有尤佳，但非必要）

12 leader

[ˋlidɚ]

(n) 領導人

- Our class leader is a model student. She is modest and always willing to help.
  我們班的班長是個模範生。她很謙虛而且總是願意幫忙。

- A leader should know how to lead.
  領導人應該知道如何領導。

13 lead

[lid]

(v) 領導

三態
lead, led, led

用法
lead to 導致

- His ignorance <u>led to</u> a disaster.
  他的無知導致了災難。

- We hope our leader will lead us to success.
  希望我們的領導人能帶領我們通往成功的道路。

延伸學習 lead to 導致（帶領……至）
→ His laziness <u>led to</u> his failure（失敗）.
（過去式：led）他的懶惰導致他的失敗。
→ Her hard work <u>led to</u> her success.
她的辛勤工作讓她成功。

14 chief

[tʃif]

(n) 主要；首領
(adj) 主要的

相似詞
main (adj) 主要的、
major (adj) 重要的

相反詞
minor (adj) 次要的

- Our Chief Executive Officer is a great leader.
  我們的 CEO 是個很棒的領導人。

- He is the chief of our tribe.
  他是我們這族的首領。

- What is the chief (main) cause of the disease?
  這個疾病的主要成因是什麼？

▶ 是非題

_____ 1. An applicant might be a person who is looking for a job.

_____ 2. If you are required to do something, it means you need to do it.

_____ 3. You can request a song.

_____ 4. To acquire means to ask.

_____ 5. To inquire means to gain.

_____ 6. You can fill in a questionnaire.

_____ 7. A prerequisite is something that can be ignored.

_____ 8. It's necessary to review new words if you want to remember them.

_____ 9. A CEO is usually a leader of a company.

_____ 10. A chief reason is a minor reason.

▶ 填空

1. Our _____ is very strict. She _____ us to be on time for work every day.

2. We are _____ to be on time for work.

3. For any _____, please contact 0910520520.

4. The _____ reason for their divorce is that they have incompatible personalities.

5. Excuse me, can you help us fill out a _____?

6. The _____ has submitted her files, hoping that she'll become one of the candidates.

7. It's sunny outside. Is it really _____ to bring an umbrella?

8. She has _____ great knowledge by reading extensively.

9. Your recklessness _____ to a disaster! Now everything is screwed!

Answer

是非題：

1. O　　2. O　　3. O　　4. X　　5. X　　6. X　　7. X　　8. O　　9. O　　10. X

填空題：

1. leader / requires　　2. required　　3. inquiries　　4. chief

5. questionnaire　　6. applicant　　7. necessary　　8. acquired　　9. led

填空題翻譯：

1. 我們的領導人很嚴格。她要求我們每天準時上班。

2. 我們被要求準時上班。

3. 如有任何問題請聯絡 0910520520。

4. 他們離婚的主要原因是個性不合。

5. 不好意思，可以請你幫忙填寫這份問卷嗎？

6. 申請人已經繳交她的文件，她希望她可以成為其中一個候選人。

7. 外面是晴天，真的有必要帶傘嗎。

8. 她藉由廣泛閱讀獲得了許多知識。

9. 你的魯莽導致了災難！現在全部事情都搞砸了！

商業一
Business 1

customer	customize	client
patron	patronage	patronize
consumer	satisfy	cater
succeed	success	successful
experience	headquarters	employ
employer	employee	unemployment rate

01 customer

[`kʌstəmɚ]
(n) 顧客

用法
meet / satisfy...needs
達成／滿足需求

- We do our very best to meet our customers' needs.
= We strive to meet our customers' requirements.
= We aim to cater to our customers' needs.
我們盡力滿足／達到顧客的需求。

02 customize

[`kʌstəmˌaɪz]
(v) 客製化

- The feature of this restaurant is that you can customize your own pizza.
這間餐廳的特色是妳可以客製化自己的披薩。

延伸學習 customized products 客製化（的）商品

補充說明
✓ "very" best 的 very 是強調用法，強調 do our best（做到最好）
✓ meet...needs / requirements / cater to...needs = 達到／滿足……需求
** 很喜歡 = I like it very much. 千萬不要說成 I very like it.
very 不會接在動詞前面喔！！

03 client

[`klaɪənt]
(n) 客戶

- The lawyer is meeting his client at 10 am.
這位律師將在早上十點和客戶見面。

04 patron

[`petrən]
(n) 老顧客；贊助者

相似詞
sponsor (n) 贊助人

- Although we cannot satisfy all of our customers, we always make sure to cater to our patrons.
雖然我們無法滿足所有的客人，但我們總是盡可能滿足老顧客。

05 patronage

[`pætrənɪdʒ]
(n) 贊助；光顧

- Dear customer, thank you for your patronage.
親愛的顧客，感謝您的光顧。

06 patronize

[`pɛtrənˌaɪz]

(v) 經常光顧

- The fancy restaurant, listed as one of the most "instagrammable" restaurants in France, is patronized by tourists around the world.
  來自世界各地的旅客經常光顧這間在法國的高級網美餐廳。

07 consumer

[kən`sjumɚ]

(n) 消費者

- The bank believed that cutting interest rates would help strengthen consumer and business confidence and keep money flowing.
  銀行相信降息可以增加消費者以及企業的信心，讓金錢持續流動。

延伸學習 consumer demand 消費者需求

08 satisfy

[`sætɪsˌfaɪ]

(v) 滿足

用法
satisfy one's needs
滿足……需求
be satisfied with
對……滿意

- Our CEO requested us to satisfy the customers' needs.
  總經理要求我們滿足顧客的需求。

- We hope the customers are satisfied with our service.
  我們希望顧客對我們的服務感到滿意。

09 cater

[`ketɚ]

(v) 備辦食物；迎合

相似詞
tailor to (v) 專門製作

用法
cater to one's needs
達成／滿足……需求

- The experienced teacher knows how to cater to her students' needs.
  這位有經驗的老師知道要如何滿足學生的需求。

延伸學習 catering service 外燴服務

10 succeed

[sək`sid]

(v) 成功

- We will definitely succeed!
  我們一定會成功！（注意：用動詞，想成 We will win!）

11 success

[sək`sɛs]

(n) 成功

- We will be a great success!
  我們會大成功！（注意：success 在這邊為可數名詞，前面要有 a）

12 successful

[sək`sɛsfəl]

(adj) 成功的

- We will be successful!
  我們會成功的！

補充說明

success 可以是可數也可以是不可數名詞

如果談的是「成功」這件事，例如：What's the key to success?（成功的關鍵是什麼？）此時 success 是不可數名詞

如果是「一個成功案例」，例如：The product is a commercial success!（那個商品是個商業成功案例！）這時就是可數名詞。

13 experience

[ɪk`spɪrɪəns]

(n) (v) 經驗

- We need someone with work experience in this field.
  我們需要在這個領域有工作經驗的人。

- I can't imagine what she had experienced.
  我無法想像她經歷了什麼。

- They have experience in taking care of babies.
  他們對照顧嬰兒有經驗。

  延伸學習 have experience in something 對什麼有經驗

14 headquarters

[`hɛd`kwɔrtəz]

(n) 總部

- The headquarters of Starbucks is in Seattle.
  星巴克的總部在西雅圖。

15 employ

[ɪm`plɔɪ]

(v) 雇用

- He has applied for several jobs, hoping to be employed soon.
  他申請了幾份工作，期望可以盡早被錄用。

16 employer

[ɪmˋplɔɪɚ]

(n) 雇主

- The employer requests his employees to satisfy their customers' demands.
  這位雇主要求他的員工滿足顧客的要求。

17 employee

[͵ɛmplɔɪˋi]

(n) 雇員

相關詞：**staff** 員工

- The employer values and respects his employees.
  那位雇主重視並尊重他的員工們。

延伸學習 contract 合約 + employee 員工 → 約聘人員

18 unemployment rate

[͵ʌnɪmˋplɔɪmənt ret]

(n) 失業率

- Due to the economic recession, the unemployment rate has risen this year.
  因為經濟蕭條，今年的失業率上升了。

 測驗

▶ 是非題

_____ 1. A customer is exactly the same with a client.

_____ 2. A greedy person might never be satisfied.

_____ 3. When we cater to someone's needs, it means we try to satisfy them.

_____ 4. 我要成功 = I want to success!

_____ 5. Have experience + on something.

_____ 6. Headquarters is another word for branch.

_____ 7. An employer is someone who employs employees.

_____ 8. A customer is a kind of consumer.

_____ 9. A contract employee usually works in the same company for more than 10 years.

_____ 10. A patron is a loyal customer.

▶ 填空題

1. If you are looking for _____ service, I highly recommend Katie's! Their salmon puff is amazing!

2. It's very hard to _____ Mandy. She is extremely hard to please.

3. Fast food stores offer food fast. They don't keep the _____ waiting.

4. Jack closed the most deals and became the _____ of the month.

5. I have a lot of _____ in the field, and I'm sure that I'm able to contribute to the team.

6. A _____ is a person who buys goods or services.

7. I would like to thank all our shareholders and investors for their support and our customers for their _____.

8. All of the employees in that global company will fly to the _____ for the annual conference next month.

9. After years of hard work, the single mother is now a _____ entrepreneur.

10. I would like to _____ my phone case by printing my name on it.

Answer

是非題：

1. X   2. O   3. O   4. X   5. X   6. X   7. O   8. O   9. X   10. O

填空題：

1. catering   2. satisfy   3. customers   4. employee   5. experience

6. consumer   7. patronage   8. headquarters   9. successful   10. customize

填空題翻譯：

1. 如果你要找外燴服務，我很推薦 Katie's！他們的鮭魚泡芙令人驚艷。

2. Mandy 很難被滿足，她很難討好。

3. 速食餐廳快速提供食物。他們不會讓顧客等待。

4. Jack 成交量最多並且成為這個月的最佳員工。

5. 我在這個領域有許多經驗，我很確定我可以為這個團隊貢獻。

6. 一位消費者是一位會買商品及服務的人。

7. 我要感謝所有股東和投資人的支持還有我們的顧客的惠顧。

8. 那間國際公司所有的員工會在下個月飛去總部參加年度會議。

9. 在努力多年後，那位單親媽媽成為了一名成功的創業家。

10. 我想要藉由把名字印在上面來客製化我的手機殼。

Track
004

project	projector	offer
professor	proficient	promote
promotion	product	produce
prototype	career	develop
development	manage	manager

01 project

[`prɑdʒɛkt]
(n) 專案

[prə`dʒɛkt]
(v) 推算；投影

相似詞
case (n) 案件；專案

- For this project, I want you to collaborate with each other.

這個專案我希望大家可以互相合作。

延伸學習 to project next year's expenses 推算明年的預算
to project the slide onto a screen
將（PPT）頁面投影到螢幕（屏幕）上

02 projector

[prə`dʒɛktɚ]
(n) 投影機

- The projector is not working. Does anyone have the manual?

投影機無法運作。有人有使用手冊嗎？

03 offer

[`ɔfɚ]
(n) (v) 供應；提供

相關詞
provide (v) 提供

- Don't wait to be offered a great salary. Ask for it and provide proof as to why it is warranted.

不要等著別人提供高薪的工作。主動要求並且提供你為什麼應該得到高薪的證明。

延伸學習 a job offer 工作機會

補充說明

pro 字首 = forward, supporting 向前、支持

promote：往前 + move 移動 → 升級

progress：往前走 → 進度

pros and cons：支持和反對（的理由）→ 優點和缺點

04 professor

[prə`fɛsɚ]
(n) 教授

相關詞
profession (n)
專業；職業
professional (n) (adj)
專業的

- A professor is an expert in a certain field. He / She is a professional in his / her profession.

一位教授即是在某個領域的專家。他／她在他／她的專業（領域）非常專業。

- He is a professional baseball player.

他是位職業棒球選手。

- Let's hire a professional to install the machine.

我們聘請一位專業人員來安裝機器吧。

05 proficient

[prə`fɪʃənt]

(adj) 精通；熟練

- She is an Australian who is proficient in Mandarin.
  她是一位精通中文的澳洲人。

06 promote

[prə`mot]

(v) 升遷；推廣

- I hope to be promoted soon! I also want to get a raise!
  我希望能被升遷！我還想要加薪！

07 promotion

[prə`moʃən]

(n) 升遷；推廣

- I hope to get a promotion soon!
  希望能趕快升遷！

08 product

[`prɑdəkt]

(n) 產品

相似詞
goods (n)
商品（恆為複數）
merchandise (n)
商品 （恆為單數）

- This store offers a wide range of / various products.
  這間店提供各式各樣的產品。

09 produce

[prə`djus]

(v) 生產

相關詞
productive (adj)
有生產力的

- The factory produces masks.
  這間工廠生產口罩。

10 prototype

[`protə‚taɪp]

(n) 原型

- The company has designed an electric car prototype.
  這間公司設計出電動車的原型。

11 career

[kə`rɪr]

(n) 職涯

相關詞
vocation (n) 職業

- What would you like to do for your career? What do you want to do for a living?
  你想要做什麼工作？

12 develop

[dɪ`vɛləp]

(v) 發展；形成

- As technology continues to develop, life gets more and more convenient.
  隨著科技不斷的發展，生活也越來越方便。

13 development

[dɪ`vɛləpmənt]

(n) 發展

- With the development of science and technology, children are living in a world that is completely different from 50 years ago.
  隨著科技的進步，現在的小孩住在跟 50 年前完全不同的世界。

延伸學習 Research and development engineer / fellow（研究員）

14 manage

[`mænɪdʒ]

(v) 掌管；順利完成

相似詞
handle (v) 處理、
deal with (phr) 處理

- Don't worry about me. I can manage it / that.
  別擔心我，我能掌控。

15 manager

[`mænɪdʒɚ]

(n) 經理
（掌管某事的人）

- I'll have to consult with my manager.
  我要諮詢我的經理。

延伸學習 a project manager 專案經理（PM）

▶ 是非題

_____ 1. It usually takes no time to finish a project.

_____ 2. To offer is another way to say to give.

_____ 3. A profession cannot be a career.

_____ 4. To be promoted means to become the executive of a company.

_____ 5. There are a variety of products in a department store.

_____ 6. A prototype is also called an antique.

_____ 7. One's job can be one's career; however, one's career can't be one's job.

_____ 8. You can develop a new hobby.

_____ 9. If you can manage something, it means you can handle it.

_____ 10. You can use "proficient" to describe a beginner.

▶ 填空題

1. If a blogger pushes a "broken" _____ or service simply because he or she is being sponsored, the blogger's credibility will permanently suffer.

2. We built a _____ to test with our potential customers.

3. Nowadays, we suggest young people to think about their future _____ as early as possible.

4. I've heard that the farmer _____ the best mangoes in Taiwan.

5. To present our presentation, we will need a _____ and a screen.

6. Due to the development of public transportation, the small town has gradually _____ into a big city.

7. To our surprise, the toddler _____ to soothe her baby sister.

8. I'm thinking about taking that job _____ because they promised to _____ me a six-figure salary.

9. We plan to _____ our company's new product by working with several celebrities.

10. It took the clown several months to become _____ at juggling balls.

Answer

是非題：

1. X　　2. O　　3. X　　4. X　　5. O　　6. X　　7. X　　8. O　　9. O　　10. X

填空題：

1. product　　2. prototype　　3. careers　　4. produces　　5. projector

6. developed　　7. managed　　8. offer / offer　　9. promote　　10. proficient

填空題翻譯：

1. 如果一個部落客僅僅是因為他被贊助就推廣不好的商品或是服務，那這個部落客的信用就會永遠受損。

2. 我們建立了一個雛形來測試潛在客戶。

3. 近年來我們建議年輕人及早思考未來的職業。

4. 我聽說那位農夫種的芒果是全臺最好吃的。

5. 為了呈現我們的報告，我們需要一臺投影機和螢幕。

6. 因為大眾運輸的發展，這個小鎮漸漸變成一個大城市。

7. 令我們驚訝的是，那個幼兒能夠安撫她還是小嬰兒的妹妹。

8. 我在考慮接受那份工作，因為他們答應給我 6 位數的薪水。

9. 我們打算和幾個名人一起推廣我們公司的新產品。

10. 小丑花了幾個月的時間精熟丟球雜技。

商業三
Business 3

manufacture	industry
control	deal
handle	appreciate
depreciate	value
valuable	grant
fund	

01 manufacture

[ˌmænjəˋfæktʃɚ]
(n) (v) 製造

- Have you ever wondered how cars are manufactured?
  你有想過車子是如何製造的嗎？

- The law limited the manufacture of weapons.
  法律限制了武器的製造。

  延伸學習 manufacturing industry 製造業

02 industry

[ˋɪndəstrɪ]
(n) 產業

- The government is trying to restart the travel and tourism industry.
  政府正試著重振觀光旅遊業。

  延伸學習 the oil and gas industry / the music industry / the entertainment industry
  石油產業／音樂產業／娛樂業

補充說明

man 字首表示和「手」相關，例如 manage（掌控、控管）、manual（手冊）、manipulate（操弄）、manufacture（製造）、manuscript（手稿），都跟「手」相關。

03 control

[kənˋtrol]
(v) 控制

- Don't worry. Everything is under control.
  別擔心，都在掌控之中。

- The situation is out of control / out of hand!
  情況已經無法控制了！

04 deal

[dil]

(n) (v) 處理；交易；
價格

相似詞
handle (v) 處理

- He made a deal with the devil.
  他跟惡魔做了交易。

- Done deal.
  已經決定了。

- They put a great deal of effort into the project.
  他們為了這專案付出很多。

- That's no big deal. Don't make a fuss over it.
  這沒什麼大不了，不要小題大作。

  延伸學習 Let me deal with / handle it. 讓我來處理。
  to make a deal with someone 與某人做個交易
  a great deal of...(a lot of) 很多
  What a great deal / price! 真棒的價格！

05 handle

[`hændl]

(v) 處理

- The babysitter is skilled at handling naughty kids.
  這保母擅長對付頑皮的小孩。

- I'll handle / deal with it.
  交給我處理。

06 appreciate

[ə`priʃɪˌet]

(v) 欣賞；感謝；增值

相反詞
depreciate (v) 貶值

- Thanks! I really appreciate your help.
  謝謝！我很感謝你的幫忙。
  = Your help is appreciated.
  = I'm grateful / thankful for your help.

- I appreciate the beauty of nature.
  我很欣賞大自然的美。

- The value of our house has appreciated by 30 percent in the last 3 years.
  我們房子的價格近三年來漲了 30%。

07 depreciate

[dɪ`priʃɪˌet]

(v) 貶值

- The value of our house has depreciated by 30 percent.
  = Our house has depreciated by 30 percent in value.
  我們房子的價格近三年來貶值了 30%。

08 value

[`vælju]
(n) (v) 價值；價值觀

相似詞
worth (n) (v) 價值

- What's the value of the car?
  = How much is it worth?
  這部車價值多少？

- The value of the diamond ring is over 1 million dollars.
  這鑽戒價值超過一百萬。

- Experts have valued the diamond ring at 1 million dollars.
  專家估算這戒指價值一百萬。

- I'm glad that we share the same values.
  很高興我們有一樣的價值觀。

- I value her advice / opinions.
  我很重視她的建議／意見。

09 valuable

[`væljʊəbl̩]
(adj) 有價值的

- The ring is very valuable.
  這戒指很有價值。

10 grant

[grænt]
(n) (v)
撥款；補助金；答應

相似詞
award (n) 獎金、
scholarship (n) 獎學金

- The teacher granted our request.
  老師同意了我們的請求。

- Do not take your parents for granted.
  不要把父母（的好）視為理所當然。

延伸學習 research grant 研究補助款
take something for granted 視為理所當然

11 fund

[fʌnd]
(n) (v) 資金；經費；
給予經費

- We hope that funds will be granted by the board of directors soon.
  我們希望董事會能夠盡快同意給予經費。

- The board of directors has agreed to fund the project.
  董事會已經同意資助專案的經費。

延伸學習 a fundraiser 募款活動

測驗

▶ 是非題

_____ 1. To manufacture something means to produce something.

_____ 2. An industry involves a certain type of business or area.

_____ 3. To control means you have the power over something or someone.

_____ 4. To deal with a situation means to give in and take no further action.

_____ 5. If you handle a task poorly, chances are that it exceeds your capability.

_____ 6. It feels pleasant when someone appreciates the work you do.

_____ 7. If the value of the car you own depreciates, you are able to sell it at a higher price.

_____ 8. If you value something, you consider it important.

_____ 9. To grant means to give or to allow.

_____ 10. A fund is an amount of money used for a certain purpose.

▶ 填空

1. This company is very well-known in the service _____ .

2. He works in a factory that _____ fabrics.

3. In the story <Aladdin>, the genie in the lamp _____ Aladdin three wishes.

4. Jane feels overwhelmed because her boss tries to _____ everything.

5. The organization has set up a _____ in order to buy more equipments.

6. My roommate always listens to loud rock music at night without headphones - I can't _____ with it anymore!

7. If the place where your house is located is convenient enough, its value will not _____ over time.

8. He was the most _____ player in the baseball team last year.

9. Even under stressful circumstances, Tracy is still able to _____ the situation calmly.

10. I sincerely _____ your hard work and effort.

Answer

是非題：

1. O　　2. O　　3. O　　4. X　　5. O　　6. O　　7. X　　8. O　　9. O　　10. O

填空題：

1. industry　　　2. manufactures　3. grants / granted（現在過去皆可）

4. control　　　5. fund　　　6. deal　　　7. depreciate　　8. valuable

9. handle　　　10. appreciate

填空題翻譯：

1. 這間公司聞名於服務業界。

2. 他在一間製造布料的工廠工作。

3. 《阿拉丁神燈》故事中，在神燈裡的精靈給予阿拉丁 3 個願望。

4. Jane 感到無力，因為她的上司總是想掌控一切。

5. 此組織成立了基金會，藉此添購設備。

6. 我室友總喜歡不戴耳機在晚上聽吵雜的搖滾樂，我無法忍受了！

7. 如果你住的地點交通便利，你的房子就不會隨時間貶值。

8. 他是去年最有價值的棒球選手。

9. 即使在充滿壓力的情況下，Tracy 仍能冷靜地處理問題。

10. 我真心感謝你的努力與用心。

升遷
Promotion

raise	directors	executive
execute	conduct	authorize
authority	résumé	advise
advice	consult	consultant
recruit	hire	retire

01 raise

[rez]

(v) 舉起；增加；養育

- I hope to either get a promotion or get a raise.
  我希望能升遷或是加薪。

  延伸學習 raise your hand / raise a baby / raise a question
  舉手／養育孩子／提問
  a fundraiser / a fund-raising event 募資活動

02 directors

[də`rɛktə]

(n) 主管

- The Board of Directors will make the final decision.
  董事會會做最後決定。

- For a limited company, the responsible person should be a director of the company or a person authorized by the Board of Directors.
  有限公司的負責人應是這間公司的其中一位管理者或是一位由董事會授權的人。

  延伸學習 Board of Directors 董事會

03 executive

[ɪg`zɛkjʊtɪv]

(n) 行政主管；經理

- Do you know who the chief executive of Apple is?
  你知道蘋果的執行長是誰嗎？

  延伸學習 Chief Executive Officer 首席執行長

04 execute

[`ɛksɪ͵kjut]

(v) 執行；處死

相似詞
perform (v) 施行、
conduct (v) 執行

- The criminal was executed for murder.
  罪犯因謀殺被處死。

  延伸學習 to execute a plan 執行計畫

05 conduct

[kən`dʌkt]

(v) 執行

相關詞
a misconduct (n) 疏失

- The police moved swiftly to conduct an investigation.
  警方迅速展開調查。

  延伸學習 to conduct a plan / an experiment / an investigation / a survey / an analysis
  執行計畫／實驗／調查／檢查／分析

06 authorize

[ˈɔθəˌraɪz]

(v) 授權

- The Board of Directors has authorized the executive to conduct the plan.
董事會已授權執行長執行計畫。

07 authority

[əˈθɔrətɪ]

(n) 官方；當局；
有權力的人

- The authorities are losing control over the situation.
官方逐漸失去對此情形的掌控。

延伸學習 the local / health authorities 地方當局／衛生當局
give sb. authority → authorize 授權

08 résumé

[ˈrezəmeɪ]

(n) 簡歷

- What should be included in one's résumé?
簡歷裡面要寫什麼呢？

- Here's a sample résumé for your reference.
這裡有一個簡歷的範例給你參考。

09 advise

[ədˈvaɪz]

(v) 建議

相似詞
suggest (v)
recommend (v)
建議、推薦

- I highly advise you to read English novels if you want to improve your English reading ability.
如果你想要加強英文閱讀能力，我強烈建議你閱讀英文小說。

延伸學習 I highly/stongly advise / suggest you to...
強烈建議你……

10 advice

[ədˈvaɪs]

(n) 建議

相似詞
suggestion (n) 建議、
recommendation (n)
推薦

- I'd like to listen to your advice / suggestion.
我想聽聽你的建議。

延伸學習 advice 建議不可數，要用 a piece of advice

11 consult

[kənˈsʌlt]

(v) 諮詢；請教

- I'd like to consult with an advisor.
我想要諮詢顧問。

延伸學習 a consulting firm 顧問公司

12 consultant

[kən`sʌltənt]

(n) 顧問

相似詞
advisor (n) 顧問

- The consultant advised me to keep a diary.
  顧問建議我寫日記。

13 recruit

[rɪ`krut]

(v) 招聘

相關詞
recruiter (n) 招聘人員

- We are <u>recruiting / hiring</u>!
  我們在徵人！

  延伸學習 recruit new members 徵新會員

14 hire

[haɪr]

(v) 聘請

- We are planning to hire talented engineers.
  我們計畫招收有才華的工程師。

15 retire

[rɪ`taɪr]

(v) 退休

- The principal is almost seventy years old, so we are guessing that she might retire soon.
  校長快要七十歲了，所以我們猜想她可能快要退休了。

▶ 是非題

_____ 1. You can raise a question.

_____ 2. An executive has a higher position than the board of directors.

_____ 3. To execute a plan means to end it.

_____ 4. A student can conduct an experiment.

_____ 5. To authorize means to give permission to.

_____ 6. A résumé is a document that you submit when you're looking for a job.

_____ 7. You can ask someone for many advices.

_____ 8. To consult someone means to help someone.

_____ 9. You can recruit a person who is about to retire.

_____ 10. To retire means to be laid off.

▶ 填空

1. My supervisor has the _____ to sign and approve this document.

2. The charity plans to _____ funds for victims of the hurricane disaster.

3. Students nearing graduation have started to prepare their _____ in order to find a job.

4. The _____ was chosen by shareholders.

5. Whenever Peter feels lost, he asks his professor for _____.

6. Researchers have been _____ experiments in the lab to develop the vaccine for COVID-19.

7. Once we have the manager's approval, we can _____ the plan.

8. John admires the candidate's experiences and decides to _____ him immediately.

9. She will _____ next year and take part in voluntary work.

10. The company plans to hire a _____ to help establish their public image.

(Answer)

是非題：

1. O   2. X   3. X   4. O   5. O   6. O   7. X   8. X   9. X   10. X

填空題：

1. authority   2. raise   3. résumés   4. board of directors

5. advice   6. conducting   7. execute   8. hire   9. retire

10. consultant

填空題翻譯：

1. 我的主管擁有權力簽核此文件。

2. 這個慈善機構計劃募資以幫助颱風的受害者。

3. 即將畢業的學生們開始準備他們的履歷並找工作。

4. 董事會由股東選出。

5. 每當 Peter 感到迷惘，他總詢問教授的建議。

6. 研究人員正在實驗室中執行不同試驗，希望開發出 COIVD-19 的疫苗。

7. 我們一取得經理的核准就會執行計劃。

8. John 非常青睞此候選人的經歷並立刻決定錄用他。

9. 她將於明年退休並參與志工服務。

10. 此公司計劃聘請顧問來幫助其建立公眾形象。

人才招募
Recruiting

manager	resource	assist
assistant	secretary	description
depict	candidate	nominate
nomination	qualify	qualification
quality	quantity	

01 manager

[`mænɪdʒɚ]

(n) 經理；管理人員

- The human resource manager is in charge of that.
  那是人資主管負責的。

- Human resource management should be improved.
  人事管理需要加強。

延伸學習 human resource manager 人資主管

02 resource

[rɪ`sors]

(n) 資源；來源

補充
resourceful (adj)
足智多謀的

- natural resources, renewable resources
  自然資源、可重複使用的資源

- We don't have the resources to conduct the plan.
  我們沒有資源可以執行此計畫。

03 assist

[ə`sɪst]

(v) 協助

用法
assist in / with + N
補充
assistance (n) 援助

- I need you to assist me in doing the project.
  這個企劃我需要你的幫助。

- Do you need any assistance?
  需要幫忙嗎？

04 assistant

[ə`sɪstənt]

(n) 助理

- My smartphone is my virtual assistant.
  我的智慧型手機是我的虛擬助理。

延伸學習 a personal assistant / a virtual, digital assistant
私人助理／虛擬、數位助理

05 secretary

[`sɛkrə͵tɛrɪ]

(n) 祕書

- Please schedule an appointment with my secretary.
  請找我的祕書安排會議。

- The executive relies heavily on his secretary's assistance.
  執行長非常依賴他的祕書的協助。

延伸學習 Secretary General 祕書長

06 description

[dɪˋskrɪpʃən]

(n) 描述

- You can find more information in the description box.
  你可以在資訊欄（描述欄）找到更多資訊。

延伸學習 job description 工作描述

07 depict

[dɪˋpɪkt]

(v) 形容

相似詞
describe (v) 描述

- How is Lucifer depicted / described in the Bible?
  路西法在聖經中是如何被描述的呢？

08 candidate

[ˋkændədet]

(n) 候選人

- There are several candidates in the race for promotion.
  有好幾位候選人在為了升遷競爭。

- The candidates all hoped to be selected / chosen.
  所有候選人都希望被選中。

延伸學習 presidential candidates 總統候選人

09 nominate

[ˋnɑməˏnet]

(v) 提名

- Taylor Swift was nominated for the Grammy Awards.
  泰勒斯被提名葛萊美獎。

- She was one of the nominees.
  她是其中一個被提名人。

10 nomination

[ˏnɑməˋneʃən]

(n) 提名

- Taylor Swift has won 10 awards since her first nomination at the 2008 ceremony.
  泰勒斯在 2008 年第一次被提名之後至今贏得了 10 個獎項。

11 qualify

[ˋkwɑləˏfaɪ]

(v) 有資格

相似詞
certify (v) 證明

- I am qualified for this position.
  我有擔任此職位的資格。

12 qualification

[ˌkwɑləfəˋkeʃən]

(n) 資格證明

相似詞
certificate 證明

- A summary of qualifications is one of the many types of résumé introductions.
資格簡介是多種履歷開頭的其中一種。

延伸學習 a list of qualifications 一系列資格證明
teaching / medical / academic...qualifications
教師／醫療／教育……等專業資格證明

---

13 quality

[ˋkwɑlətɪ]

(n) 人格特質；品質

- What are some of the qualities that a good teacher should possess?
一位好老師應該要有什麼樣的特質？

- Our notebook is made of high-quality paper.
我們的筆記本是用高品質的紙張製作的。

---

14 quantity

[ˋkwɑntətɪ]

(n) 數量

相似詞
capacity (n)
容量；能力、
amount (n) 量

- Quality is more important than quantity.
質比量更重要。

延伸學習 It's quality, not quantity, that really counts.
是品質，不是數量，才是真正重要的。
用法有兩種：
1. a...quantity of
a large / small quantity of... food / water / information
大量／少量的……食物／水／資訊

2. quantities of...
quantities of food / water/ pumpkins
大量的食物／水／南瓜

▶ 是非題

_____ 1. The human resource department is responsible for recruitment.

_____ 2. Natural resources are limited.

_____ 3. A student can ask for a teacher's assistance.

_____ 4. A secretary can also be an assistant.

_____ 5. You can always find information about compensation in the job description.

_____ 6. Only presidents can be candidates.

_____ 7. A nominee is likely to win an award.

_____ 8. You need a qualification or a certification to be a good mom.

_____ 9. Another word for quantity is amount.

▶ 填空題

1. Over two thousand _____ are competing for this position.

2. If you have any questions regarding the product, please contact our customer service department for _____.

3. The young actor was _____ for the Academy Award.

4. The _____ journalist knows who to approach in order to get the information she needs.

5. The CEO is not available right now, but her _____ will take a message and notify her later.

6. The _____ in the textbook clearly explains the meaning of the vocabulary.

7. Our company values the _____ of our products and always inspect them carefully before shipping them to customers.

8. The _____ requires all employees to attend the training program.

9. The factory manufactures a large _____ of garments every year.

10. The procedure requires your birth _____ and financial proof.

Answer

是非題：

1. O　　2. O　　3. O　　4. O　　5. O　　6. X　　7. O　　8. X　　9. O

填空題：

1. candidates　　2. assistance　　3. nominated　　4. resourceful　　5. secretary

6. description　　7. quality　　8. human resources manager　　9. quantity

10. certificate

填空題翻譯：

1. 超過兩百名候選人欲競爭此職位。

2. 若您對於產品有任何疑問，請向客服部門尋求協助。

3. 這位年輕的演員被奧斯卡提名。

4. 這位機智的新聞記者知道該透過誰才能取得她所需要的資訊。

5. 執行長目前沒空，但她的祕書可以幫您留言並晚點通知她。

6. 課本中的敘述清楚地解釋此單字的意思。

7. 我們公司重視產品的質量，出貨前也都會仔細地檢驗。

8. 人資經理要求所有員工都要參加訓練。

9. 此工廠每年皆製造大量的成衣。

10. 這項程序會需要您的出生與財力證明。

履歴準備
Résumé

Track
008

motive	motivate	motivation
expert	expertise	specialty
specialize	relevant	characteristics
organize	arrange	financial
scholarship	recommendation	recommend

01 motive

[`motɪv]

(n) 動機

- What is your motive?
  你的動機是什麼？

- A weasel giving New Year's greetings to a hen has ulterior motives.
  黃鼠狼給雞拜年沒安好心。

02 motivate

[`motə,vet]

(v) 使……有動力

相似詞
drive (v) 使……有動力

- What motivates you?
  什麼使你有動力？

03 motivation

[,motə`veʃən]

(n) 動力

- I believe that this will not only improve efficiency but will indeed provide better motivation to those who work in the department.
  我相信這不只會增加部門員工的效率也會讓他們更有動力。

- A high level of motivation makes workers efficient and productive.
  很高的動力會使員工更有效率及生產力。

04 expert

[`ɛkspɚt]

(n) 專家

- An expert is a person with a high level of knowledge in a certain field.
  專家是在某方面擁有高度知識的人。

05 expertise

[,ɛkspɚ`tiz]

(n) 專業

- What is your expertise?
  你的專業／專長是什麼？

- I'm afraid that consulting is really not my area of expertise.
  恐怕我真的不擅長幫別人諮詢。

06 specialty

[`spɛʃəltɪ]

(n) 專業；特色；特產

- What's your specialty?
  你們的專長是什麼？

- Stinky Tofu is a local specialty.
  臭豆腐是當地的特別菜色。

07 specialize

[ˋspɛʃəˌlaɪz]

(v) 專精

用法
specialize + in
補充
specialist (n) 專家

- What do you specialize in?
  你的專長是什麼？

- I specialize in English teaching / mechanical engineering.
  我專精於英語教學／機械工程。

08 relevant

[ˋrɛləvənt]

(adj) 相關的

相似詞
related (adj) 相關的
相反詞
irrelevant (adj) 不相關的
unrelated (adj) 無關的

- Do you have any relevant experience?
  你有相關經驗嗎？

- How is this relevant to our case?
  這個和我們的案子有關連嗎？

延伸學習 relevant job experience 相關工作經驗

09 characteristic

[ˌkærəktəˋrɪstɪk]

(n) 特質；特色

相似詞
quality (n) 特質、
trait (n) 特性、
personality (n) 個性

- What are the characteristics of the main characters?
  主角們的人格特質是什麼？

10 organize

[ˋɔrgəˌnaɪz]

(v) 整理；籌備；安排

- You should organize your desk properly.
  你應該好好整理桌子。

- How do I organize my résumé sections?
  要如何安排我的簡歷欄位？

延伸學習 a well-organized person 一個有條理的人
organize a fundraising event / party
籌備募款活動、派對

11 arrange

[əˋrendʒ]
(v) 安排

- The executive's assistant arranges meetings for her.
  那位執行長的助理會幫她安排會議。

- My books are arranged in alphabetical order.
  = are arranged alphabetically.
  我的書依照字母順序排列。

  延伸學習 an arranged marriage 安排好的婚姻

12 financial

[faɪˋnænʃəl]
(adj) 財務的

- The Financial Statement is required for international undergraduate applicants who live outside the U.S.
  國際大學生需要提供財務證明。

- The city's annual financial statement has been presented for public review.
  這座城市的財務報告已提供給大眾檢視。

  延伸學習 financial statement 財務證明、財務報告

13 scholarship

[ˋskɑləˌʃɪp]
(n) 獎學金

- Financial aid may include scholarship funds and student employment.
  財務資助方式可能包含獎學金以及工讀。

  延伸學習 apply for scholarship / win a scholarship
  申請獎學金／贏得獎學金

14 recommendation

[ˌrɛkəmɛnˋdeʃən]
(n) 推薦

相似詞
suggestion (n) 建議、
advice (n) 建議

- Any recommendations?
  有推薦的嗎？

  延伸學習 recommendation letters 推薦信

15 recommend

[ˌrɛkəˋmɛnd]
(v) 推薦

相似詞
suggest (v) 建議、
advise (v) 建議

- Cindy was recommended for a job as a teacher.
  有人推薦老師的工作給 Cindy。

- Beef noodles are highly recommended.
  = I highly recommend that you try beef noodles.
  我強烈推薦牛肉麵。

  延伸學習 highly recommended 強烈推薦

測驗

▶ 是非題

_____ 1. To motivate someone means to stop someone from doing something.

_____ 2. An expert usually specializes in a particular area and has high-level knowledge of it.

_____ 3. A specialist is someone who has lots of experiences and expertise in a particular area.

_____ 4. If two subjects are relevant, they are related to each other.

_____ 5. A characteristic is a noticeable feature of a person or a thing.

_____ 6. You can organize your thoughts.

_____ 7. You can arrange a phone call, so you can also organize a phone call.

_____ 8. A financial statement shows the cash flow, profit, and loss in a company.

_____ 9. You can apply for a scholarship.

_____ 10. You can recommend a restaurant if the food there is tasty.

▶ 填空題

1. Since studying abroad costs a large amount of money, he decides to apply for a _____.

2. We need _____ and persistence to achieve our goals.

3. I got the job on my former supervisor's _____.

4. He's a marketing _____ and is capable of understanding the preference of customers.

5. My colleague will help to _____ shipment when the goods are ready.

6. Humility is a valuable _____.

7. Shareholders usually refer to a company's _____ to decide whether to make more investments or not.

8. The company _____ in financial management and helps to analyze the investment risk of its clients.

9. In order to have an efficient meeting, please only discuss details that are
_____ to the topic.

10. I need to _____ the files on my desk.

Answer

是非題：

1. X   2. O   3. O   4. O   5. O   6. O   7. X   8. O   9. O   10. O

填空題：

1. scholarship   2. motivation   3. recommendation   4. expert   5. arrange

6. characteristic   7. financial statement   8. specializes   9. relevant

10. organize

填空題翻譯：

1. 因為出國唸書的費用較高，他打算申請獎學金。

2. 我們需要動力並且堅持不懈才能達成目標。

3. 我因為前主管的推薦而得到工作。

4. 他是個行銷專家，能夠了解客戶的喜好。

5. 我的同事會在貨物準備好時協助安排出貨。

6. 謙虛是一項珍貴的特質。

7. 股東們通常會根據一間公司的財務狀況決定是否增加投資。

8. 這間公司專攻財務管理並協助分析客戶的投資風險。

9. 為了提升會議效率，請討論與主題相關的細節即可。

10. 我需要整理書桌上的文件。

Track
009

efficient	efficiency	effective
effect	valid	validate
validation	productive	productivity
competent	competence	responsible
responsibility	accountable	liability
achieve	accomplish	fulfill

01 efficient

[ɪˈfɪʃənt]

(adj) 有效率的

- An efficient worker is more likely to get a raise.
  有效率的員工更有可能被加薪。

02 efficiency

[ɪˈfɪʃənsɪ]

(n) 效率

- She works with efficiency.
  她工作很有效率。

03 effective

[ɪˈfɛktɪv]

(adj) 有效的

- We've proved that this is an effective approach.
  我們證明了這是個有效的方法。

  延伸學習 an effective method, way (to do something), strategy
  有效的方法／策略
  effective date（有效期限）→ expiration date
  effective treatment 有效的治療方式

04 effect

[ɪˈfɛkt]

(n) 效果

- The order takes effect immediately.
  此命令立即生效。

- The sound and visual effects blew me away!
  這音效和視覺效果令我驚豔！

補充說明

effect (n) 效果 vs affect (v) 影響
注意！大部分的時候 effect 是名詞，affect 是動詞！（只有極少數的情況會相反，而考試通常不會出。）只要記得 sound effects 叫做音效，是名詞，那麼 affect 就是動詞囉！

05 valid

[ˈvælɪd]

(adj) 有效的；正當的

相似詞
legal (adj) 合法的、
logical (adj) 合理的

- I have a valid reason for this.
  我有一個合理的原因。

  延伸學習 a valid parking permit / reason / email address
  有效的停車證／原因／郵件地址

06 validate

[`væləˌdet]

(v) 使……有效；認可

- Do you validate parking?
  你們可以免費停車嗎？

- Many antibody kits are not validated.
  許多抗體試劑還未經認可。

07 validation

[ˌvæləˈdeʃən]

(n) 認同

- In Selena Gomez's speech, she says that she doesn't seek nor need validation anymore.
  在 Selena Gomez 的演講中，她說她已經不需再尋求也不再需要別人的認同。

08 productive

[prəˈdʌktɪv]

(adj) 多產的

- I'm more productive in the morning.
  我在早上的生產力比較高（工作效率較高）。
- = I'm a morning person.
  （我適合早上工作。）

09 productivity

[ˌprodʌkˈtɪvətɪ]

(n) 生產力

- Research shows that great office amenities help boost productivity in the workplace.
  研究顯示好的辦公室設施能夠增加員工的生產力。

- As employees spend most of their time at the workplace, a good culture is crucial to team productivity and a company's success.
  因為員工花大部分的時間在公司，一個好的文化對團隊的生產力和公司的成功很重要。

10 competent

[`kɑmpətənt]

(adj) 有能力的

相似詞
capable of doing sth
有能力做某事

相反詞
incompetent (adj)
沒能力的

- We need competent managers to assist us in reaching these objectives both efficiently and effectively.
  我需要有能力的經理幫助我們有效率且有效地達成這些目標。

11 competence

[ˈkɑmpətəns]

(n) 能力

相反詞
incompetence (n) 無能

- His competence as an engineer is unquestionable; however, can he be a leader?
他當工程師的能力無庸置疑，然而，他可以當一位領導者嗎？

- I'm not interested in the details of your incompetence.
我對你有多無能的細節沒興趣。

12 responsible

[rɪˈspɑnsəbl]

(adj) 負責的

相反詞
irresponsible (adj)
不負責任的

- We all know that she is a responsible employee.
我們都知道她是一位有責任感的員工。

延伸學習 a responsible worker / student / parent
負責的員工／學生／家長
be responsible for... 對……有責任

13 responsibility

[rɪˌspɑnsəˈbɪlətɪ]

(n) 責任

相似詞
duty (n) 責任、
obligation (n)
責任；義務

- It's our responsibility to protect the Earth / our planet together.
保護地球是我們共同的責任。

14 accountable

[əˈkɑuntəbl]

(adj) 負責的

- Teachers would be held accountable for students' safety.
老師需要對學生的安全負責。

- The government is accountable to taxpayers.
政府對納稅人有責任。

- The government is accountable for the taxes it spent.
政府對稅務開銷有責任。

延伸學習 be held accountable for... 對……負責

補充說明

responsible：任何責任均適用

accountable：多指跟工作相關的責任

liable：多指會牽涉到法律的責任

15 liability

[ˌlaɪə`bɪlətɪ]

(n) 法律責任；累贅

- Don't let your weakness become your liability.
  不要讓你的弱點成為你的累贅。

16 achieve

[ə`tʃiv]

(v) 達成

相似詞
reach (v) 達到、
fulfill (v) 完成、
obtain (v) 達成、
achievement (n) 成就

- The responsible secretary always achieves her goals.
  那位負責的祕書總是能達成目標。

17 accomplish

[ə`kɑmplɪʃ]

(v) 完成

相關詞
accomplishment (n)
成就

- It's a relief to accomplish the task on time!
  幸好可以在時間內完成任務！

18 fulfill

[fʊl`fɪl]

(v) 實現

相關詞
fulfilling (adj) 充實的

- One of my dreams was fulfilled when I visited Universal Studios last year.
  我其中一個夢想在我去年去環球影城的時候達成了。

延伸學習 to fulfill one's dream / promise / obligation
實現夢想／約定／義務

 測驗

▶ 是非題

_____ 1. If you're an efficient person, you use your time well and produce good results.

_____ 2. If something is effective, it gives you the results you expect.

_____ 3. If something is valid, it can be accepted legally.

_____ 4. Fruitful is a synonym for productive.

_____ 5. To be competent means to be able to handle something well.

_____ 6. To take responsibility means to take over all of the tasks and handle them on your own

_____ 7. In a company, the CEO is usually accountable to the board of directors.

_____ 8. You can effortlessly achieve your goal if you manage your time poorly.

_____ 9. To accomplish means to successfully complete a task or a goal.

_____ 10. Eating too much can make you feel fulfilling.

▶ 填空

1. The new law will be _____ next year.

2. Employees need to prepare ahead in order to have a _____ meeting.

3. Sandy is very _____ and always completes tasks in a timely manner.

4. As the direct contact person of this project, I will be held _____ if any thing goes wrong.

5. The company's sales revenue has increased by 10% this month, and the employees decide to celebrate the _____ .

6. He's _____ at his job and has earned respect from his team members.

7. After working in the new company for two months, Judy realized that the job didn't _____ her expectations.

8. George has spent ten years establishing his own company and finally _____ his dream.

9. The department is _____ for shipping the products on time.

10. This coupon is no longer _____ and cannot be accepted.

是非題：

1. ○　　2. ○　　3. ○　　4. ○　　5. ○　　6. X　　7. ○　　8. X　　9. ○

10. X（應為 full）

填空題：

1. effective	2. productive	3. efficient	4. accountable	5. accomplishment
6. competent	7. fulfill	8. achieved	9. responsible	10. valid

填空題翻譯：

1. 新法令將於明年生效。

2. 員工需事先準備才能開一個有成效的會議。

3. Sandy 非常有效率，他能夠妥善安排時間並完成許多任務。

4. 身為此計劃的聯絡窗口，若發生任何問題將由我負責。

5. 公司本月的銷售總額提升了 10%，員工打算慶祝這項成就。

6. 他能夠勝任這份工作並且得到同事們的尊敬。

7. 在新公司任職兩個月後，Judy 發現這份工作並未達到自己的期待。

8. George 花了十年成立自己的公司，最終達成了夢想。

9. 此部門負責將產品準時出貨。

10. 這張優惠券已經無效且無法使用。

Unit 10

面試預約
Appointment

Track 010

complete	completion	attach
attached	refer	referral
revise	revision	express
expect	reply	response
feedback	receive	advertise
advertisement	commercial	appointment

01 complete

[kəm`plit]

(v) 完成

- You complete me.
  你使我完整。

- We've completed the project with efficiency.
  我們很有效率地完成了報告。

02 completion

[kəm`pliʃən]

(n) 完成

- Let's celebrate the completion of the task!
  我們來慶祝任務完工！

03 attach

[ə`tætʃ]

(v) 連接、附著

相似詞
connect (v) 連結
相反詞
detach (v) 拆除

- Please refer to the attached file.
  請見附檔。

- The attached file is my résumé.
  附件是我的簡歷。

- The hood is easy to attach and detach.
  （外套）帽子可以輕易接上或是拆下。

- The coupon will not be effective if detached from the slip.
  如果從紙條上撕下來這張折價券就會無效。

04 attached

[ə`tætʃt]

(adj) 喜歡；依戀

相反詞
detached (adj) 不在乎

- The child is very attached to her mother.
  這孩子非常依賴她母親。

- When he heard the bad news, he somehow managed to look detached and emotionless.
  當他聽到壞消息，他不知為何能夠表現得不在乎且毫無情緒。

05 refer

[rɪ`fɝ]

(v) 參考；稱為

相關詞
reference (n) 參考
用法
refer + to

- For questions 6 to 9, please <u>refer to</u> the following paragraph.
  關於第 6 到第 9 題請參閱以下段落。

- She always <u>refers to</u> her husband as her "prince charming."
  她總是把她老公稱為她的「白馬王子」。

06 referral

[rɪˋfɝəl]

(n) 轉介

- The teacher gave me a referral to the consultant.
  老師將我轉介給諮商師。

  延伸學習 a referral code 推薦碼

07 revise

[rɪˋvaɪz]

(v) 修改

- Make sure to revise your essay before you submit it.
  在交作文之前請先確定已經修改過了。

08 revision

[rɪˋvɪʒən]

(n) 修改

- Here is the revision of my essay.
  這是修改過後的作文。

09 express

[ɪkˋsprɛs]

(v) 表達

(n) 快遞

- He doesn't know how to express anger properly.
  他不知道如何適當地表達自己的怒氣。

  = He is poor at controlling his anger.
  他不會控制怒氣。

- He has difficulty expressing himself.
  他不太會表達自己。

  延伸學習 to express gratitude 表達感謝
  to express oneself: You can express yourself freely.
  你可以自由表達自己（想說什麼都可以）。
  express delivery (panda express) 快遞（熊貓快餐）

10 expect

[ɪkˋspɛkt]

(v) 預計；期望

相關詞
expectation (n) 期待

- I expect you to hand in the report by Friday.
  我希望你在星期五前交出報告。

- What do you expect?
  你期望什麼？

expect 跟 look forward to 雖然都翻譯成「期待」，但意思不同。

expect 是「預期」，例如父母的期待：I find it very hard to reach my parents' expectations. 我覺得要達成父母的期待很困難；或是 I expect you to become a doctor. 我期望你成為醫生。

而 look forward to 是「期待做某事」，例如：I look forward to seeing you. 期待見到你。

---

11 reply
[rɪ`plaɪ]
(v) 回覆

- I haven't received your reply.
  我還沒收到你的回覆。

---

12 response
[rɪ`spɑns]
(n) 回應

- I haven't heard any response. Please respond asap.
  我還沒收到任何回應。請盡快回應。

---

13 feedback
[`fid͵bæk]
(n) 回饋

- Thank you for your feedback.
  謝謝你的回饋。

---

14 receive
[rɪ`siv]
(v) 收

- Responsible parents make sure that their children receive an effective education.
  有責任感的父母會確保他們的小孩接受有效的教育。

- I received the acceptance letter this morning.
  我今天早上收到了入學許可通知書／公司聘用通知書。

  延伸學習 receive a package/ a letter / a phone call / education
  收到包裹、信件、電話、受教育

---

15 advertise
[`ædvɚ͵taɪz]
(v) 打廣告

- How are you planning to advertise the new product?
  你要怎麼宣傳新的商品？

16 advertisement

[ˌædvɚˋtaɪzmənt]

(n) 廣告

- I saw your advertisement (ad).
  我有看到你的廣告。

- The advertisement of the makeup product is very appealing.
  那化妝品的廣告非常吸引人。

17 commercial

[kəˋmɚʃəl]

(n) 電視廣告

(adj) 商業的

相關詞
commerce (n) 商業

- The product is a commercial success.
  這商品是個商業成功案例。

- This is a commercial company; not a charity.
  這是一間營利企業，不是慈善公司。

- We designed the dress from a commercial perspective.
  我們從商業的角度來設計這件洋裝。

延伸學習 TV commercial / a commercial break 電視廣告

18 appointment

[əˋpɔɪntmənt]

(n)（正式的）約會；
預約

相關詞
reservation (n) 預約、
date (n) 約會

- The assistant is responsible for scheduling appointments for the boss.
  助理負責幫老闆安排約會（會議）。

延伸學習 make an appointment with a dentist / doctor / manager
跟牙醫、醫生、經理 預約
cancel / miss an appointment 取消、錯過約會

 測驗

▶ 是非題

_____ 1. The completion of a project is usually the start of it.

_____ 2. You can attach a document in your email.

_____ 3. To make a reference to something means to mention it.

_____ 4. You can revise a paragraph in order to make it easier to read.

_____ 5. To express is to show an opinion or feeling.

_____ 6. To expect means to believe something may happen.

_____ 7. You can reply to someone without giving him / her a concrete answer.

_____ 8. To receive means to give.

_____ 9. To advertise something is to make something more well-known.

_____ 10. The purpose of a commercial enterprise is to make money.

▶ 填空

1. I need to _____ this urgent task by the end of the week.

2. We will _____ the proposal and submit it to our manager for approval tomorrow.

3. They _____ satisfaction by yelling "hurrah" !

4. I have _____ the shipping documents in this email for your reference.

5. The package was sent yesterday. Please let me know when you _____ it.

6. Jason gave Steve a _____ to a physician who has more expertise in the symptoms he described.

7. The Internet has made it easier for people to _____ what they want to sell as well as promote their ideas.

8. This company sells popular products and has reached _____ success.

9. Please remember to _____ the customer's email since she's still waiting for your response.

10. It's good to have _____, but you still have to be realistic.

(Answer)

是非題：

1. X　　2. O　　3. O　　4. O　　5. O　　6. O　　7. O　　8. X　　9. O　　10. O

填空題：

1. complete　　2. revise　　3. expressed　　4. attached　　5. receive

6. referral　　7. advertise　　8. commercial　　9. reply　　10. expectation(s)

填空題翻譯：

1. 我必須在本週末前完成這項緊急任務。

2. 我們會修正提案並於明天提交給經理審核。

3. 他們大喊「萬歲」來表達滿足。

4. 我已經將出貨文件都夾帶在本信中給您參考。

5. 包裹已於昨天寄出，收到時請通知我。

6. Jason 轉介了一位更了解 Steve 症狀的醫生給他。

7. 網路使人們能夠更容易宣傳他們想賣的產品以及想提倡的點子。

8. 這間公司賣許多熱門的產品，在商業領域非常成功。

9. 請記得回覆客人的信件，她還在等你的回應。

10. 抱有期待固然好，但也要現實一點。

Unit 11

工作面試一
Job Interview 1

Track
011

accept	acceptable	obtain
gain	acquire	attain
secure	security	position
rehearse	communicate	communication
connection	confirm	confirmation
conform	interview	

01 accept

[ək`sɛpt]

(v) 答應；接受

- Congratulations! You are accepted!
  恭喜！你錄取了！

  = You made a request and we said yes! You are in!
  你提出請求而我們答應了！你進了！

- I accept you for who you are.
  我接受你做你自己。

02 acceptable

[ə`sɛptəbl]

(adj) 可接受的

相反詞
reject 拒絕、
unacceptable 無法接受

- The plan is not perfect but acceptable.
  這計畫不完美但尚可接受。

- Your hurtful words are unacceptable.
  你傷人的話語令人無法接受。

補充說明

字尾 able：

able 本身是「能夠」的意思，他也是許多單字的字尾

depend (v) 依靠 + able → 能夠依靠的

wash (v) 洗 + able → 能夠洗的

03 obtain

[əb`ten]

(v) 得到

- I worked hard to obtain my diploma.
  我努力獲得我的學位證書。

  延伸學習 obtain / gain / acquire knowledge 獲得知識
  obtain information / funding 得到資訊／資金

04 gain

[gen]

(v) 得到

相似詞 get 得到

- I've gained valuable experience by working in relevant industries.
  在相關產業工作讓我獲得有價值的經驗。

- I've gained weight in the past few months.
  在過去幾個月我增重了。

05 acquire

[ə`kwaɪr]

(v) 獲得

- After continuous practice, I've eventually acquired juggling skills.

  在持續練習之後，我終於習得花式踢球技巧。

  延伸學習 acquire a skill / experience / a certificate

  獲得技能、經驗、證書

06 attain

[ə`ten]

(v) 獲得；實現

- After years of hard work, he has finally attained a degree.

  在努力多年之後他終於獲得學位

  延伸學習 attain / reach one's goal 實現、達成目標

07 secure

[sɪ`kjʊr]

(v) 獲得；使安全

(adj) 安全的

- He will do anything to secure the position.

  他為了得到這個職位會不顧一切。

08 security

[sɪ`kjʊrətɪ]

(n) 安全

- Considering recent incidents, I think we should hire a security guard.

  考慮到最近的事件，我覺得我們應該聘一位保全。

- Have you checked the security (camera) footage?

  你檢查過監視錄影畫面了嗎？

09 position

[pə`zɪʃən]

(n) 職位；位置

- I'm writing to apply for the teaching position which was advertised on Facebook.

  來信申請在臉書上廣告的教職工作。

- You put me in a difficult / awkward position.

  你讓我的處境很困難／尷尬。

10 rehearse

[rɪ`hɝs]

(v) 排演

You had better rehearse for a job interview before you go to one.

你最好在工作面試前先演練過。

- To give yourself a leg up on your job search competition, you should rehearse your job interviews.

  為了在找工作中更勝一籌，你最好在面試之前先演練過。

11 communicate

[kə`mjunəˌket]

(v) 溝通

- I find it difficult to communicate with him in English.
  我發覺和他很難用英文溝通。

12 communication

[kəˌmjunə`keʃən]

(n) 溝通

- I wanted to improve my communication skills, so I read a book called Crucial Communications.
  我想增進我的溝通技巧，所以我讀了一本叫做 Crucial Communications 的書。

13 connection

[kə`nɛkʃən]

(n) 聯繫；關係

相關詞
connect (v) 聯絡；連接

- I have a few connections.
  我有幾個人脈。

- I can feel a connection between us.
  我感覺我們來電了。

14 confirm

[kən`fɝm]

(v) 確認

- They confirmed that they have tested positive.
  他們確診了。

- The government claims that the country has only four confirmed cases of the disease and one death.
  政府宣稱國內只有 4 起確診及 1 死亡案例。

15 confirmation

[ˌkɑnfə`meʃən]

(n) 確認

- We are waiting for your confirmation.
  我們在等你確認。

16 conform

[kən`fɔrm]

(v) 順從

- Students are expected to conform to school rules.
  我們期待學生遵守校規。

  延伸學習 con 一起 + firm 確定 → 確認
  con 一起 + form 形式 → 一樣的形式 → 順從

17 interview

[`ɪntɚˌvju]

(n) 面試

- There were more than three hundred applicants, but we only interviewed twenty of them.
  有超過三百位申請者，但我們只有面試二十位。

  延伸學習 have an interview for a job 有個工作面試

▶ 是非題

_____ 1. If you are accepted by a school, you are able to study there.

_____ 2. When you gain weight, you become lighter.

_____ 3. To acquire can also mean to buy.

_____ 4. To feel secure means to feel safe.

_____ 5. You can apply for a position.

_____ 6. To rehearse means to practice and prepare before a performance.

_____ 7. Communication is usually one-sided.

_____ 8. You can draw a line to connect two dots.

_____ 9. You can conform to your client's request, and also confirm to someone's request.

_____ 10. A hiring manager can interview candidates to see if they qualify for a position.

▶ 填空題

1. Our team _____ the goal of increasing the sales revenue by 15% last month.

2. She worked her way up and finally attained a high-level _____.

3. It is essential for a team to have good _____ so that work can be done efficiently.

4. People working in the same fields often _____ with each other.

5. Sara needs to _____ more information in order to complete her article.

6. The working environment is stressful because the CEO requires every employee to _____ to a set of rules.

7. It is best to _____ several times before you deliver a presentation to the vice president so that you don't forget the details.

8. The annual review shows that the performance of our department is
_____, but not excellent enough.

9. The reporter is very excited because she is going to _____ a famous
actor.

10. We installed another lock on the door to make sure it is _____.

Answer

是非題：

1. O   2. X   3. O   4. O   5. O   6. O   7. X   8. O   9. X   10. O

填空題：

1. attained   2. position   3. communication   4. connect   5. obtain

6. conform   7. rehearse   8. acceptable   9. interview   10. secure

填空題翻譯：

1. 我們團隊上個月達到了增加 15% 的銷售額這個目標。

2. 她努力往上並且終於得到高階職位。

3. 良好溝通對團隊很重要，如此工作才能有效率地完成。

4. 在同領域工作的人常常互相聯繫。

5. 為了寫完她的文章，Sara 需要取得更多資訊。

6. 這個工作環境很有壓力，因為 CEO 要求每個人都要遵守一套規則。

7. 在妳給副總簡報之前最好先預演才不會忘記細節。

8. 年度審核顯示我們部門的表現還可以接受但是還不夠好。

9. 這位記者很興奮因為她即將要訪問一位有名的演員。

10. 我們在門上面安裝了另一道鎖以確保安全。

工作面試二
Job Interview 2

Track
012

strength	weakness	introduce
supervise	supervisor	supervision
superior	capable	capability
income	compensation	pension
benefits	beneficial	bonus
admission	admit	

01 strength

[strɛŋθ]

(n) 強項；力量

- What are your strengths and weaknesses?
  你的優點（強）和缺點（弱）是什麼？

02 weakness

[`wiknɪs]

(n) 弱點

- What is your greatest weakness?
  你最大的缺點是什麼？

- The key to preparing for this question is to identify weaknesses that still communicate strength.
  回答這個問題的關鍵是找出一個可以顯現優點的缺點。

03 introduce

[ˌɪntrə`djus]

(v) 介紹

相關詞
introduction (n) 介紹

- Let me introduce you to Cindy.
  讓我介紹 Cindy 給你認識。

- Please briefly introduce yourself.
  請簡短介紹自己。

04 supervise

[`supɚˌvaɪz]

(v) 監督

- A leader should know how to manage, supervise, and motivate his / her subordinates.
  領導人應該知道如何管理、監督以及鼓勵下屬。

05 supervisor

[ˌsupɚ`vaɪzɚ]

(n) 監督者；管理者

相似詞
guardian 監護人、
superior 上級
相反詞
subordinate 下屬

- You should report directly to your supervisor.
  你應該直接向你的管理者報告。

06 supervision

[ˌsupɚ`vɪʒən]

(n) 監督

- This team is under my supervision.
  這個團隊由我監督。

07 superior

[sə`pɪrɪə]

(n) (adj) 上級；優越

- Don't act as if you're my superior!
  不要表現得好像你是我的上級！

- Dark chocolate is superior to white chocolate.
  黑巧克力優於白巧克力

08 capable

[`kepəbl]

(adj) 有能力的

用法
capable + of

- I am capable of doing the job.
  我有能力做這份工作。

- You don't know what he is capable of (doing)!
  妳不知道他能夠做出什麼事！（通常是恐懼的狀態下說出這句話）

09 capability

[ˌkepə`bɪlətɪ]

(n) 能力

- He showed us that he has the capability to attain goals efficiently.
  他向我們展現了他有能力有效率地達成目標。

10 income

[`ɪnˌkʌm]

(n) 收入

相關詞
salary and wage 薪水、
hourly wage 時薪
相似詞
salary (n) 薪水、
wage (n) 薪資

- Don't forget to pay your income tax!
  別忘了繳所得稅！

延伸學習 monthly / annual income / gross income
月收入、年收入、總收入

11 compensation

[ˌkɑmpən`seʃən]

(n) 報酬

- Compensation is defined as the total amount of the monetary and non-monetary pay provided to an employee.
  報酬是指公司提供給員工金錢及非金錢的總額（包含分紅、股票等等）。

延伸學習 annual compensation 年度報酬

12 pension

[`pɛnʃən]

(n) 退休金

- We can receive our pensions when we retire.
  退休的時候可以得到退休金。

  (延伸學習) receive / get / draw / collect pension
  得到、提領退休金
  retirement / personal pension
  退休計畫、個人退休計畫

13 benefit

[`bɛnəfɪt]

(n) (v) 好處

(相似詞)
perk (n) 好處、
advantage (n) 好處

- (n)：What are the health benefits of bananas?
  香蕉對健康有什麼好處？

- (v)：Eating bananas benefits your health.
  吃香蕉對健康有好處。

  (延伸學習) be of benefit to... 有幫助……
  例：The new program will be of great benefit to our
  customers. 這個新活動對我們的顧客有幫助。

  employee benefits 員工福利
  例：Benefits are any perks offered to employees in
  addition to salary. 福利即是薪資之外提供的補貼。

14 beneficial

[ˌbɛnəˋfɪʃəl]

(adj) 有利的

- Apples are beneficial to your health.
  蘋果對健康有好處。

15 bonus

[`bonəs]

(n) 分紅；獎金

- Would you prefer a higher base salary or an annual
  bonus?
  你比較喜歡高一點的底薪還是多一點分紅？

16 admission

[əd`mɪʃən]

(n) 許可；認可

- His action was a tacit admission of his incompetence.
  他的行為是其無能的默認。

  (延伸學習) apply for admission 申請許可
  a tacit admission 默認（沉默的承認）

17 admit

[əd`mɪt]

(v) 承認；允許進入

- It's not shameful to admit your mistakes.
  承認自己的錯誤並不可恥。

- Congratulations! You are admitted to the intensive training course!
  恭喜！妳已被許可參加密集課程！

 測驗

▶ 是非題

_____ 1. If you have a weakness for something, it is difficult for you to resist it.

_____ 2. You introduce yourself to let others know more about you.

_____ 3. Supervision means great eyesight.

_____ 4. A superior is a person who is older than you.

_____ 5. If you are capable of something, you have the ability or the potential to do something.

_____ 6. Income is the result of something you do.

_____ 7. You can claim compensation if someone damages your belongings.

_____ 8. A pension usually refers to the amount of money someone gets after retirement.

_____ 9. A bonus is an extra amount of money paid in addition to your salary.

_____ 10. Admission is another word for administration.

▶ 填空題

1. These products contain corrosive substances and need to be manufactured under strict _____ .

2. He shows no sign of _____ when facing difficulties.

3. Meg has strong leadership skills and is _____ of building a team.

4. The retired man receives his _____ every month.

5. Sherry is new to the company; please _____ her to your colleagues.

6. Those who perform well will receive a _____ by the end of the year.

7. Aside from his full time job, he also works part time on weekends to make extra _____.

8. Mother never _____ that she is wrong.

9. We need a QR code to gain _____ to the exhibition.

10. She treats me dinner as _____ for breaking my stuff accidentally.

(Answer)

是非題：

1. O   2. O   3. X   4. X   5. O   6. X   7. O   8. O   9. O   10. X

填空題：

1. supervision   2. weakness   3. capable   4. pension   5. introduce

6. bonus   7. income   8. admits   9. admission   10. compensation

填空題翻譯：

1. 那些產品含有腐蝕性物質，在製造的時候需要嚴格的監督。

2. 他在面對困難的時候沒有顯示任何的弱點。

3. Meg 有很強的領導能力而且也有能力組織團隊。

4. 那位退休的男人每個月會收到他的退休金。

5. Sherry 是新來的，請把她介紹給你的同事。

6. 表現好的人會在年底得到獎金。

7. 除了他的全職工作，他在週末還會兼差賺額外的薪水。

8. 媽媽從不承認她做錯了。

9. 我們需要掃條碼才能進入展覽。

10. 她請我吃晚餐當做不小心把我的東西弄壞的賠禮。

新工作
Getting a New Job

Track
013

orientation
reception
ambience
schedule

administration
brief
morale
agenda

clerical
boost
process

01 orientation

[ˌorɪɛnˈteʃən]

(n)

（新工作、新環境的）
培訓；介紹；傾向

- The Human Resource manager arranged a job orientation for new employees.
  人資經理安排了工作介紹（培訓）給新進員工。

- What should I prepare for the orientation?
  新進培訓我需要準備什麼？

延伸學習 a job / college / school orientation
工作、大學、學校的介紹
sexual / political orientation 性／政治取向

02 administration

[ədˌmɪnəˈstreʃən]

(n) 行政

相關詞
administrative (adj)
行政的

- You can go to the administration office for paperwork assistance.
  你可以去行政處尋求書面資料協助。

延伸學習 administration official 行政官員
business administration 企業管理

03 clerical

[ˈklɛrɪkl̩]

(adj) 文書的

- The assistant's superior clerical skills amazed the manager.
  那位助理傑出的文書處理技術驚豔了經理。

延伸學習 clerk → clerical work
店員／（處理文書的）職員 → 文書工作

04 reception

[rɪˈsɛpʃən]

(n) 接待

- They held a reception party to welcome the new employees.
  他們舉辦了接待派對來歡迎新進員工。

延伸學習 check in at the reception desk 在前臺報到

05 brief

[brif]

(adj) 簡短的

- I'll give you a brief introduction of the company.
  我簡短向妳介紹一下這間公司。

06 boost

[bust]
(v) 提升

- We hope that the refreshment can boost your energy.
  希望這些點心能提振你的精神。

- A positive work environment boosts employee productivity.
  正向的工作環境會提升員工的產能。

  延伸學習 boost the economy / the immune system / one's confidence 提振經濟、免疫系統、自信心

07 ambiance

[`æmbɪəns]
(n) 氣氛

相關詞
atmosphere (n) 氣氛

- I love the romantic ambience / atmosphere of the restaurant.
  我喜歡這間餐廳浪漫的氣氛。

- We believe that the ambience / atmosphere of a workplace influences worker productivity.
  我們相信工作環境的氣氛會影響員工的生產力。

08 morale

[mə`ræl]
(n) 士氣

- Due to the recent incident, morale is fairly low. Managers are looking for ways to boost morale.
  因為最近的事件士氣很低落。經理們在想辦法提升士氣。

- How's the morale?
  士氣如何？

  延伸學習 good / bad for morale, high / low morale
  對士氣有正向／負面影響，高／低士氣
  boost morale 提升士氣

09 process

[`prɑsɛs]
(n) (v)
程序；處理；加工

- You will learn during the process.
  妳在過程中會有所學習。

- What have you learned in the process?
  妳在過程中學到了什麼？

  延伸學習 processed food
  加工食品（經過加工的食品，使用被動態）

10 schedule

[`skɛdʒʊl]

(n) (v)

行程；安排行程

- I have a tight schedule.
  我的行程很滿。

- Let's schedule a meeting.
  我們來安排一個會議。

11 agenda

[ə`dʒɛndə]

(n) 議程

- There are several items on the agenda today.
  今天的議程有好幾個項目。

- Let's move on to discuss the next item on the agenda.
  我們來討論議程上的下一個項目。

 測驗

▶ 是非題

_____ 1. Orientation can refer to a person's preference for something.

_____ 2. Clerical is similar to clinical.

_____ 3. A reception desk is usually where guests are welcomed in a hotel.

_____ 4. You can write a brief essay by adding more long sentences.

_____ 5. To boost means to increase or to lift.

_____ 6. You can measure the pressure of the atmosphere as well as the ambience of surroundings.

_____ 7. A team tends to have better performance when its morale is high.

_____ 8. If something is being processed, it is going through a set of methods or rules.

_____ 9. If a project is ahead of schedule, it means its progress is going faster than expected.

_____ 10. An agenda is similar to an advertisement.

▶ 填空題

1. Mike prefers not to discuss his political _____.

2. Ever since the CEO announced that the company is going to downsize, the _____ in the office has become very tense.

3. The _____ is bad here; let me call you back in ten minutes.

4. Your application will take two weeks to _____.

5. Please send a _____ version of the report you presented yesterday to me.

6. We expect the task to be completed on _____.

7. Remember to go over the details on the _____ before attending the meeting.

8. Please contact the _____ department if you have any questions regarding your attendance record.

9. The manager tries to raise the team's _____ by encouraging his subordinates.

10. The revenue of the company _____ after the latest product was launched.

Answer

是非題：

1. O   2. X   3. O   4. X   5. O   6. X   7. O   8. O   9. O   10. X

填空題：

1. orientation   2. atmosphere   3. reception   4. process   5. brief

6. schedule   7. agenda   8. administrative   9. morale   10. boosted

填空題翻譯：

1. Mike 傾向於不討論他的政治取向。

2. 自從 CEO 宣布公司要縮編，辦公室氣氛就變得很緊張。

3. 這邊收訊不好，我 10 分鐘後再回電。

4. 我們需要兩週的時間處理你的申請作業。

5. 請把你昨天報告的簡短版本傳給我。

6. 我們期望任務能按時程完成。

7. 在參加會議前請先看過議程的細節。

8. 對於你的出席紀錄有任何問題請聯絡行政部門。

9. 經理試著藉由鼓勵下屬來提振團隊的士氣。

10. 公司的營業額在最新產品發布之後提升了。

Unit 14

公司環境一
Workplace 1

Track 014

supply	demand
facilities	printer
cafeteria	fitness
folder	staple
cabinet	stationery

01 supply

[sə`plaɪ]

(n) (v) 供應；供給品

- Employees are supplied with free folders.
  我們會提供員工免費資料夾。

  延伸學習 office supplies / food and medical supplies
  辦公室補給品／食品及醫療補給
  supply and demand 供給和需求

02 demand

[dɪ`mænd]

(n) (v) 要求；需求

相似詞
need (n)、
requirement (n) 需求

- We must do our best to fulfill customers' demands.
  我們盡力達成客戶的需求。

- The bossy executive demanded us to be on time.
  那愛指使人的執行長要求我們要準時。

03 facility

[fə`sɪlətɪ]

(n) 設施

相關詞
amenity (n) 便利設施

- I love the hotel facilities, including a swimming pool, sauna, gym, and so on.
  我喜歡這飯店的設施，包含游泳池、三溫暖、健身房等等。

04 printer

[`prɪntɚ]

(n) 印表機

- This new printer has several capabilities.
  新的印表機有很多功能。

- Please print the flyer with the new printer.
  請用新的印表機印傳單。

05 cafeteria

[ˌkæfə`tɪrɪə]

(n)（學校；員工）餐廳

- We had lunch at the cafeteria.
  我們在學校餐廳吃過飯了。

  延伸學習 college / university / company / employee cafeteria
  大學／公司／員工餐廳

06 fitness

[`fɪtnɪs]

(n) 健康

- Our office amenities include a fitness center.
  我們辦公室的設施包含健身房。

- Having a fitness center in the office helps employees stay energetic.
  公司有健身房會讓員工更有活力。

延伸學習 fitness center 健身中心

07 folder

[`foldɚ]

(n) 資料夾

相關詞
binder (n) 活頁夾

- You can find the file in a folder named "Teacher Cindy."
  妳可以在一個名為「Teacher Cindy」的資料夾中找到檔案。

- There are several binders on the desk.
  桌上有活頁夾。

08 staple

[`stepḷ]

(v) 裝訂

- After you print the documents out, staple them on the top left corner (with a stapler).
  把文件印出來之後，請（用釘書機）將他們從左上角裝訂起來。

09 cabinet

[kæbənɪt]

(n) 櫃子

- Please organize the folders in the file cabinet.
  請整理資料櫃中的檔案夾。

延伸學習 file cabinet 資料櫃

10 stationery

[`steʃənˌɛrɪ]

(n) [U] 文具

同音字
stationary (adj)
靜止的；不變的

- I got those highlighters from the stationery store around the corner.
  我在轉角的文具店買到這些螢光筆。

延伸學習 stationery store 文具店

 **測驗**

▶ **是非題**

_____ 1. To supply means to provide.

_____ 2. To demand means to ask for something.

_____ 3. The word amenities has exactly the same meaning as the word facilities.

_____ 4. An example of a hotel's facility is a swimming pool.

_____ 5. You can use a printer to copy a document.

_____ 6. A waiter will serve your food in a cafeteria.

_____ 7. A fitness center is similar to a gym.

_____ 8. You can categorize documents using a binder.

_____ 9. A stapler can fasten several pieces of paper together.

_____ 10. Stationery and stationary are interchangeable.

▶ **填空題**

1. During the pandemic, face masks are in great _____.

2. There's a _____ in the office building and most employees dine there during lunch time.

3. This hotel has a lot of _____, including a swimming pool and a golf course.

4. The _____ in the resort are quite old and shabby and the Internet connection is very poor.

5. I like to use _____ to categorize important documents.

6. This vendor _____ most of the materials of our products.

7. The company has its own _____ for employees to do exercises after work.

8. I ran out of _____, so instead I used paper clips to hold the files together.

9. I bought these paper and pens in the _____ store.

10. You can use the _____ in the office to scan documents.

Answer

是非題：

1. O   2. O   3. X   4. O   5. O   6. X   7. O   8. O   9. O   10. X

填空題：

1. demand   2. cafeteria   3. amenities/ facilities   4. facilities   5. folders

6. supplies   7. fitness center 8. staples   9. stationery   10. printer

填空題翻譯：

1. 在疫情期間，口罩的需求量大。

2. 公司有員工餐廳，大部分員工都在那邊吃午餐。

3. 這間飯店有很多設施，包含游泳池和高爾夫球場。

4. 這渡假村的設施滿破舊的，而且他的網路連不太上。

5. 我喜歡用資料夾分類重要檔案。

6. 這供應商提供我們產品大部分的材料。

7. 這公司有自己的健身中心給員工在下班後運動。

8. 我的訂書針用完了，所以我改用迴紋針把文件夾在一起。

9. 我在文具店買這些紙和筆。

10. 你可以用印表機掃描文件。

公司環境二
Workplace 2

Track
015

access	electronic
identify	identification(ID)
badge	recognize
install	software
heater	air conditioning
manual	manually

01 **access**

[ˋæksɛs]
(v) (n)
連接;通道;途徑

- How can I access the Internet?
  要如何連到網路?

- We don't have access to the Internet.
  我們不能連到網路。

- How can we access (enter) the bar?
  要如何進入那間酒吧?

- How do I gain access to the building?
  我要如何獲得進入大樓的權限/方式?

延伸學習 Internet access 互聯網

02 **electronic**

[ɪlɛkˋtrɑnɪk]
(adj) 電子的

- Be careful with electronic devices. They can be dangerous.
  使用電子設備要小心,他們很危險。

延伸學習 electronic devices: TV, mobile phones, laptops, desktops...
電子設備:電視、手機、筆電、桌上型電腦……
electrical engineering / engineer / current / system
電子工程/工程師/電流/電子系統
electric fan / mixer / car 電扇/電動攪拌器/電動車

03 **identify**

[aɪˋdɛntəˌfaɪ]
(v) 認出;識別;發現

- He is identified as a thief.
  他被發現是個小偷。

- Due to the way you dress, you will be identified as the homeless.
  因為你的穿著,你會被認為是遊民。

延伸學習 identify an item 認出/發現一個東西
identify oneself / someone as... 識別某人為……
identify someone with... 認同/產生共鳴

04 **identification (ID)**

[aɪˌdɛntəfəˋkeʃən]
(n) 識別

- Please present a valid form of identification.
  請提供有效的證件。

延伸學習 national identification card 身分證。

05 badge

[bædʒ]

(n) 徽章

- The undercover policeman showed the thieves his badge.
  便衣警察給小偷看了他的警徽。

延伸學習 a police badge 警徽
wear a badge / turn in a badge 戴徽章／交回徽章

06 recognize

[`rɛkəɡ͵naɪz]

(v) 認出；認同

相關詞
recognition (n) 認同

- I didn't recognize her because I haven't seen her for more than ten years.
  我沒認出她因為我已經超過十年沒看到她了。

- We recognize your hard work and we appreciate it.
  我們認同你的努力，而我們也很感謝。

07 install

[ɪn`stɔl]

(v) 安裝

相反詞
remove (n) 移除

- You don't need to install anything to play the game. You can play it on your browser.
  你不需要下載任何東西就能玩這款遊戲。你可以在瀏覽器上玩。

延伸學習 to install the new software system 安裝新的軟體系統
install an application 安裝程式

08 software

[`sɔft͵wɛr]

(n) 軟體

- It's time to renew the software system!
  更新軟體的時間到了！

- There seems to be a failure in the software system.
  軟體中好像有個地方無法運作。

延伸學習 software system 軟體系統

09 heater

[`hitɚ]

(n) 暖氣機

相關詞
heating (n) 暖氣

- It's freezing! Why don't you turn on the heater? Is the heating on?
  好冷喔！為什麼不開暖氣機？暖氣有開嗎？

延伸學習 heating system / facility 暖氣系統／設備

10 air conditioning (AC) [ɛr kən`dɪʃənɪŋ] (n) 冷氣	• It's hot and humid in here. Do you mind me turning on the air conditioning? 這裡又熱又悶。你介意我開冷氣嗎？
11 manual [`mænjʊəl] (n) 手冊	• Please read the manual carefully before using a product. 在使用任何一個產品之前請詳讀使用手冊。
12 manually [`mænjʊəlɪ] (adv) 手動的	• It won't move on its own. You'll have to do it manually. 它不會自己動。它是手動的。

 測驗

▶ 是非題

_____ 1. To have access to something means to have the right to use it.

_____ 2. Electronic devices include cell phones and laptops.

_____ 3. To identify means to ignore.

_____ 4. A badge is used to show others who you are.

_____ 5. A flower is easy to recognize among a bunch of leaves.

_____ 6. To install means to put something together in order to use it.

_____ 7. The computer screen is an example of a software system.

_____ 8. The function of a heater is similar to that of a fireplace.

_____ 9. Air conditioning helps to keep the air in a building cool.

_____ 10. You can find the best sightseeing spots in a tourist manual.

▶ 填空

1. We always hire people who are able to _____ problems and can think of ways to resolve them.

2. She gave me a key so I can gain _____ to the conference room.

3. Each competitor wears a _____ with a number on it.

4. The winter is so cold that I decided to buy a _____ to warm up the house.

5. The _____ in the office stops working and the temperature becomes extremely high.

6. The store sells all kinds of _____ such as televisions and printers.

7. He lost so much weight that it is difficult to _____ him now.

8. The bank clerk suggested me to _____ the application so that I can pay the bills online.

9. This machine is very old. You'll need to power it up _____.

10. The _____ of the computer will be upgraded.

Answer

是非題：

1. O　　2. O　　3. X　　4. O　　5. O　　6. O　　7. X　　8. O　　9. O　　10. O

填空題：

1. identify　　　2. access　　　3. badge　　　4. heater　　　5. air conditioning

6. electronic devices　　　7. recognize　　　8. install　　　9. manually

10. software system

填空題翻譯：

1. 我們錄用可以指出問題並且想辦法解決的人。

2. 她給我鑰匙好讓我進到會議室。

3. 每一個參賽者都戴著一個有數字的徽章。

4. 冬天好冷所以我決定買一個暖爐來溫暖房子。

5. 辦公室的冷氣壞掉使得溫度變得異常地高。

6. 這間店賣各種電器用品例如電視機還有影印機。

7. 他瘦了好多以至於我們現在很難認出他。

8. 銀行行員建議我安裝 APP 才能在線上繳帳單。

9. 這機器很舊了，它需要手動發電。

10. 電腦的軟體系統會被升級。

公司環境三
Workplace 3

equipment | defect
defective | repair
maintain | maintainance
malfunction | fail
failure | mechanic
bulletin | calculate
renew

01 equipment

[ɪˋkwɪpmənt]

(n) [U] 配備

- Computers and printers are essential office equipment.
  電腦和列印機（印表機）是辦公室必備的設備。

  延伸學習 electronic / electrical equipment 電子配備
  office / kitchen equipment 辦公室、廚房配備

02 defect

[dɪˋfɛkt]

(n) 缺點；瑕疵

用法
defect in sth
某部分有瑕疵

- However excellent, everyone has his / her defect.
  Nobody is perfect.
  不管多優秀，每個人都有自己的缺點。沒有人是完美的。

  延伸學習 birth / heart / mental / genetic defect
  出生／心臟／心理／基因缺陷

03 defective

[dɪˋfɛktɪv]

(adj) 有瑕疵的

- When you purchase a product on Amazon, if the item is damaged or defective, you can return your product through the Online Return Center during the return period (most items can be returned within 30 days of receipt of shipment.)
  當你在亞馬遜網站購買產品，如果商品有損傷或是缺陷，你可以在退貨時限內透過線上退貨中心退還（大部分商品可以在到貨後 30 天內退貨）。

04 repair

[rɪˋpɛr]

(v) 修理

- I found a defect in the item, and I'll have it repaired / replaced.
  我在這個東西上發現瑕疵，我會請人修理它／替換它。

05 maintain

[menˋten]

(v) 維持；維護

相似詞
remain (v)、retain (v)
sustain (v) 保持、維持

- It costs a lot to maintain a car.
  維護一臺車要花很多錢。

  延伸學習 maintain eye-contact / friendship / control / a healthy diet
  維持眼神交流／友誼／控制／健康飲食

06 maintenance

[`mentənəns]

(n) 維持、維護

- The old car needs a lot of maintenance.
  這臺舊車需要經常維修。

  延伸學習 high / low maintenance 很難／很好維護
  Monica is high maintenance.
  （口語：Monica 很難搞。）

07 malfunction

[mæl`fʌnʃən]

(n) (v) 壞掉

- There's a malfunction in the system.
  系統有一處壞掉。

- The system malfunctions sometimes.
  系統有時候會壞掉。

08 fail

[fel]

(v) 失敗

相反詞
succeed (v) 成功

- You'll definitely fail the exam if you don't study at all.
  如果妳完全不唸書一定會不及格。

- "If you don't try at anything, you can't fail... it takes backbone to lead the life you want." - Richard Yates
  「如果你不做任何嘗試，你就不會失敗。我們需要勇氣追尋自己想要的生活。」—理察・葉慈

  延伸學習 fail to V → I failed to pass the math test.
  無法做某事：我沒辦法通過數學考試。
  fail (in) N → I failed (in) math.
  做某事失敗了：我數學不及格。

09 failure

[`feljɚ]

(n) 失敗

相反詞
success (n) 成功

- Failure is the Mother of Success.
  失敗為成功之母。

10 mechanic

[mə`kænɪk]

(n) 技師

相似詞
technician (n) 技工

- A mechanic would probably know how to repair it.
  技師可能會知道該如何修理它。

11 bulletin [`bʊlətɪn] (n) 公告	• I will post <u>the notice / announcement</u> on the bulletin board. 我會把通知／告示張貼在布告欄。 延伸學習 bulletin board 公佈欄
12 calculate [`kælkjə͵let] (v) 計算 相關詞 **calculator (n)** 計算機	• You don't have to calculate by hand. Use a calculator to speed things up! 你不需要用手計算。用計算機來加快速度吧！
13 renew [rɪ`nju] (v) 更新 相似詞 **refresh (v)** 刷新（網頁）	• Your software system is outdated. You should renew it. 你的軟體系統過期了。你應該更新。 延伸學習 renew membership / software system 更新會員／軟體系統

 測驗

▶ 是非題

_____ 1. A piece of equipment is a machine used for a certain purpose.

_____ 2. A defect is similar to a flaw.

_____ 3. To repair means to retain.

_____ 4. To maintain means to continue to do something.

_____ 5. If a machine malfunctions, it does not work properly.

_____ 6. If you fail the exam, you receive a great score.

_____ 7. A technician has the skills to repair machines when there's a problem.

_____ 8. You can use a marker to write on a bulletin board.

_____ 9. To calculate means to judge or count to number of something.

_____ 10. You can refresh yourself by drinking a cup of coffee, so you can also renew yourself by doing the same thing.

▶ 填空題

1. The printer _____ and cannot work normally right now.

2. The theory is _____ and many researchers have found evidence to prove that it is wrong.

3. A projector is a necessary piece of _____ for presentations.

4. He _____ to enter the final round of the competition and was very disappointed.

5. I saw an advertisement on the _____, saying there's a new coffee shop around the block. Let's go there after class.

6. A pension is _____ based on a person's earnings and his/her length of service.

7. My computer is broken and my friend can help to _____ it.

8. I have to _____ my passport since it expired last month.

9. As an account manager, I strive to _____ a good partnership with my clients.

10. The skillful _____ can always assist me when I encounter computer problems.

Answer

是非題：

1. O   2. O   3. X   4. O   5. O   6. X   7. O   8. O   9. O   10. X

填空題：

1. malfunctions   2. defective   3. equipment   4. failed   5. bulletin board

6. calculated   7. repair   8. renew   9. maintain   10. technician / mechanic

填空題翻譯：

1. 影印機目前故障沒辦法正常運作。

2. 這個理論有缺陷，很多研究人員有證據可以證明它是錯的。

3. 投影機是報告的必備設備。

4. 他非常失望因為他沒能順利進到比賽的最後一關。

5. 我在公告欄上看到附近有新咖啡廳的廣告。下課後一起去吧。

6. 退休金是根據一個人的所得和年資來計算的。

7. 我的電腦壞了，我的朋友可以幫忙修理。

8. 我需要更新護照因為它上個月過期了。

9. 身為客戶經理，我努力維繫和客戶之間良好的合作關係。

10. 當我遇到電腦相關的問題，這位熟練的技師總是能幫我。

Unit 17

電話英文
On the Phone

Track
017

extension	transfer
message	wonder
signal	return
dial	verify
code	operator
receptionist	

01 extension

[ɪk`stɛnʃən]

(n) 分機

- My extension (number) is 243.
  我的分機是 243。

02 transfer

[træns`fɚ]

(n) (v) 轉接；轉學；
轉機

- Please hold. I'll transfer you.
  請稍後，我為您轉接。

  延伸學習 a transfer student: transfer into a new school
  轉學生：轉到新學校

  transfer a flight: Arriving at the hotel after a long flight and transfer, the participants immediately headed for the conference room.
  轉機：在長途飛行及轉乘，到達飯店後，參加者立刻前往會議室。

03 message

[mɛsɪdʒ]

(n) 訊息

- May I take a message?
  請問要留言嗎？

- He is not available now. Would you like to leave a message?
  他不在／他不方便接聽。請問要留言嗎？

  延伸學習 leave a message 留言

04 wonder

[`wʌndɚ]

(v) 想知道

- I wonder if I can sit next to you.
  請問我能坐你旁邊嗎？（禮貌說法）

  延伸學習 I'm wondering if... 我想知道……（禮貌說法）

05 signal

[`sɪgn!]

(n) 訊號

相關詞
bad reception 訊號不良

- There is no signal here! The reception is poor.
  這裡沒有訊號！這邊收訊不好。

06 return

[rɪ`tɝn]

(v) 回答；回報

- The manager left a message. You might want to return the call soon.
  經理有留言。你可能要盡快回電。

  延伸學習 return a book / a favor 還書／還人情
  return a phone call 回電

07 dial

[`daɪəl]

(v) 撥打

- You've dialed the wrong number.
  你打錯了。

  延伸學習 dial the number 撥打號碼

08 verify

[`vɛrə͵faɪ]

(v) 確認

- Please verify that you are not a robot by entering the numbers below.
  請藉由輸入以下數字來確認你不是機器人。

- Click "allow" to verify that you are not a robot.
  點選「允許」以確認你不是機器人。

  延伸學習 verify information / your email address / your identity
  確認資訊／電子郵件／身分

09 code

[kod]

(n) 密碼；代碼

- The message was written in Morse code.
  這訊息是用摩斯密碼寫的。

- Is there a dress code for the party tomorrow?
  明天的派對有服裝規定嗎？

  延伸學習 verification code / dress code / code name / zip code
  確認碼／服裝規定／代號／郵遞區號

  doctors' code for "prepare to die" (Steve Job's Speech) 醫生說「準備死吧」的暗示（賈伯斯的演講）

10 operator

[`ɑpə͵retɚ]

(n) 接線員；操作員

- The operator has a sweet voice.
  那位接線員的聲音很好聽。

  延伸學習 phone operator / machine operator
  電話接線員／機臺操作員

11 **receptionist**

[rɪˋsɛpʃənɪst]

(n) 接待員

- A hotel receptionist should be able to communicate with travelers effectively.
  飯店的接待員應能夠有效地和旅客溝通。

- A receptionist is also sometimes referred to as an administrative assistant.
  接待員有時也被稱作行政助理。

 測驗

▶ 是非題

_____ 1. An extension number is an additional telephone wired to the same telephone line.

_____ 2. People, money, and information can all be transferred.

_____ 3. If Andy calls and asks for Mary, who is currently not at her desk, you should tell Andy to "take a message."

_____ 4. If you are wondering about something, you think it is wonderful.

_____ 5. Having poor reception means very little signal can be received by the device.

_____ 6. To return a favor means to do something considerate for someone because he / she has done it for you before.

_____ 7. To dial someone's number means to call someone.

_____ 8. To verify something is to make sure it is true or correct.

_____ 9. A code is usually a set of numbers or words used to represent a message.

_____ 10. A receptionist is the person working in a hotel that welcomes guests when they arrive.

▶ 填空題

1. She asked the senior manager whether she can _____ to another department or not.

2. My _____ number is on the name card. Please call me if you have any inquiries.

3. The _____ in the tunnel is bad; let me call you later.

4. Sorry, Sandra is not at her desk. May I _____?

5. He told me to _____ his number whenever I need him.

6. I have to enter a _____ to read the email because it is encrypted.

7. I received an anonymous email and _____ who sent it.

8. The _____ will give you the keys when you check in at the hotel.

9. You need to enter a code to _____ your identity.

10. I'm in the middle of a conference right now and will _____ as soon as I get back to my desk.

Answer

是非題：

1. O   2. O   3. X   4. X   5. O   6. O   7. O   8. O   9. O   10. O

填空題：

1. transfer   2. extension   3. reception / signal   4. take a message

5. dial   6. code   7. wonder / wondered   8. receptionist

9. verify   10. return the call

填空題翻譯：

1. 她問資深經理她是否能轉到另一個部門。

2. 我的分機號碼在名片上。如果有任何問題請打給我。

3. 隧道裡的訊號不好，我待會打給你。

4. 不好意思，Sandra 不在位子上。要留言嗎？

5. 他說我需要他的時候就打給他。

6. 我在讀這封郵件之前需要輸入密碼因為它有加密。

7. 我收到一封匿名信件，我想知道是誰寄的。

8. 飯店接待員在你入住的時候會給你飯店鑰匙。

9. 你需要輸入密碼以確認身分。

10. 我在會議中。當我回到座位上時會立刻回電。

Unit 18

簽合約
Sign a Contract

Track
018

certify	certificate
eligible	tenure
provide	sign
contract	term
select	procedure
staff	

01 certify

[`sɝtə͵faɪ]

(v) 認證

- Cindy is a certified English teacher.
  Cindy 是一位通過認證的英文老師。

  延伸學習 a certified teacher 經過認證的老師

02 certificate

[sə`tɪfəkɪt]

(n) 證書；證明

相似詞
**license: driver's
license** 執照；駕照
certification (n) 證書

- To apply for this position, one should <u>obtain / submit</u> relevant certificates.
  要申請這個職位，申請者須要獲得／繳交相關證明。

  延伸學習 birth / death / marriage certificate
  出生／死亡／結婚證書

03 eligible

[`ɛlɪdʒəbl̩]

(adj) 合格的；
有資格的

- Eligible applicants will be informed before next Monday.
  合格的申請人會在下週一前被通知。

  延伸學習 eligible bachelors / bachelorettes / applicants
  黃金（有條件的）單身漢／單身女郎／合格的申請人

04 tenure

[`tɛnjʊr]

(n) 任期

- He strengthened international relations during his tenure as president.
  在他當總統的期間，他加強了國際關係。

  延伸學習 job tenure 工作任期

05 provide

[prə`vaɪd]

(v) 提供

用法
provide sb with sth
提供某人某物
provide sth for sb / sth
提供某物給某人／事
provide sth to sb
提供某物給某人

- Please provide the administration office with relevant certificates.
  請提供行政處室相關的證明。

  延伸學習 provide bonus to / for the best employee
  提供紅利給最好的員工

  provide venue for the fund-raising event
  提供場地給募款活動

06 sign

[saɪn]

(v) 簽署

- Please sign your name here.
  請在這裡簽名。

07 contract

[`kɑntrækt]

(n) 合約

- Before you sign a contract, make sure to read the terms carefully and thoroughly.
  在簽屬合約之前，請詳閱條款。

  延伸學習 draw up a contract 擬定合約
  例：When we draw up a contract, we'll take views expressed by both parties into consideration.
  當我們擬定合約時，我們會將雙方提出之見解納入考量。

08 term

[tɝm]

(n) 期；條款

- We will need a long-term plan to solve the problems brought by global warming.
  我們會需要一個長遠的計劃來解決全球暖化帶來的問題。

  延伸學習 long / short term 長／短期
  spring / fall term: first / second semester
  第一／二學期
  terms and conditions / terms of contract 條款

09 select

[sə`lɛkt]

(v) 挑選

相似詞
pick (v)、choose (v)、elect (v) 選

- After careful consideration, we have selected two candidates.
  在仔細考慮過後，我們選出了兩位候選人。

- She was selected / chosen based on her professional credentials.
  她因為她的專業資格而獲選。

10 procedure

[prə`sidʒɚ]

(n) 流程

相似詞
process (n) 程序

- We must follow the procedure.
  我們需要遵守流程。

11 **staff**

[stæf]

(n) 員工（全體）

相似詞
employee 一位員工

• Welcome to join the staff! All staff <u>is / are</u> required to finish the training.

歡迎成為員工！全體員工都需要完成訓練。

延伸學習 Staff only / a staff meeting
只有員工（可以進入）／員工會議

 測驗

▶ 是非題

_____ 1. If you obtain a certification, you have reached a standard in a certain profession.

_____ 2. To be eligible is to be qualified to do something.

_____ 3. Tenure refers to the period of time when someone owns a position.

_____ 4. You can provide someone to something or provide something with someone.

_____ 5. Sigh is a synonym for sign.

_____ 6. A contract is a document agreed by two people or two parties.

_____ 7. A short term is a short period of time.

_____ 8. Choose is a synonym for select.

_____ 9. A process is usually included in a procedure.

_____ 10. A customer can ask a staff for assistance.

▶ 填空題

1. He earned the respect from the students during his _____ as a teacher.

2. The manager needs to _____ the document to indicate that he approves of it.

3. I will be 20 years old next month and will be _____ to vote.

4. We finally reached an agreement and had the client sign the _____.

5. Among hundreds of competitors, the judges could only _____ three winners.

6. Checking one's identity is the institution's standard operating _____.

7. Before these products become available in the market, the lab needs to _____ them first.

8. The room is for _____ only. Please prevent customers from entering.

9. I work hard to _____ my family with food and clothing.

10. He listed his short and long _____ goals.

(Answer)

是非題：

1. O   2. O   3. O   4. X   5. X   6. X   7. O   8. O   9. X   10. O

填空題：

1. tenure   2. sign   3. eligible   4. contract   5. select

6. procedure   7. certify   8. staff   9. provide   10. term

填空題翻譯：

1. 在他當老師的任期內他贏得了學生的尊敬。

2. 經理需要在文件簽名表示他同意。

3. 我下個月就 20 歲了，到時就會有資格投票。

4. 我們終於達成共識並且讓客人簽署合約。

5. 在上百個參賽者當中裁判只能選出三個優勝者。

6. 檢查每個人的身份是這個機構的基本作業流程。

7. 在產品可以進到市場之前，實驗室必須先審核它們。

8. 這個房間只有員工可以進去，請避免客人進入。

9. 我努力工作以提供家人溫飽。

10. 他寫下了短期和長期的目標。

撰寫合約
Write a Contract

draft	detail	modify
modification	adjust	adjustment
amend	agree	abide
conform	assure	conclude
finalize		

01 draft

[dræft]
(n) 草稿
(v) 起草

- The lawyer drafted a contract for us.
  律師幫我們草擬了一份合約。

- This is just <u>a rough draft</u>. I will revise it.
  這只是草稿,我還會修改。

延伸學習 a rough draft 草稿

02 detail

[`ditel]
(n) 細節

相關詞
detailed (adj) 詳細的

- Let's go over the details of the contract.
  我們來細看一下合約的細節。

- Let's discuss the issue in detail later.
  我們等會來詳細討論一下問題。

延伸學習 go over the details 細看細節
         in detail 詳細地

03 modify

[`madə,faɪ]
(v) 修改

相關詞
review (v) 審核、
revise (v) 修改

- Can we modify a few terms in the contract?
  可以修改合約中幾個條款嗎?

04 modification

[,madəfə`keʃən]
(n) 修改

- I want to make a few modifications.
  我想要修正幾個事項。

05 adjust

[ə`dʒʌst]
(v) 調整

- Is it possible to adjust the contract?
  有可能調整合約嗎?

延伸學習 adjust your car seat / seat belt 調整安全帶

06 adjustment

[ə`dʒʌstmənt]
(n) 調整

- Is it possible to make adjustments to the contract?
  有可能調整合約嗎?

07 amend

[ə`mɛnd]

(v) 修改

相關詞
amendment (n) 修改

- Please read the contract carefully and let us know if you want to amend anything.
  請仔細閱讀合約並讓我們知道您是否想修改任何地方。

- Protesters went on strike, hoping that their move would urge the legislators to amend the law.
  抗議者罷工了，他們希望這樣的做法能促使立法者修改法律。

延伸學習 amend the law / constitution / settlement
修改法條、憲法、協定
make amends 進行修正

08 agree

[ə`gri]

(v) 同意

相反詞
disagree (v) 意見不合

相關詞
agreement (n) 合約

- Please sign your name here if you agree.
  同意請在此簽名。

延伸學習 agree with someone / something 同意某人／某事
agree to 接受、認可；agree to V 同意做某事
agree on something 對某事意見一致

09 abide

[ə`baɪd]

(v) 遵守

- The compliant worker always abides by the rules.
  這順從的員工總是遵守規定。

延伸學習 abide by the rules / the restrictions 遵守規定

10 conform

[kən`fɔrm]

(v) 遵循

相似詞
comply (v) 遵守

- Employees should conform to the company's dress code.
  員工應遵守公司服儀規定。

延伸學習 conform to government regulations / requirements
遵循政府的規定、要求

11 assure

[ə`ʃʊr]

(v) 保證

相關詞
assurance (n) 保證

- I assured him that I will keep my promise.
  我跟他保證我會守信用。

補充說明

assure (v) 保證、ensure (v) 確保、insure (v) 投保、reassure (v) 使安心

assure + 人：I can assure you that the roller coaster is safe.
　　　　　　我向你保證這雲霄飛車是安全的。

ensure + 事：Please fasten your seatbelt to ensure safety.
　　　　　　為了確保安全請繫上安全帶。

insure：insure your car 為車子投保

reassure：Mom reassured me that everything will be alright.
　　　　　媽媽安慰我說一切都會沒事的。

---

12 conclude

[kən`klud]

(v) 議定、結束

- Before I conclude the speech, does anyone have any questions?

在我總結今天的演講之前，有人有問題嗎？

延伸學習 conclude / finalize a contract or an agreement
完成一份合約
In conclusion,... 總之

---

13 finalize

[`faɪnḷˌaɪz]

(v) 最後定下

- We finalized the contract after negotiations were successfully completed.

我們在協商順利結束後定下了合約。

延伸學習 finalize the agreement / deal / divorce
最後決定／定下合約、約定、離婚

測驗

▶ 是非題

_____ 1. To draft something means to write a document without including all the details yet.

_____ 2. If you modify a document, you change or revise certain points of it.

_____ 3. When a person is adjusting to the environment, he / she knows the place very well.

_____ 4. To amend a legal document is to admit and approve of the terms it states.

_____ 5. If you can't agree with someone more, you disagree with their opinions.

_____ 6. When you abide by the rules, you follow them.

_____ 7. A compliant student complains all the time.

_____ 8. When you assure someone of something, your attitude is confident.

_____ 9. To conclude a speech is similar to wrapping up a speech.

_____ 10. When something is finalized, there is still room for negotiation.

▶ 填空題

1. During the economic depression, companies need to make some _____ to keep business operating.

2. She's a _____ employee and never breaks the rules.

3. His lawyer already _____ the legal document but has not gotten into the details yet.

4. I just started my new job and I'm still trying to _____ to the environment.

5. There are some errors in the report and I'll have to make some _____ to it.

6. I cannot disclose the _____ stated in the contract.

7. We have to keep our promises once the deal is _____.

8. The meeting will end in 10 minutes, so please _____ your speech soon.

9. You can't be mad simply because I don't _____ with you.

10. We can only proceed after we reach an _____.

Answer

是非題：

1. ○   2. ○   3. X   4. X   5. X   6. ○   7. X   8. ○   9. ○   10. X

填空題：

1. adjustments   2. compliant   3. drafted   4. adjust   5. amendments

6. details   7. finalized   8. conclude   9. agree   10. agreement

填空題翻譯：

1. 在經濟不景氣的時候，公司需要做些調整才能讓公司持續經營。

2. 她是一個很遵守規定的員工並且從不違規。

3. 他的律師已經擬訂了法律文件，但是還沒有寫到細節。

4. 我才剛開始我的新工作，還在適應新環境當中。

5. 在這份報告當中有些錯誤，而我需要做些修正。

6. 我不能公開合約中的細節。

7. 在合約決定之後我們必須要遵守約定。

8. 會議會在 10 分鐘內結束，所以請盡快總結你的演講。

9. 你不能僅僅因為我不同意就生氣。

10. 我們只有在達成共識之後才能繼續進行。

Unit 20

合約
Contract

Track
020

fulfill   consequence   consequently

penalty   lawsuit   sue

terminate   terminal   condition

circumstances   clause   discharge

fraud   rectify

01 fulfill

[fʊl`fɪl]

(v) 履行義務

- If you <u>fail to fulfill / perform your duties</u>, I'm afraid that there will be consequences.
  如果你無法達成義務，恐怕會有不好的後果。

  延伸學習 fail to fulfill / perform obligations / duty
  無法履行義務

02 consequence

[`kɑnsə͵kwɛns]

(n) 後果

相關詞
result (n) 結果、
effect (n) 效果

- The consequences are too frightening to imagine.
  後果太可怕以至於無法想像。

- He didn't work hard when he was young and is now suffering the consequences in his old age.
  少壯不努力，老大徒傷悲。

03 consequently

[`kɑnsə͵kwɛntlɪ]

(adv) 結果

- He refused to listen to the experienced old man's advice; consequently, he is suffering now.
  不聽老人言，吃虧在眼前。

04 penalty

[`pɛnl̩tɪ]

(n) 懲罰

相似詞
punishment (n) 懲罰

- The man faced penalties for drunk driving.
  那男人因為酒駕被懲處。

  延伸學習 face penalty / impose penalty 面對懲處／處以懲罰

05 lawsuit

[`lɔ͵sut]

(n) 訴訟

- You might face lawsuits for the violation of copyright law.
  侵犯著作權法你可能會吃上官司。

  延伸學習 face lawsuit 吃官司

06 sue

[su]

(v) 提告

- It's possible for you to be sued when you breach a contract.
  如果違約有可能會被告。

07 terminate

[ˋtɝməˌnet]

(v) 終止

相似詞
end (v) 結束

- I'm looking for ways to terminate the contract.
  我在找方法終止合約。

08 terminal

[ˋtɝmən̩]

(adj) 最後的

(n) 航廈

- The next station is the terminal station.
  下一站是終點站。

延伸學習 next station is the terminal station 下一站是終點站
airport terminal 機場航廈

09 condition

[kənˋdɪʃən]

(n) 情況

- The contract should be terminated because conditions / circumstances have changed.
  因情況已經變了，合約應當終止。

- I will fund your project on one condition.
  只有在一個條件下我才會贊助你的專案計畫。

延伸學習 on one condition 在一個條件下

10 circumstance

[ˋsɝkəmˌstæns]

(n) 情況

（通常為複數：circumstances）

- Under no circumstances should you drunk drive.
  在任何情況之下都不應該酒駕。

延伸學習 under certain circumstances 在某些情況之下
under the circumstances 在那種情況之下

11 clause

[klɔz]

(n) 法律條文

- They have finally agreed to amend a clause in the contract.
  他們終於同意修改合約中一項條文。

12 discharge

[dɪsˋtʃɑrdʒ]

(v) 允許離開；
履行（義務、職責）

- When both parties fulfilled their duties, the contract is then discharged.
  當雙方都履行義務，合約就解除了（合約已履行）。

- The Prime Minister is discharged from the hospital.
  首相已出院（已被允許離開醫院）。

13 **fraud**

[frɔd]

(n) 詐騙

相關詞
fraudulent (adj)
假；偽造的、
phone scams 詐騙電話
相似詞
fake (adj) 假的、
scam (n) 詐騙
相反詞
real (adj)、**true (adj)**、
genuine (adj)、
bona fide (adj) 真的

- You can terminate the contract if the other party commits fraud.
  如果合約中任一方犯了詐欺罪即可終止合約。

- I'm calling regarding a fraud case.
  我打來是為了一樁詐欺案。

  延伸學習 commit fraud 犯詐欺罪
  accuse sb. of fraud 指控某人詐欺

14 **rectify**

[ˋrɛktəˌfaɪ]

(v) 修正

- We should draw up a plan to rectify the current problems.
  為了修正現在的問題，我們應該要擬定一個計畫。

  延伸學習 rectify a situation / a problem 修正一個狀況／問題

▶ 是非題

_____ 1. To perform your duties is to do what you're supposed to do.

_____ 2. Consequence is similar to result but has a more negative meaning.

_____ 3. A penalty is similar to a punishment.

_____ 4. To terminate a contract means to renew it.

_____ 5. A terminal station is the first station.

_____ 6. The word "circumstance" is uncountable.

_____ 7. A clause refers to the statement written in a legal document.

_____ 8. If a person is discharged from the hospital, he / she can leave.

_____ 9. A fraud is a crime of stealing money without people noticing.

_____ 10. To rectify a problem is to correct it.

▶ 填空題

1. You will suffer the _____ if you continue to spend money without discipline!

2. Under no _____ should you accept a drink from a stranger.

3. He faced _____ for parking at an illegal spot.

4. That woman was sued for committing _____ by deceiving people and asking them for money.

5. If the financial _____ of this company continue to worsen, it will go bankrupt soon.

6. We have to add one more _____ to the contract to make it more complete.

7. The employee is filing a _____ against his former employer for wrongful termination.

8. Just take the bus and get off at the _____ stop; you'll see my house on the right side.

9. The CEO will take certain steps to _____ the situation and correct the mistake.

10. We have to _____ our obligations according to the contract.

Answer

是非題：

1. ○   2. ○   3. ○   4. X   5. X   6. X   7. ○   8. ○   9. X   10. ○

填空題：

1. consequences 2. circumstances 3.penalty   4. fraud   5. condition

6. clause   7. lawsuit   8. terminal   9. rectify   10. fulfill / perform

填空題翻譯：

1. 如果你繼續毫不節制地花錢，你將會承擔後果。

2. 在任何情況之下你都不應該接受陌生人給的飲料。

3. 他因為違規停車接受處分。

4. 那個婦人因為詐欺別人並且向人要錢而被告。

5. 如果這間公司的財務狀況持續惡化，它很快就會破產。

6. 我們需要在合約當中再加一個條款讓它更完整。

7. 這員工因為前雇主沒有正當理由辭退他而提告。

8. 只要搭公車並且在終點站下車，你就會看到我家在右手邊。

9. 執行長會採取一些步驟來改正目前的情況並且修正錯誤。

10. 我們必須按照合約履行義務。

協商
Negotiation

negotiate	compromise
promise	settle
settlement	reconcile
moderate	judge
judgement	violate
breach	infringe

01 negotiate

[nɪ`goʃɪ͵et]
(v) 協調

- Our prices are non-negotiable.
  我們的價格是不二價的。

  延伸學習 negotiate a deal / settlement / price
  協調約定／和解／價格

02 compromise

[`kamprə͵maɪz]
(v) 妥協

- After a great deal of communication and negotiation, they finally compromised and modified the contract.
  在大量溝通和協調後他們終於讓步並且修改合約。

03 promise

[`pramɪs]
(v) 承諾

- When you make a promise, you should keep it.
  當你做出承諾，你就應該守住它。

  延伸學習 make / break a promise 做出／違反承諾
  a promising future 美好的未來

04 settle

[`sɛtl̩]
(v) 確定；穩定下來

- If you haven't found it yet, keep looking. Don't settle.
  (Steve Jobs)
  如果你還沒找到（內心所愛的工作），繼續追尋。不要屈就。

  延伸學習 everything is settled then 這樣全部事情都確定了
  settle down 定居

05 settlement

[`sɛtl̩mənt]
(n) 和解

- After a series of negotiations, they both compromised and reached a settlement.
  在一番協商之後，雙方都妥協了並且達成和解。

  延伸學習 reach a settlement 達成和解（法律）

06 reconcile

[`rɛkənsaɪl]
(v) 和解

相關詞
reconciliation (n)
和解

- They finally reconciled with each other after not speaking for a whole year.
  在一年都沒有跟對方講話之後他們終於和解了。

  延伸學習 to reconcile with someone 和某人和解（生活）

07 moderate

[`mɑdərɪt]

(v) 主持；管控
(adj) 適中的

相關詞
moderator (n)
調解人；仲裁者

- The chairperson will moderate the meeting.
  主席會主持會議。

  延伸學習 moderate a meeting 主持會議
  mild and moderate 溫和而適中的
  moderate or severe 溫和的還是嚴重的

08 judge

[dʒʌdʒ]

(n) (v) 裁判

- The judge will judge the situation and make the final judgment.
  裁判／法官會判斷狀況並且做最後決定。

09 judgement

[`dʒʌdʒmənt]

(n) 判斷；審判

相關詞
judgemental (adj)
愛評價別人的

- Players should respect the referee's judgement.
  選手應尊重裁判的判決。

- Don't be so judgemental.
  不要這麼喜歡評價別人。

10 violate

[`vaɪəˌlet]

(v) 違反；侵犯

相似詞
invade (v) 侵犯

- How do I make sure what I post doesn't violate copyright law?
  要如何確定我張貼的內容不會侵犯著作權？

  延伸學習 violate a contract / privacy / orders / copyright law
  違反合約／隱私權／規定／版權

11 breach

[britʃ]

(v) 違反

- I don't want to be sued for breach of agreement.
  我不想要因為違約而被告。

  延伸學習 breach an agreement 違反合約

12 infringe

[ɪn`frɪndʒ]

(v) 違反；違背

- We may infringe someone else's copyright when we post a photo onto Facebook.
  當我們張貼照片到臉書的時候有可能侵害了別人的版權。

  延伸學習 infringe copyright / the rights of... / regulations
  違反版權／侵權／違反規定

 測驗

▶ 是非題

_____ 1. You negotiate with someone by telling him/her what to do.

_____ 2. To compromise means to commit and promise someone something.

_____ 3. People break up sometimes, so they also break up promises sometimes.

_____ 4. To settle something means to arrange something and reach a decision.

_____ 5. If two people fail to reach a settlement in a lawsuit, they will have to go to trial.

_____ 6. To reconcile with someone is similar to recognize someone.

_____ 7. An antonym for moderate is severe.

_____ 8. A judgemental person is usually objective and make conclusions based on facts.

_____ 9. To violate means to act against something.

_____ 10. If someone does not abide by the contract he / she signed, the person might be sued for breach of contract.

▶ 填空

1. Think hard before you make a _____ or you'll suffer the consequences as well as lose your credit.

2. It took some time for her to _____ down in the new environment.

3. Some requirements raised by my client are too difficult, and I've decided to _____ with them to see if we can make some amendments.

4. You should not post my picture online without my permission. You're _____ my privacy!

5. We are determined to go with our way and will not _____ this time.

6. We need to double check whether we're allowed to use this article in case we _____ the copyright of its author.

7. They finally _____ after fighting for 3 months.

8. The market has finally shown some _____ growth after the economic decline.

9. Don't _____ a book by its cover.

10. You're losing your _____ and simply acting impulsively!

Unit 22

法律相關
Law

Track
022

measure	implement
policy	liability
liable	given
patent	insurance
insure	trustee

131

01 measure

['mɛʒɚ]

(n) 措施

(v) 衡量

- The government has adopted numerous measures to fight the disease.
  政府已經採取了許多措施來對抗這疾病。

- Please measure the ingredients properly before you mix them together.
  將它們混合在一起之前，請先正確測量食材。

延伸學習 take / adopt / implement measures 採取／實施措施

02 implement

['ɪmpləmənt]

(v) 實施

- Local leaders are working to implement the policy.
  當地的領導人合作實施政策。

延伸學習 implement the law / policy / program / recommendations 實施法規／政策／計畫／建議

03 policy

['pɑləsɪ]

(n) 政策；方針

相似詞
rule (n) 規定、
guideline (n) 指導方針

- Where can I find the return and refund policy on the website?
  在哪裡可以找到網站上的退貨和退款規定？

- Honesty is the best policy.
  誠實為上策。

04 liability

[ˌlaɪə`bɪlətɪ]

(n) 責任；累贅（負擔）；弱點

- They think that they won't have (legal) liability if they hire an agent.
  他們覺得如果請代理商他們就沒有責任。

- The airline has liability to your luggage.
  航空公司對你的行李有責任。

- Get rid of him. He is a liability.
  擺脫他，他是個負擔。

- What's your liability?
  你的弱點是什麼？

05 liable

['laɪəbl]

(adj) 有責任

- The airline is liable for your luggage.
  航空公司對你的行李有責任。

06 given

[ˈgɪvn]

(n) (prep.) 有鑑於；
假定事實

- Given the situation, we better run!
  考慮到目前的情況，走為上策！

- Given (the fact) that one's work can be easily stolen nowadays, you better have your invention patented right away.
  考慮到現在的作品很容易被偷，你最好立刻幫你的發明申請專利。

  延伸學習 taken as a given 視為既定

---

07 patent

[ˈpætnt]

(n) 專利 (v) 申請專利

- Your invention should be patented immediately.
  你的發明應該立刻申請專利。

  延伸學習 patent law 專利法

---

08 insurance

[ɪnˈʃʊrəns]

(n) [U] 保險

- Have you bought health insurance?
  你有買健康保險嗎？

- Cancer is not covered by this insurance.
  這個保單不包含癌症。

---

09 insure

[ɪnˈʃʊr]

(v) 保險

- Make sure to insure your car.
  = Make sure that your car is insured.
  請記得幫你的車子保險。

補充說明

ensure 保證事情、assure 對人保證

Please fasten your seatbelt to ensure safety.
為了安全請繫上安全帶。

I can assure you that your baby will be safe here.
我可以跟你保證你的寶寶在這裡很安全。

---

10 trustee

[trʌsˈti]

(n) 受託人

- The board of trustees will make the final call.
  董事會會做最後決定。

  延伸學習 board of trustees 董事會

 測驗

▶ 是非題

_____ 1. A ruler can be used to measure things.

_____ 2. You can implement a policy or a task.

_____ 3. A policy is a rule followed by the police.

_____ 4. The phrase "call for" has something to do with phone calls.

_____ 5. If someone is a liability, that person is very reliable.

_____ 6. Given is a synonym for regarding.

_____ 7. You can protect something if you patent it.

_____ 8. Insure is a synonym for ensure.

_____ 9. A trustee is someone who trusts you.

_____ 10. A trust fund is a type of fundraiser.

▶ 填空題

1. Many citizens are urging the government to adopt _____ to reduce drunk driving.

2. He applied for a _____ for the handy gardening tool that he made.

3. A stupid guy like Edward will become a _____ in our team.

4. They are considering setting up a _____ as a long-term investment for their children.

5. A ruler can be used to _____ things.

6. A _____ helps people manage money and assets.

7. Several industries _____ restrictions to be eased.

8. Many people in developing countries don't even have access to health

_____ .

9. The board has _____ new measures to cut costs.

10. _____ that Ms. Sung is a controlling shareholder, we should probably consult her.

Answer

是非題：

1. O   2. O   3. X   4. X   5. X   6. X   7. O   8. X   9. X   10. X

填空題：

1. policies / measures   2. patent   3. liability   4. trust fund   5. measure

6. trustee   7. called for   8. insurance   9. implemented   10. Given

填空題翻譯：

1. 很多市民督促政府採取政策以減少酒駕。

2. 他為他製作的好用花園工具申請專利。

3. 像 Edward 這樣的笨蛋會成為我們團隊的累贅。

4. 他們在考慮為他們的小孩設立信託當作長期投資。

5. 尺可以用來衡量東西。

6. 受託人幫別人管理錢和資產。

7. 好幾個產業呼籲放鬆限制。

8. 很多開發中國家的人甚至沒有辦法使用健保。

9. 董事會採取新的措施來減少成本。

10. 考慮到宋小姐是控股股東，我們或許應該詢問她的意見。

商業書信一
Business Email 1

Track
023

audience	specific
purpose	urgent
message	update
additional	forward
clerical	confidential

01 audience
[`ɔdɪəns]
(n) 觀眾

相似詞
recipient (n) 接受者

- When you write a business email, first consider who your audience / recipient is.
  幫你寫一封工作的電子郵件時，請先思考你的對象／收信人是誰。

02 specific
[spɪ`sɪfɪk]
(adj) 特定的；明確的

相反詞
general (adj) 概括的

- To make your email stand out, you should keep the subject simple and specific.
  要讓你的信件突出，你應該讓你的標題簡單而明確。

03 purpose
[`pɝpəs]
(n) 目的

- You should present the purpose of your email in the subject.
  你要在標題中寫出你的目的。

04 urgent
[`ɝdʒənt]
(adj) 緊急的

- If you want to talk about an urgent matter, you probably shouldn't send an email.
  如果你想要講的是比較緊急的事情，你可能不應該用電子郵件。

05 message
[`mɛsɪdʒ]
(n) 訊息

- You should send a message instead.
  你應該要傳訊息。
  = Instead, you should send a message.
  = Instead of an email, you should send a message.

延伸學習 send a message 傳訊息

06 update
[ʌp`det]
(n) (v) 最新消息更新

- I'm in charge of providing weekly updates for the board of directors.
  我負責提供每週更新事項給董事會。

- We keep each other updated on the project by sending emails.
  我們藉由電子郵件讓彼此知道專案的最新消息。

- I will keep you updated / posted!
  我會讓你知道最新消息！

延伸學習 keep sb. updated 通知最新消息

07 additional [ə`dɪʃən̩l] (adj) 額外的	• You can offer additional information at the end of an email. 你可以在電子郵件的最後提供額外資訊。 **延伸學習** additional information 額外資訊
08 forward [`fɔrwɚd] (v) 轉寄	• Please forward the email to me. 請把電子郵件轉寄給我。
09 clerical [`klɛrɪkl̩] (adj) 文書的	• Writing emails is a kind of clerical work. 寫信是一種文書工作。
10 confidential [͵kɑnfə`dɛnʃəl] (adj) 機密的	• Please note that the information in this letter is confidential and should not be shown to anyone outside our team. 請注意這封信的資訊是機密，不應該對團隊以外的人公開。

 **測驗**

▶ 是非題

_____ 1. The word "audience" is countable.

_____ 2. To be more specific means to be clearer and more exact.

_____ 3. If you do something on purpose, you do it intentionally.

_____ 4. An urgent task should be on the top of your list.

_____ 5. To update someone means to let someone know your latest schedule.

_____ 6. Extra is a synonym for additional.

_____ 7. You can forward an email, so you can also backward it.

_____ 8. A clerical job usually involves writing emails and organizing files.

_____ 9. If a document is confidential, it can be shown to the public with confidence.

▶ **填空題**

1. The contract is _____ and only our team members are allowed to read it.

2. Please remember to _____ me a _____ when you arrive at the airport so I can pick you up.

3. The dancer is always developing new dance moves in order to surprise her faithful _____ .

4. The meeting was so long and boring; in fact, I didn't even know what the _____ of the meeting was.

5. We stay in touch and keep each other _____ .

6. I realized that you were not included in the email, so I will _____ it to you later.

7. During the pandemic, you need a _____ reason to travel to another country.

8. We can customize the product according to your needs, but it will require some _____ charges.

9. I just received an _____ meeting notification and will probably work overtime tonight.

10. She got a _____ job and is responsible for filing records.

Answer

是非題:

1. O 2. O 3. O 4. O 5. X 6. O 7. X 8. O 9. X

填空題:

| 1. confidential | 2. send / message | 3. audience | 4. purpose | 5. updated |
| 6. forward | 7. specific | 8. additional | 9. urgent | 10. clerical |

填空題翻譯:

1. 這合約是機密的,只有我們團隊成員可以看。

2. 在你到達機場的時候記得傳訊息給我,好讓我去接你。

3. 那舞者為了驚艷她忠誠的觀眾,總是不斷發想新的舞蹈。

4. 會議又長又無聊;事實上,我甚至不知道這會議的目的是什麼。

5. 我們保持聯絡並且讓彼此知道近況。

6. 我發現你沒有被包含在信件當中,所以我待會會把信轉寄給你。

7. 在流行病大爆發期間,你需要明確的理由才能出國。

8. 我們可以依照你的需求將商品客製化,但是會需要一些額外的費用。

9. 我剛收到一個緊急會議通知,今天有可能要徹夜加班。

10. 她得到一個文書處理工作,並且負責檔案紀錄。

distribute	delegate
division	divide
assign	appreciate
respond	correspondence
mention	claim
remark	feedback

01 **distribute**

[dɪ`strɪbjʊt]

(v) 分配

- The manager distributed his work to several colleagues.
  經理把工作分配給幾個同事。

- The intern is in charge of distributing brochures.
  那位實習生負責發手冊。

02 **delegate**

[`dɛlə,get]

(n) (v) 代表；分配

- As a team leader, you should learn to delegate tasks to your team members! Don't do everything by yourself!
  身為一個領導人,你應該要學習把工作分配給團隊成員!不要全部事情都自己做!

- I was the delegate of Sri Lanka when I first participated in a Model United Nations' meeting.
  我第一次參加模擬聯合國會議時是斯里蘭卡的代表。

03 **division**

[də`vɪʒən]

(n) 部門

相似詞
department (n) 部門、
sector (n) 部門

- The company is divided into several departments / divisions.
  公司被分成幾個部門。

04 **divide**

[də`vaɪd]

(v) 分開

- I'll divide you into 6 groups.
  我會把你們分成 6 組。

05 **assign**

[ə`saɪn]

(v) 指派

相關詞
assignment (n)
作業；任務

- "I have an assignment for you!" said the teacher cheerfully as she assigned us 50 pages for homework.
  「我有出作業給你們!」老師開心地說著,一邊分配 50 頁給我們當作業。

06 appreciate

[əˋpriʃɪˌet]

(v) 感謝、欣賞

相似詞
grateful (adj) for 感謝、
thankful (adj) for 感謝

- I really appreciate your help.
  我很感謝你的幫忙。

- I feel like you don't appreciate my hard work.
  我覺得你不在乎我的努力。

- We'd really appreciate it if you could lower your voice.
  如果你可以降低音量我們會很感激。

- I appreciate the beauty of nature.
  我欣賞大自然的美麗。

07 respond

[rɪˋspɑnd]

(v) 回應

相關詞
response (n)
回答;答覆

- I'm very anxious because I don't know <u>how they will respond / what their response will be</u>.
  我很緊張因為我不知道他們會怎麼回答。

08 correspondence

[ˌkɔrəˋspɑndəns]

(n) 信件

- We communicate by phone and correspondence.
  我們透過電話和信件溝通。

- Email correspondence has become extremely important in business nowadays.
  電子郵件在今日的商場中變得極為重要。

  延伸學習 email correspondence 電子郵件

09 mention

[ˋmɛnʃən]

(v) 提到

- Why didn't you mention anything about your ex-girlfriend?
  為什麼你完全沒有提到你的前女友?

10 claim

[klem]

(v) 聲稱;拿

相關詞
alleged (adj) 據稱

- Don't forget to claim your luggage at the baggage claim.
  不要忘了去行李領取處拿你的行李。

- He claims that his duffel bag is stolen.
  他聲稱他的行李袋被偷了。

11 remark

[rɪ`mɑrk]

(n) 發言；評語

(v) 評論

相關詞
remarkable (adj)
極好的、
comment (v) (n) 評論

- The writer is known for his humorous remarks.
  那作家因他幽默的說話方式聞名。

- He made a remark about the movie after watching it.
  在看了電影之後他給了一個評論。

- He remarked that she looked tired.
  他說她看起來很累。

補充說明

remark VS comment VS observation

這三個字都有「評論」的意思，但是卻是不同的評論。

remark 是簡短且快速、未經過深思熟慮的評論。

comment 是評語、建議，帶有一點想法或是批評。

ex: The teacher's comments on my essay helped me greatly!
老師給我的評語對我幫助很大。

observation 是經過仔細觀察之後做出的評論。

ex: May I make an observation about the meeting?
我可以對會議做一些評論嗎？

12 feedback

[`fid͵bæk]

(n) [U] 回饋

- Thank you for your feedback.
  謝謝你的回饋。

- I would love it if you can give me some feedback.
  如果你可以給我一點回饋我會很開心。

 **測驗**

▶ 是非題

_____ 1. You can distribute a book to several people.

_____ 2. A boss can delegate tasks or jobs to his/her subordinates.

_____ 3. If something has been divided, it has been separated into parts.

_____ 4. If you assign a document to someone, you sign it and approve it.

_____ 5. You can be thankful to someone, so you can also appreciate for someone.

_____ 6. To respond is to react to something.

_____ 7. Correspondence refers to the communication via letters or emails.

_____ 8. When people say "Don't mention it," they want you to stop talking about a certain subject.

_____ 9. To claim is to prove something is truthful or correct.

_____ 10. The word remark can be both a noun and a verb.

▶ 填空題

1. You have too much on your plate! Please _____ some tasks to other team members so we can complete them sooner.

2. He just went through a break-up, so please do not _____ anything about relationships when you see him.

3. He has not replied to my emails since last week, and when I knocked on his door this morning, there was no _____.

4. I was so glad when I received the _____ about the job offer.

5. These brochures will be _____ to the attendees tomorrow.

6. My boss will _____ a new project for me next week.

7. He is famous for his witty _____, and people love to listen to his talk show.

8. Joe _____ that he completed the work all by himself but his colleagues did not agree.

144

9. Feel free to use our company's free sample and please let us know your
_____ after you use it.

10. I forgot to bring my wallet. Can you lend me some money? I'll really
_____ it.

Answer

是非題：

1. X　　2. O　　3. O　　4. X　　5. X　　6. O　　7. O　　8. X　　9. X　　10. O

填空題：

1. delegate　　　2. mention　　　3. response　　　4. correspondence

5. distributed　　6. assign　　　7. remarks　　　8. claimed　　　9.feedback

10. appreciate

填空題翻譯：

1. 你有太多事情了！請把一些工作分配給其他成員，我們才能盡快完成。

2. 他剛分手，所以見到他的時候請不要談到任何有關感情的事。

3. 自從上週他就沒有回覆我的電子郵件，而且當我今天早上敲他的門時也沒有任何回應。

4. 當我收到工作通知的信件我非常開心。

5. 這些手冊明天會發給參加者。

6. 下禮拜我的老闆會指派一個新的專案給我。

7. 他因為他機智的言論而出名，大家都喜歡去聽他的脫口秀。

8. 他聲稱他自己完成全部的工作，但他的同事不同意。

9. 請自由使用我們公司的免費樣本，並且在使用過後讓我們知道你的回饋。

10. 我忘記帶錢包了，可以借我一點錢嗎？我會很感激的。

購買與付款
Purchasing and Payment

Track
025

purchase   merchandise
payment   transaction
track   remit
reimburse   warranty

01 purchase

[`pɝtʃəs]

(n) 購買物

(v) 購買

相似詞

buy (v) 購買

- How are you going to pay for your purchases?
  請問您要如何付款？

  延伸學習 purchase goods 購買商品
  place a purchase order 下訂單

02 merchandise

[`mɝtʃənˌdaɪz]

(n) [U] 商品

相似詞

products (n) 商品、

goods (n) 商品

相關詞

merchant (n) 商人

- A merchant sells merchandise / products / goods.
  商人賣商品。

  延伸學習 a wide selection of merchandise 各式各樣的商品
  merchandising and marketing 銷售與行銷

03 payment

[`pemənt]

(n) 款項

- I almost forgot that my credit card payment is due this Wednesday.
  我差點忘記信用卡帳單繳款截止時間是這週三。

  延伸學習 monthly / mortgage / down payment
  月費、房貸、頭期款

04 transaction

[træn`zækʃən]

(n) 交易

用法

conduct (v) +

transaction

執行／進行交易

- I want you to act as our agent in a business transaction.
  我要你當我們交易的仲介。

- The agent will conduct a transaction between the firm and its suppliers.
  代理商將在公司及其供應商之間進行交易。

  延伸學習 business / financial / commercial transactions
  業務／金融／商業交易
  conduct transactions 進行交易

05 track

[træk]
(n) 紀錄
(v) 追蹤

- Make sure to invest firms with good track records.
  要確保你投資的公司有良好的紀錄。

- The police use special equipment to track criminals.
  警察用特別的配備追蹤犯人。

- I'll track him down someday!
  有一天我一定會追查（抓）到他！

  延伸學習 keep track of 紀錄；追蹤
  track record 成績紀錄
  track sb. / sth. down 追查

06 remit

[rɪ`mɪt]
(v) 匯款

- When you go on a business trip, you remit payment first, then you submit a claim for reimbursement.
  當你在出差的時候，你要先支付款項，之後再報帳。

  延伸學習 remit payment and submit a claim for reimbursement 支付款項以及提出退款要求

07 reimburse

[ˌrim`bɝs]
(v) 退費；補償

相關詞
reimbursement (n)
退的費用

用法
reimburse + for

- Each individual will be reimbursed for his / her participation.
  我們會退費給每位參加者。

- I was reimbursed by the airline for the cancelation of the flight.
  因班機取消航空公司退費給我。

- Our company will reimburse all travel expenses.
  我們公司會補助所有旅行支出。

補充說明

reimburse 來自 re + in + purse 重新放進錢包→退費、補償

08 warranty

[ˈwɔrəntɪ]

(n) 保固

- A car warranty does not cover accidental damage.
  車子的保固不包含意外傷害。

- If you find a defect in the product, you can return it with a warranty.
  如果在商品中發現缺陷，您可以憑保證書退貨。

延伸學習 under warranty 有保固
offers a lifetime warranty 提供終身保固
warranty covers... 保固包含……

補充說明

補充資訊：receipt VS invoice

a receipt is a proof of payment

發票是付費的證明

an invoice is a request for payment

付費清單是要求付款的單據

commercial invoice 商業發票：

Commercial invoices are required for all the shipments.

這裡所有的運輸貨物都需要開商業發票。

commercial invoice for shipping 運輸貨物需要的商業發票

測驗

▶ 是非題

_____ 1. To acquire something can also mean to purchase something.

_____ 2. A merchant sells goods to others.

_____ 3. A down payment refers to the entire amount of money of something.

_____ 4. You can conduct transactions by using a laptop.

_____ 5. If you keep track of something, you have records of it.

_____ 6. To remit means to pay someone again.

_____ 7. To reimburse means to charge someone a certain amount of money.

_____ 8. If a product is still under warranty, you can ask the company to fix a problem without paying.

_____ 9. You can send your customer a receipt in order to ask for payment.

_____ 10. The seller usually sends the commercial invoice to the buyer after shipping out the goods.

▶ 填空題

1. The electric bill is one of my monthly _____.

2. The Internet allows people to conduct online _____, so people often shop online now.

3. I've made up my mind to only _____ things I need.

4. Please remember to send the _____ for her to remit payment.

5. I love going to shopping centers because they always have a wide selection of _____.

6. Make sure to take notes during meetings in order to keep _____ of the topics we covered.

7. My customer said he would _____ the payment by the end of the week.

8. Our latest product has a three-year _____ and our technicians can come to your house if there are any problems.

9. The conference has been canceled and every participant will be _____.

10. He applied for _____ after returning from the business trip.

是非題：

1. O　　2. O　　3. X　　4. O　　5. O　　6. X　　7. X　　8. O　　9. X　　10. O

填空題：

1. payments　　2. transactions　　3. purchase　　4. invoice　　5. merchandise

6. track　　7. remit　　8. warranty　　9. reimbursed　　10. reimbursement

填空題翻譯：

1. 電費是我每月的支出之一。

2. 網路使人們能夠在線上交易，所以現代人經常在線上購物。

3. 我已經決定只買我需要的東西。

4. 請記得寄發票請她付款。

5. 我喜歡去購物中心因為它們總有非常多商品。

6. 為了記錄我們在會議中涵蓋的主題請記得要做紀錄。

7. 我的客人說他會在週末之前付款。

8. 我們最新的產品有三年保固，如果有任何問題我們的技師可以去你家處理。

9. 會議被取消了，它們會退費給每一位參加者。

10. 他在出差後申請報銷。

貨品運送
Shipping

Track
026

ship	shipping
shipment	package
cargo	freight
port	import
export	customs
inventory	stock

01 ship

[ʃɪp]

(n) 大船 (v) 運輸

- Your order will be shipped soon.
  你的訂單即將出貨。

02 shipping

[ˋʃɪpɪŋ]

(n) 運輸

- This online store offers free shipping to orders over 1000 dollars.
  這間網路商店在消費金額超過 1000 塊的時候免運費。

  延伸學習 shipping industry 運輸業

03 shipment

[ˋʃɪpmənt]

(n) 運輸物品

- Please note that your shipment will arrive soon.
  請注意你的物品即將抵達。

04 package

[ˋpækɪdʒ]

(n) 包裹

相似詞
parcel (n) 包裹

- It's a package deal.
  整批交易／須整套購買。

  延伸學習 deliver a package 運送包裹
  join / take a package tour 參加旅行團／套裝行程

05 cargo

[ˋkɑrgo]

(n) 貨物

- This is the area where the workers unload the cargo.
  這是工人卸貨的地方。

  延伸學習 a cargo ship / plane 貨船／貨機

06 freight

[fret]

(n) 貨物

- This ship / train carries freight as well as passengers.
  這艘船／輛火車載貨也載乘客。

- The goods will be sent / delivered by freight trains.
  商品會由載貨火車運送。

07 port

[port]

(n) 港；插槽

相似詞
dock (n) 碼頭、
harbor (n) 港

- The ship has left the port.
  那艘船已離港。

  延伸學習 come into / leave port 進入／離開港口
  (plug it into) a USB port（插入）USB 插槽

port：to carry 攜帶、移動

portable：port + able → 可移動的

transport：trans（橫越）+ port → 運輸

deport：de（離開）+ port → 驅逐

---

08 import

[ˋɪmport]

(n) (v) 進口

- The Customs department will continue to monitor the import and export of merchandise.
  海關會繼續管控商品的進出口。

- They import goods from foreign countries to Taiwan.
  他們將國外商品進口至臺灣。

  延伸學習 imported goods 進口商品

---

09 export

[ˋɛksport]

(n) (v) 出口

- We export products from Taiwan to foreign countries.
  我們將臺灣的商品出口至海外。

---

10 customs

[ˋkʌstəmz]

(n) 海關

- You must carry your passport to go through customs.
  你必須帶護照才能過海關。

  延伸學習 go through customs 通過海關

---

11 inventory

[ˋɪnvənˌtorɪ]

(n) [U]

（商店的）存貨

(n) [C] 商品的清單

- I'm looking for someone to manage inventory and shipping.
  我在找人管理貨品和運送。

- This car is the best among our inventory.
  這是在我們存貨當中最好的車。

  延伸學習 an inventory of rare items 一系列稀有商品

12 stock

[stɑk]

(n) (v) 存貨;儲備

- We don't have it <u>in stock</u> / We are all <u>out of stock</u>, but I can order one in for you.
  我們沒有存貨了,但我可以幫你調貨。

- I sold the rest of the stock at lower prices.
  我把剩下的存貨用較低的價格售出了。

- Our grocery store stocks a wide range of products.
  我們的雜貨店儲備了各式商品。

- Many people rushed to <u>stock up</u> toilet paper during the novel coronavirus outbreak.
  在新冠肺炎爆發期間,許多人急著去儲備廁所衛生紙。

  延伸學習 <u>in / out of</u> stock 有/沒有存貨
  stock up 儲備
  stock market 股票市場

 測驗

▶ 是非題

_____ 1. We can buy and sell merchandise.

_____ 2. A backpacker is someone who joins a package tour.

_____ 3. Cargo containers are usually tiny.

_____ 4. Freight trains always carry passengers.

_____ 5. A portable phone is also called a mobile phone.

_____ 6. Imported goods is another way of saying local specialties.

_____ 7. To export something means to send products to another country for sale.

_____ 8. When you go through customs, you usually get a health check.

_____ 9. An inventory is something that you invented.

_____ 10. When a product is out of stock, it's sold out.

▶ 填空題

1. Houses made of _____ containers can be found in many foreign countries.

2. Jane likes electric appliances that are _____ from Japan. She thinks they are better than those made in other countries.

3. You can find a wide variety of _____ in the department store.

4. "Here's a _____ for Mr. Lin," said the mailman.

5. The criminal hid in a _____ train when he escaped.

6. Many business owners are complaining that the new policy had a bad impact on _____, making it difficult for them to transport goods abroad.

7. It might be risky to invest in the _____ market.

8. The man was caught at _____ for carrying illegal drugs.

9. Hit by panic-buying, Ben has about a month's worth of _____.

10. The _____ of Kaohsiung is the largest harbor in Taiwan.

Answer

是非題：

1. O   2. X   3. X   4. X   5. O   6. X   7. O   8. X   9. X   10. O

填空題：

1. cargo	2. imported	3. merchandise	4. package / parcel	5. freight
6. export	7. stock	8. customs	9. inventory	10. port

填空題翻譯：

1. 在外國可以看到用貨櫃做的房子。

2. Jane 喜歡日本進口的電子產品。她覺得它們比其他國的產品好。

3. 你可以在百貨公司找到許多商品。

4. 郵差說：「這裡有林先生的包裹。」

5. 犯人逃跑的時候躲在貨櫃火車裡。

6. 很多老闆抱怨新的政策對出口有不好的影響，導致他們很難將貨物運送到國外。

7. 投資股票市場有風險。

8. 那個男人在海關因為攜帶非法藥品而被抓。

9. 因為恐慌而購物，班買了一個月的貨物。

10. 高雄港是臺灣最大的海港。

Unit 27

採購
Purchasing

Track
027

budget	revenue	renowned
reimburse	disburse	expense
loan	mortgage	accurate
accuracy	accurately	priority
prior		

01 budget

['bʌdʒɪt]

(n) (v) 預算;定預算

- I use Filmora to edit my videos because it's simple and within my budget.
  我使用 Filmora 剪輯影片因為它很簡單又在我的預算內。

- 50 billion dollars has been budgeted to stimulate the economy.
  已編列 500 億美元的預算用於刺激經濟。

  延伸學習 annual / travel / marketing / advertising budget
  年預算／旅遊預算／行銷預算／廣告預算
  on / over / under budget
  在預算內／超過預算／低於預算

02 revenue

['rɛvə‚nju]

(n) 收入

注意
不要跟 "avenue"（大道）搞混

- Due to the recession, revenues plummeted this year.
  因為經濟不景氣，收入大幅降低。

- Revenue is the income made by a business.
  收入是企業的收入。

03 renowned

[rɪ'naʊnd]

(adj) 有名的

- Some people believe that it's safer to buy goods from renowned brands.
  有些人相信跟有名的品牌買商品比較安全。

- Bill Gates is a renowned business magnate, software developer, investor, and philanthropist.
  比爾・蓋茨（Bill Gates）是著名的商業巨頭、軟件開發人員、投資者和慈善家。

04 reimburse

[‚riɪm'bɝs]

(v) 補償;退款

相關詞
refund (v) 退費

- I want to know if our company will reimburse my travel expenses for the business trip.
  我想知道我們公司是否會報銷出差的旅行費用。

- Please keep your receipts if you want to be reimbursed by the company.
  如果你想由公司補償（差旅費），請保留你的收據。

refund (v) (n) VS reimburse (v) / reimbursement (n)

refund 是商品有瑕疵或是活動取消等等的退費

reimburse 是公司出差的時候由你先付款，公司之後補給你的費用

05 disburse

[dɪs`bɝs]

(v) 支付

- The renowned firm disburses charitable funds annually.
  這家著名的公司每年都會撥付慈善資金。

06 expense

[ɪk`spɛns]

(n) 費用

相關詞
budget (n) (v) 預算、
charge (n) (v) 費用

- You will be reimbursed after you get your expenses approved.
  在您的費用被批准後，您將獲得報銷。

延伸學習 medical / travel / personal / living / basic expenses
醫療／旅遊／私人／生活／基本／費用

07 loan

[lon]

(v) 貸款；借錢

相關詞
borrow (v) 借

- The bank loaned me some money.
  銀行貸款給我。

- I borrowed money from the bank.
  我跟銀行借錢。

延伸學習 get a loan from the bank 向銀行貸款

08 mortgage

[`mɔrgɪdʒ]

(n) 房貸

- I wonder if they have paid off their mortgage.
  我想知道他們是不是已經還清了房貸。

延伸學習 a 30 year / 10 million mortgage
30 年房貸／1 千萬的房貸

09 accurate

[`ækjərɪt]

(adj) 精準；正確的

- I'm not sure if this is the accurate number.
  我不確定這是不是正確的數字。

10 accuracy

[`ækjərəsɪ]

(n) 準確性

- We want to know the accuracy of the test.
  我們想要知道這個測驗的準確性。

- The system can mimic your voice with pinpoint accuracy.
  該系統可以精確地模仿您的聲音。

11 accurately [`ækjərɪtlɪ] (adv) 正確地	• I hope I did it accurately this time. I don't want to fail again! 希望我這次做對了！我不想再次失敗！
12 priority [praɪˋɔrətɪ] (n) 優先順序	• Getting your priorities right is one of the keys to happiness. 正確安排優先事項是幸福的關鍵之一。
13 prior [`praɪɚ] (adj) 之前	• No prior knowledge of the subject is required. 此課程不需要先備知識。 • We didn't receive prior notice. 我們沒有收到事前通知。 • Prior to the incident, did anything strange happen? 在事件發生之前，有發生奇怪的事情嗎？ 延伸學習 prior to... 在……之前

 測驗

▶ 是非題

_____ 1. To go over the budget means to acquire more money.

_____ 2. You can walk on the revenue.

_____ 3. If someone is renowned, he / she is well-known.

_____ 4. To reimburse is to pay back the money someone has spent it for you first.

_____ 5. To disburse means to reject the application for reimbursement.

_____ 6. Expense can refer to money, effort, or time.

_____ 7. When you borrow an amount of money from the bank, you get a loan from it.

_____ 8. A mortgage is a type of loan.

_____ 9. Approximate is a synonym for accurate.

_____ 10. Priorities usually need to be dealt first.

▶ 填空題

1. I will purchase the flight ticket for the business trip first and my company will _____ me when I get back.

2. In order to remain within budget, we need to start cutting down on our _____.

3. Thanks for _____ me the money. I promise to pay you back with interest.

4. The newlywed plans to take a 30-year _____ to buy the house they want.

5. We only have a certain amount of money, so we need to make sure to spend it carefully in order to stay within _____.

6. Please prepare all of the relevant documents _____ to the meeting.

7. Sam helped to increase the department's sales _____ by 15%.

8. This place is _____ for its picturesque scenery.

9. The students checked to make sure that the figures on their final reports were _____ before submitting them to the professor.

10. The government decided to _____ 2 million dollars to support the minorities.

Answer

是非題：

1. X   2. X   3. O   4. O   5. X   6. O   7. O   8. O   9. X   10. O

填空題：

1. reimburse   2. expenses   3. loaning   4. mortgage   5. budget

6. prior   7. revenue   8. renowned   9. accurate   10. disburse / budget

填空題翻譯：

1. 為了商務旅行我會先買機票，之後公司會讓我報銷。

2. 為了不要超出預算，我們需要降低成本。

3. 謝謝你借我錢，我保證會連本帶利還你。

4. 那對新婚夫妻計劃要用 30 年房貸來買他們想要的房子。

5. 我們的錢有固定的量，所以我們要小心的使用不能超出預算。

6. 在會議前請準備好所有相關文件。

7. 他幫助這個部門增加了 15% 的業績收入。

8. 這個地方以它如詩如畫的風景聞名。

9. 學生在交最後報告給教授之前，先檢查他們的數字是否準確。

10. 政府決定撥兩百萬資助少數族群。

稽核
Assessment

colleague	associate	incumbent
compete	competition	contest
contender	assess	assessment
weigh	evaluate	determined
determine	approve	approval

01 colleague

[kɑ`lig]

(n) 同事

相似詞
co-worker (n) 同事

- I'm having dinner with a colleague.
  我正和一位同事一起吃晚餐。

02 associate

[ə`soʃɪet]

(n) (v) 同事；關聯

用法
associate with：
associate A with B
be associated with

- People often associate pigs with laziness.
  Pigs are often <u>associated with</u> laziness.
  人們經常將豬跟懶惰聯想再一起。

  延伸學習 a business associate （一位同事）工作往來之人
  associate A with B 把 A 跟 B 連在一起

03 incumbent

[ɪn`kʌmbənt]

(n) 在職者

- The incumbent should report to the secretary general.
  在職者應向祕書長報告。

04 compete

[kəm`pit]

(v) 競爭

用法
compete with / against
sb. compete for sth.

- You will <u>compete with</u> designers from all around the world in the contest for the first prize.
  在競賽中你會跟來自世界各地的設計師爭奪第一名。

05 competition

[͵kɑmpə`tɪʃən]

(n) 競爭

相關詞
competitor (n) 競爭者、
competitive (adj) 有競
爭力的

- This is not a competition. But if it were, I would win.
  這不是一場比賽。但如果是的話，我會贏。

- This is the best burger in town! There's no competition.
  這是這裡最好的漢堡！沒人能競爭！

06 contest

['kɑntɛst]

(n) 競賽

相關詞
contestant (n) 參賽者

- Have you participated in any contests before?
  你有參加過任何比賽嗎？

  延伸學習 enter a contest 參賽
  a writing / singing / speech...contest
  寫作／歌唱／演講比賽

07 contender

[kən`tɛndɚ]

(n) 競爭者

- I am the strongest contender!
  我是最強的競爭者！

08 assess

[ə`sɛs]

(v) 評估

- We will assess the candidates based on their experiences.
  我們會根據候選人的經驗來評估他們。

09 assessment

[ə`sɛsmənt]

(n) 評價；評量

- You'll need at least a score of 60 to pass the final assessment.
  你至少要考 60 分才能通過評量。

10 weigh

[we]

(v) 秤重；權衡

相關詞
overweight (adj) 過重、
weight scale (n)
體重機

- How much do you weigh?
  你體重多重？

- How much does your luggage weigh?
  行李多重？

- Weigh the options carefully before you make your decision.
  在決定之前先仔細衡量所有的選項。

- We might ask some experts to weigh in on the issue.
  我們可能會請一些專家參與這個議題的討論。

  延伸學習 weigh in 積極參與

11 evaluate

[ɪ`væljʊˌet]

(v) 評估；評價

- Your performance will be evaluated by your supervisor.
  你的表現會由你的監督者來評量。

12 **determined**

[dɪˋtɝˍmɪnd]

(adj) 有決心的

- I am determined to do this.
  = I've <u>decided / made up my mind</u> to do this.
  我有決心要做這件事。

13 **determine**

[dɪˋtɝˍmɪn]

(v) 決定

相似詞
decide (v) 、 **resolve (v)**
決定

- The executive will determine who will get a raise.
  執行長會決定誰可以加薪。

- The judges will determine who shall leave the competition.
  評審會決定誰要離開比賽。

14 **approve**

[əˋpruv]

(v) 認同；許可

相似詞
permit (v) 許可、
agree (v) 同意

- The executive's proposal is approved by the board of directors.
  執行長的提案被董事會認可了。

- She doesn't approve of my boyfriend.
  她不認同我的男友。

15 **approval**

[əˋpruvl̩]

(n) 認可

- I'm not seeking for her <u>approval / validation / permission</u>.
  我不是在尋求她的認同／許可。

▶ 是非題

_____ 1. A colleague is someone whom you work with - your manager is an example.

_____ 2. To associate two things together means to connect them in your mind.

_____ 3. An incumbent president has already retired.

_____ 4. A competition is an event where people try to win a prize by being better than others.

_____ 5. A contender is someone who is content.

_____ 6. You can gain assess to the room with the right key.

_____ 7. To evaluate means to judge the quality or value of something or someone.

_____ 8. If you're determined, you have already made a decision.

_____ 9. If someone does not approve of your opinion, he / she disagrees with you.

_____ 10. To seek for approval can mean asking for permission.

▶ 填空題

1. My _____ will take over the project after I leave the company.

2. The organization will hold a piano _____ and welcome students around the world to join.

3. The _____ vice president plans to retire in two years.

4. Do not ask girls how much they _____.

5. He brought the jewelry to the shop to let the expert _____ its worth.

6. My boss _____ of our plan and told us to start taking action immediately.

7. The brand has established an excellent image. When customers see its logo, they _____ it with high quality.

8. All employees are required to take an online _____ and their managers will delegate tasks according to the result.

9. The budget will _____ the amount of money we're allowed to spend during the business trip.

10. The company is our greatest _____ and we're constantly planning strategies to win the hearts of customers.

Answer

是非題：

1. X   2. O   3. X   4. O   5. X   6. X   7. O   8. O   9. O   10. O

填空題：

1. colleague   2. contest / competition   3. incumbent   4. weigh

5. evaluate / assess 6. approved   7. associate   8. assessment

9. determine   10. competitor

填空題翻譯：

1. 在我離開公司之後我的同事會把專案接過去。

2. 那個組織會舉辦一個鋼琴比賽並且邀請全世界的學生參加。

3. 現任的副總計劃在兩年內退休。

4. 不要問女生的體重多少。

5. 他把珠寶帶到店裡讓專家衡量它的價值。

6. 我的老闆同意了我們的計劃並且要求我們立刻行動。

7. 這個品牌建立了優良的形象。當客人看到他的商標他們會聯想到高品質。

8. 所有員工都必須做一個線上測驗，接著他們的經理會依照結果分配工作。

9. 我們商務旅行能花多少錢將由這個預算決定。

10. 這間公司是我們最大的競爭者，我們不斷計畫新的策略想要贏得顧客的心。

工作表現一
Job performance 1

volunteer	solve
solution	contribute
donate	affect
effect	impact
influence	convince
convinced	persuade

01 volunteer

[ˌvɑlən`tɪr]

(n) (v) 志願者；自願

- Any volunteers?

  有志願者嗎？

  延伸學習 volunteer to do sth. 自願做某事

02 solve

[sɑlv]

(v) 解決

- Can you help me solve this difficult math problem?

  可以幫我解這題困難的數學題嗎？

03 solution

[sə`luʃən]

(n) 解決方案

用法
solution to sth.

- I think I've found a solution to this problem.

  我想我找到問題的解決方案了。

04 contribute

[kən`trɪbjut]

(v) 付出；貢獻

相關詞
contribution (n) 付出；貢獻

用法
contribute + to

- The teacher asked her students to think about how they can contribute to the society.

  老師請學生思考他們能如何對社會有所貢獻。

  延伸學習 contribute (a lot / greatly) to the society / this project 為社會／這個專案付出很多

05 donate

[`donet]

(v) 捐

相關詞
donation (n) 捐獻

- To contribute to the global society, we've donated a million face masks.

  為了貢獻給全球的社會，我們捐了一百萬個口罩。

06 affect

[ə`fɛkt]

(v) 影響

- My new job deeply affects my life.

  我的新工作深深影響了我的生活。

- How does climate change affect us?

  氣候變遷會如何影響我們？

07 effect

[ɪˋfɛkt]

(n) 影響

用法
effect + on

- My new job has an <u>effect on</u> my life.
  我的新工作對我的生活有影響。

- What are the effects of global warming?
  全球暖化的影響是什麼？

08 impact

[ˋɪmpækt]

(n) 影響

[ɪmˋpækt]

(v) 影響

用法
impact + on

- My new job greatly impacts my life.
  = My new job has a great <u>impact on</u> my life.
  我的新工作大大影響了我的生活。

- What are the impacts of climate change?
  氣候變遷的影響是什麼？

- Climate change is here, and it's causing a wide range of impacts that will affect every human on Earth in severe ways.
  氣候變遷確實存在，它會對地球上每個人類造成許多嚴重影響。

09 influence

[ˋɪnflʊəns]

(n) (v) 影響

用法
influence + on

- My new job influences my life.
  我的新工作影響了我的生活。

- I hope you can influence his decision.
  我希望你能影響（改變）他的決定。

- I think he has a bad <u>influence on</u> you.
  我覺得他對你有不好的影響。

  延伸學習 an influencer 有影響力的人

10 convince

[kənˋvɪns]

(v) 使……信服

- I need to convince my superior that I can be trusted.
  我需要讓我的上級知道我是可以信任的。

- I need to convince my parents to trust me.
  我要讓我的父母信任我。

11 convinced

[kənˋvɪnst]

(adj) 確信的

- I'm convinced that I'm able to complete the task.
  我有自信我能完成這任務。

12 persuade

[pɚ`swed]

(v) 說服

- I'm planning to persuade the manager to give me another chance.
  我計畫說服經理再給我一次機會。

- The little boy persuaded his mom to buy him the toy.
  小男孩說服了媽媽買玩具給他。

 測驗

▶ 是非題

_____ 1. A volunteer does his/her work due to responsibility.

_____ 2. A solution is the answer to a problem.

_____ 3. To make contributions means to give money or make efforts in order to achieve a goal.

_____ 4. A person can donate blood to help others.

_____ 5. The word affect and effect are interchangeable.

_____ 6. A good song can effect people.

_____ 7. To impact someone means to create a powerful effect on someone.

_____ 8. To have an influence on someone means to catch a flu.

_____ 9. To convince means to make someone believe something.

_____ 10. It usually takes a lot of effort to persuade someone.

▶ 填空題

1. It is wrong to take credits without making any _____.

2. The successful entrepreneur _____ a huge amount of money to the charity.

3. Please think before you do something because your actions might _____ other people.

4. YouTubers have expanded their _____ on the society.

5. My grandma worked as a _____ in the charity after retirement.

6. The sales person tried to _____ me that the quality of his product is better.

7. Last week when I visited the restaurant, the waiter _____ me to order a dish on the menu by describing how good it tasted.

8. The _____ of this medicine is very strong and it makes you sleepy in 10 minutes.

9. It is difficult to find a _____ to this complicated problem.

10. The virus had a huge _____ on global economy and totally changed people's lives.

Unit 30

工作表現二
Job performance 2

perform	performance
range	rise
rank	status
retain	senior
capacity	command
review	

01 perform

[pɚˋfɔrm]

(v) 進行；實施；表演

- That talented engineer can perform multiple tasks simultaneously.
  那位有才華的工程師可以同時進行很多任務。

- The surgeon performed several operations today.
  那位外科醫師今天動了好幾個手術。

- The rapper can perform music without using any instrument(s).
  那位饒舌歌手可以不用任何樂器表演音樂。

延伸學習 perform a task /an operation / music
進行任務／動手術／表演音樂
performed well / badly / poorly
表現得很好／不好／很糟

02 performance

[pɚˋfɔrməns]

(n) 表現

- My parents care about my academic performance very much.
  我的父母很在乎我的學業表現。

延伸學習 job / academic performance 工作／學業表現

03 range

[rendʒ]

(n) (v) 範圍

用法
range from...to

- A salary range is the amount of compensation a candidate would accept for a position.
  薪資範圍是指候選人願意接受一個職位的薪資範疇。

- The price of the train ticket ranges from 20 to 50 dollars.
  火車票的價格範圍是 20 到 50 元。

延伸學習 long / short – range plan 長程／短程計畫

04 rise

[raɪz]

(v) 升起

- Rise and shine! Time to wake up!
  要起來囉！該起床囉！

- It's time (for you) to rise up and make your voice heard.
  是時候站起來為自己發聲了。

延伸學習 watch the sunrise 看日出

05 rank

[ræŋk]
(n) (v) 位階;等級;
排序

相關詞
ranking (n) 等級;順序

- Tzu-ying Tai, a strong contender, is in the first rank of international badminton players.
  戴資穎,一位很強的選手,是世界一流的羽球選手。

- The rookie, a fast learner, rose through the ranks and became a manager in merely 6 months.
  那位新人學習力很強,在僅僅六個月內就爬上階級晉升為經理。

  延伸學習 ranked first in the class 班排第一
  a top-ranked business 排名很前面的企業
  rise through the ranks 往上爬

06 status

[`stetəs]
(n) 狀態

- You can check the current status of your flight on our application.
  您可以在我們的應用程式上面查詢您的航班目前的狀況。

  延伸學習 social status / current status / marital status / economic status
  社交狀態╱目前的狀態╱婚姻狀態╱經濟狀況
  status quo 現狀
  to maintain the status quo 維持現狀

07 retain

[rɪ`ten]
(v) 保持;保留

相似詞
maintain (v) 維持

- The company offers bonuses in order to retain outstanding employees.
  公司提供獎勵以留住優秀的員工。

  延伸學習 retain memory / talented employees
  保留記憶╱優秀員工

08 senior

[`sinjɚ]
(adj) 資深的

相反詞
rookie (n) 菜鳥

- Whenever the newcomer has questions, he consults the senior worker for advice.
  每當那位新人有問題,他就諮詢資深員工的意見。

  延伸學習 senior engineer / senior advisor / senior citizen
  資深工程師╱資深顧問╱年長者

09 capacity

[kə`pæsətɪ]

(n) 能力

相似詞
capability (n) 能力

- I think I have a great capacity for coding.
  我認為我對寫程式語言相當擅長。

  延伸學習 exceed the maximum limit / expectations
  超出最高限制／期待

10 command

[kə`mænd]

(n) (v) 掌握

- Since Jenny has a good command of English, her teacher commanded (demanded) her to speak English in class.
  因為 Jenny 英文很好，她的老師就要求她上課要說英文。

  延伸學習 have good command of English
  英文能力不錯（對英文有很好的掌握）

11 review

[rɪ`vju]

(n) (v) 評論；審查

- Before I send an email to my clients, I ask my supervisor to review it first.
  在我將電子郵件寄給客戶之前，我會請我的上司先審查過。

  延伸學習 book / movie / monthly performance reviews
  書評／影評／每月績效審查
  review guidelines 審查方針

 測驗

▶ 是非題

_____ 1. A doctor can perform a task or an operation.

_____ 2. A wide range of means a variety of.

_____ 3. To be given a salary increase is called getting a rise.

_____ 4. If a person ranks first in class, it means she / he is at the top of the class.

_____ 5. You can check the status of your flight online.

_____ 6. You should retain eye-contact with the person you're talking to.

_____ 7. A first – year student at college is called a college senior.

8. To exceed one's expectations means to go beyond one's expectations.

9. To have a good command of English means to be proficient in English.

10. If you are not sure whether you should watch the movie, you can read the movie reviews on Rotten Tomatoes first.

▶ 填空題

Louise has been working in the same company for five years now. However, he has never been promoted. Recently, he learned that the company has planned to downsize in personnel. To 1.＿＿＿＿＿ his position, Louise has devised a long 2.＿＿＿＿ plan to move up the 3.＿＿＿＿. First, he is determined to take on more responsibilities. Although it might be 4.＿＿＿＿ his capabilities, he's convinced that he would leave a good impression on his supervisor if he takes the initiative. Next, he will provide regular 5.＿＿＿＿ updates. He figured that if his supervisor knows that he is always on schedule, he will get a high score in the
6.＿＿＿＿ 7.＿＿＿＿. In addition, he will consult a 8.＿＿＿＿ employee who has a good 9.＿＿＿＿ of time management for advice. Louise believes that by completing the above tasks, he will not only secure his job, but might even 10.＿＿＿＿ up to a higher level.

Answer

是非題：

1. O   2. O   3. X   4. O   5. O   6. X   7. X   8. O   9. O   10. O

填空題：

1. retain   2. range   3. ranks   4. beyond   5. status
6. performance 7. review   8. senior   9. command   10. rise

填空題翻譯：

　　路易斯在同一間公司工作五年了，然而他從來沒有被升遷過。最近他得知公司計畫要裁員。為了保住他的職位，路易斯做了一個長期的計畫想要提升他的排名。首先，他決定要承擔更多責任。雖然有可能會超出他的能力範圍，但是他相信如果他更積極主動，會給他的主管好的印象。接下來他會定期提供工作紀錄（status update 狀態更新，這是提供老闆最新工作進度的英文說法）。他覺得如果他的上司知道他總是準時完成工作，他就會在考核的時候得到高分。除此之外，他會請一位時間管理良好的資深員工給他一些建議。路易斯相信藉由完成以上的任務，他不只能夠確保他的工作，甚至可能升到更高的階層。

優良員工特質
Good Workers

Track
031

devote	committed	dedicate
dedicated	dedication	initial
initiative	obligate	obligation
monitor	progress	effort
effortless	talent	

01 devote

[dɪ`vot]

(v) 把……貢獻給

用法
devote + to

- He is a devoted (adj) worker who devotes his life to his work.
他是個把生命奉獻於工作的努力員工。

02 committed

[kə`mɪtɪd]

(adj) 忠誠的；
承諾過的

相關詞
commit (v) 犯；承諾

- I am committed to learning and teaching English.
我決定要認真學習以及教英文。

- I have committed myself to improving my English.
我決心要努力加強英文。

延伸學習 be committed to sth. (N / Ving)... 忠誠地做某事
commit oneself to sb. / sth.
承諾跟某人在一起、盡忠職守地做某事
be in a committed relationship
在一段穩定的感情關係中

03 dedicate

[`dɛdə‚ket]

(v) 致力於

用法
dedicate + to

- She dedicates her life to helping the poor.
她終生致力於幫助貧窮的人。

04 dedicated

[`dɛdə‚ketɪd]

(adj) 盡心盡力的

- The non-profit organization is dedicated to protecting the environment.
那個非營利組織盡力保護環境。

05 dedication

[‚dɛdə`keʃən]

(n) 付出

- Thank you for your hard work and dedication.
謝謝你的努力和付出。

06 initial

[ɪˋnɪʃəl]

(adj) (n) 最初的；姓名的第一個字母

相關詞
initially (adv) 最初地

- Although initial reports showed that the vaccine was effective, it still requires more testing.
  雖然最初的報告顯示此疫苗有效，還是需要更多檢測。

- Cindy Sung's initials are C and S.
  Cindy Sung 的姓名首字母是 C 和 S。

- Initially (adv), I didn't know what to do.
  我一開始不知道該怎麼做。

延伸學習 initial reaction / reports / phase
最初的反應／報告／時期

07 initiative

[ɪˋnɪʃətɪv]

(n) [U] 主動性

(n) 倡議

- Cindy impressed her supervisor when she took (the) initiative and presented her ideas.
  Cindy 主動呈現她的想法，令主管印象深刻。

延伸學習 take (the) initiative 主動出擊
show initiative 展現積極主動
peace initiative 和平倡議

08 obligate

[ˋɑbləˌget]

(v) 使……有義務

相似詞
responsible (adj)
負責的、
accountable (adj)
有責任的

- The airline is obligated to compensate you under the following circumstances.
  在以下狀況下航空公司有義務賠償你。

- The following situations may obligate the airline to compensate you.
  以下的情況可能使航空公司有義務賠償你。

延伸學習 be obligated to... / obligate sb. to do sth.
有義務做某事／使某人有義務做某事

09 obligation

[ˌɑbləˋgeʃən]

(n) 義務

相似詞
responsibility (n) 責任、
accountability (n) 責任

- It's our obligation to join the military for a year.
  我們有義務從軍一年。

延伸學習 a military service obligation 當兵義務
perform compulsory military service
服義務兵役

10 monitor

[`mɑnətɚ]

(v) 監控

(n) 監督員；監測器；螢幕

相似詞
oversee (v) 監督、
supervise (v) 監督

- The manager wants to know how to monitor a project successfully.
  那位經理想要知道如何成功地控管一個專案。

- The professor assigned Cindy to be the monitor of the activity.
  教授指派 Cindy 當活動的監控員。

延伸學習 to monitor work progress 監控工作進度
a TV / computer monitor 電視／電腦螢幕

11 progress

[´prɑgrɛs]

(n) 進度

- How much progress has been made?
  進度到哪了？

12 effort

[`ɛfɚt]

(n) 努力

- I can see that you've put a lot of effort into your work.
  我看得出你在你的作品中付出很多努力。

延伸學習 put a lot of effort in(to) sth. 很努力做某事

13 effortless

[`ɛfɚtlɪs]

(adj) 不費力

- You make it seem effortless!
  你讓它看起來不費吹灰之力！

14 talent

[`tælənt]

(n) 天分

- What should we do to retain talented (adj) employees?
  我們該如何留住優秀的員工？

延伸學習 show your talents 表現你的長處

181

測驗

▶ 是非題

_____ 1. To devote means to vote for something or someone you believe in.

_____ 2. If you're committed to doing something, you spend time and energy on it.

_____ 3. To dedicate to something means to work really hard towards something you believe in.

_____ 4. A person's initial is his / her middle name.

_____ 5. Obligation is something you have to do.

_____ 6. To monitor means to watch and check something or someone carefully for a period of time.

_____ 7. If you're making steady progress with English, your English skills are improving.

_____ 8. The antonym for effortless is effortful.

_____ 9. Your talent is something you work really hard to acquire.

▶ 填空題

1. At the event, Jim thanked us for our _____ and effort throughout the year.

2. She never waits to be told what to do and always takes the _____.

3. The security guards will take turns to _____ the building 24 hours a day.

4. He _____ all of his time to work and forgets to take care of his health.

5. When we watched her play the flute, it looked _____. However, she actually worked very hard for the performance.

6. She _____ a serious crime and was sent to jail for ten years.

7. You need _____ as well as effort to be successful at/in this job.

8. If you continue to learn English every single day, I'm sure you will improve and make steady _____.

9. Make sure you read the contract carefully because once you sign it, you're under _____ to its terms.

10. You don't need to sign your full name, just your _____ should be fine.

Answer

是非題：

1. X   2. O   3. O   4. X   5. O   6. O   7. O   8. O   9. X

填空題：

| 1. dedication | 2. initiative | 3. monitor | 4. devotes | 5. effortless |
| 6. committed | 7. talent | 8. progress | 9. obligation | 10. initials |

填空題翻譯：

1. 在活動當中 Jim 感謝大家這一年的努力和付出。

2. 她從來不等別人告知她該做什麼，並且總是積極主動。

3. 警衛會全天候 24 小時輪流監控這棟大樓。

4. 他把所有時間奉獻於工作，忘記照顧自己的健康。

5. 當我們看她吹奏長笛，看起來毫不費力，然而事實上她為了這場表演非常努力。

6. 她因為犯下重罪被關 10 年。

7. 這工作需要才華和努力才能成功。

8. 如果你每天持續學習英文，我保證你的英文會進步並且穩定地成長。

9. 在簽合約之前請一定要仔細閱讀，因為一旦簽署了，你就有義務履行合約中的內容。

10. 你不需要簽全名，只要簽姓名的第一個字母即可。

agenda	address
deliver	delivery
issue	item
focus	focused
pinpoint	conference
elaborate	discuss
discussion	

01 agenda

[əˋdʒɛndə]

(n) 議程

用法
on the agenda
相似詞
schedule (n) 行程

- What's <u>on the agenda</u>?
  議程內容有什麼？

- There are several items <u>on the agenda</u>.
  今天有幾個事項要討論。

  延伸學習 a hidden agenda 隱密的動機

02 address

[ˋædrɛs]

(n) 地址；演說

- What's your email / delivery address?
  你的電郵／寄件地址是什麼？

  延伸學習 inaugural address 就職演說
  John F. Kennedy's Inaugural Address
  甘迺迪總統的就職演說

[əˋdrɛs]

(vt) 寫地址；發表演說；處理；對付

- The letter was addressed to me.
  這封信是寫給我的。

- The principal would like to address a few words to the students.
  校長想要跟同學們說幾句話。

- "W.H.O. is not only fighting Covid-19," Dr. Ghebreyesus said. "We're also working to address polio, measles, malaria, Ebola, H.I.V., tuberculosis, malnutrition, cancer, diabetes, mental health and many other diseases and conditions."
  Dr. Ghebreyesus 說世界衛生組織不僅在對抗新冠肺炎，也在努力對付小兒麻痺、麻疹、瘧疾、伊波拉、愛滋病、肺結核、糖尿病、精神疾病以及許多其他疾病和症狀。

  延伸學習 address an issue 處理議題

03 deliver

[dɪˋlɪvɚ]

(v) 發表；運送

- Your meal will be delivered by Uber Eats.
  你的餐點會由 Uber Eats 運送。

  延伸學習 deliver a speech 發表演說

04 delivery

[dɪ`lɪvərɪ]

(n) 運送；遞送

- Thanks to smartphones, the popularity of food delivery service has grown significantly.
  因為智慧型手機，食物外送服務變得非常受歡迎。

  延伸學習 delivery address / food delivery service
  運送地址／食物外送服務
  express delivery / special delivery
  快遞／特快專遞

補充說明

express [ɪk`sprɛs] (n) (adv) (adj) 快遞

an express train 高速列車

send the package (by) express 藉由快遞送包裹

05 issue

[`ɪʃʊ]

(n) 議題；
（報刊的）期

(v) 發布

相關詞
problem (n) 問題
（比 issue 負面）

- Is that an issue? What's your issue (problem)?
  那會是個問題嗎？你有什麼問題？

- You have more issues than the 17 magazines.
  你比 17 雜誌（一個年輕女性雜誌）有更多期／問題！（語意雙關）

  延伸學習 important / critical issue 重要議題
  issue fines 罰款
  issue a statement 發布聲明

06 item

[`aɪtəm]

(n) 項目

- Let's move on to the next item on the agenda.
  我們來討論議程上的下一個項目。

- There are so many items on the menu!
  菜單上有好多選項！

07 focus

[`fokəs]

(v) 專注

(n) 重點

相似詞
concentrate (v) 專注

- Please focus on me.
  請把注意力給我。

- Let's focus on this chart.
  我們來仔細看這表格。

- What's the focus of the report?
  這個報告的重點是什麼？

  延伸學習 focus on sth. / concentrate on sth. 專注於某事

08 focused

[`fokəst]

(adj) 專注的

- It's difficult to stay focused in the lecture.
  這演講很難讓人保持專注。

補充說明

concentrate 由字首 con（一起）＋字根 center（中心）組成＝一起來到中間，延伸成專注於……的意思。center 這個字根也有許多相關單字，例如 self-centered 自我中心、Eurocentric 歐洲中心主義。

09 pinpoint

[`pɪn͵pɔɪnt]

(v) 明確指出

相似詞
identify (v) 指認

- I don't understand why the Board of Directors refused to pinpoint the problem and insisted on using their own ways.
  我不懂為什麼董事會拒絕指出問題並堅持使用他們的方式。

延伸學習 pinpoint an issue 明確指出問題

10 conference

[`kɑnfərəns]

(n) 會議

相似詞
meeting (n) 會議

- I have a conference / meeting at 3 o'clock.
  我三點有個會議。

延伸學習 a conference call 電話會議

11 elaborate

[ɪ`læbə͵ret]

(v) (adj) 詳述；詳細的

用法
elaborate + on

相反詞
brief (v) 簡述

- Can you please elaborate on that?
  你可以詳細說明嗎？

- I will elaborate on this issue later.
  我待會會詳細說明這個議題。

延伸學習 an elaborate address / speech 詳細的演說

12 discuss

[dɪ`skʌs]

(v) 討論

用法
discuss 後不接介係詞

相似詞
talk about 討論

- Shall we discuss the last item on the list?
  我們要討論清單上最後一個項目嗎？

- I will discuss with them.
  我會跟他們討論。

13 discussion

[dɪ`skʌʃən]

(n) 討論

- I will have a discussion with them.
  我會跟他們討論。

- Let's have a brief discussion about the issue (which was) addressed in the conference just now.
  我們快速討論一下剛剛會議中提到的議題。

- The matter is still under discussion.
  這問題還在討論中。

測驗

▶ 是非題

_____ 1. An agenda is similar to a schedule.

_____ 2. To address a problem can mean to begin to deal with a problem.

_____ 3. You can deliver a speech.

_____ 4. An issue is similar to a problem.

_____ 5. The word "item" is uncountable.

_____ 6. When a student dozes off in class, he is focused.

_____ 7. To pinpoint a problem means to solve the problem.

_____ 8. You can have a conference in the toilet.

_____ 9. You can briefly elaborate on a topic.

_____ 10. You can talk about something, so you can also discuss about something.

► 填空題

1. The professional officers were able to _____ the cause of the accident in a short period of time.

2. We need to _____ the issue and look for ways to solve it.

3. There are only two _____ on the agenda; it's going to be a short meeting.

4. We will go over the items on the _____ before the meeting.

5. I can't _____ because you're making so much noise!

6. Please _____ with me before you make the final decision.

7. I will _____ a speech about e-commerce next week.

8. They put a lot of effort and made _____ preparations for this event.

9. This _____ caught people's attention and now everyone is talking about it.

10. Phillip and I will represent our company to attend the business _____ tomorrow.

Answer

是非題：

1. O   2. O   3. O   4. O   5. X   6. X   7. X   8. X   9. X   10. X

填空題：

1. pinpoint   2. address   3. items   4. agenda   5. focus

6. discuss   7. deliver   8. elaborate   9. issue   10. conference

填空題翻譯：

1. 那些專業的警官能夠在短時間內指出造成意外的原因。

2. 我們需要處理這個議題並且尋找解決方式。

3. 議程上面只有兩個事項，這會是一個很短的會議。

4. 在會議開始之前，我們會先一起看過議程上面的事項

5. 我沒辦法專心因為你太吵了！

6. 在做最後決定之前請先和我討論。

7. 下禮拜我有一個關於電子商務的演講。

8. 他們很努力為這個活動作最詳盡的準備。

9. 這個議題吸引到大家的注意，現在所有人都在談論它。

10. Phillip 和我會代表公司去參加明天的會議。

會議與簡報二
Presentation 2

Track
033

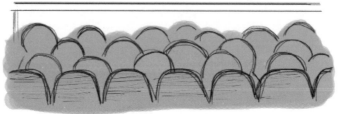

proceed	continue
interrupt	disrupt
session	postpone
cancel	summary
minutes	clarify

01 **proceed**

[prə`sid]

(v) 繼續

- Let's proceed to the next item.
  請繼續討論下一個項目。

- Sorry for the interruption. Please proceed.
  剛剛不好意思干擾到大家了，請繼續。

- This is the final boarding call for passengers Cindy and Jenny Sung for flight 101A to Taipei.
  Please <u>proceed to</u> gate 5B immediately.
  搭乘航班 101A 前往臺北的旅客 Cindy Sung 和 Jenny Sung，
  這是最後一次登機的廣播，請盡速前往閘門 5B。

  延伸學習 proceed to 前往

02 **continue**

[kən`tɪnjʊ]

(v) 繼續

- Let's continue to discuss the issue.
  我們繼續討論這議題吧。

- Shall we continue?
  要繼續嗎？

- I'm not able to continue this conversation.
  我沒辦法繼續這個對話。

  延伸學習 continue to do sth. 繼續做某事
  to be continued... 未完待續……

03 **interrupt**

[͵ɪntə`rʌpt]

(v) 干擾；打擾

- Please don't interrupt me when I'm talking. There will be time for you to ask questions.
  我在講話的時候請不要干擾我。會有時間讓你問問題。

- Sorry for the interruption. Please <u>proceed / continue</u>.
  不好意思干擾到大家了，請繼續。

04 **disrupt**

[dɪs`rʌpt]

(v) 破壞

相關詞
disturb (v) 打擾
(Do not disturb.)
（請勿打擾。）

- Our travel plans were disrupted by the <u>typhoon / virus</u>.
  我們的旅遊計畫被颱風／病毒破壞了。

rupt 字根：爆發

erupt: e + rupt → 出來＋爆發 → 爆發

disrupt: dis + rupt → 分開＋爆發 → 使中斷、打擾

interrupt: inter + rupt → 之間＋爆發 → 打斷

bankrupt: bank + rupt → 銀行帳戶＋爆炸 → 錢全部流失＝破產

corrupt: core（核心）+ rupt → 良心＋爆炸 → 道德敗壞

---

05 session

[`sɛʃən]

(n) 會議；課程

- Can our meeting be scheduled in the afternoon? I already have a morning session today.
  我們的會議可以安排在下午嗎？我今天早上已經有會議了。

  延伸學習 morning session / training session
  早晨的會議／訓練課程

---

06 postpone

[post`pon]

(v) 延後；延期

補充
take a rain check 延期
put off 拖延
procrastinate 拖延

- If you want to postpone the wedding, I'd rather cancel it.
  如果你想要把婚禮延後，我寧願取消。

- Something came up. Can I take a rain check?
  我突然有事，可以下次再約嗎？

- Never put off till tomorrow what you can do today.
  永遠不要把今天可以做的事拖到明天再做。

---

07 cancel

[`kænsl]

(v) 取消

- Due to the torrential rain, we had to cancel the picnic.
  因為大雨，我們必須取消野餐。

- The dinner is canceled.
  晚餐取消了。

---

08 summary

[`sʌmərɪ]

(n) 摘要

相關詞
summarize (n) 總結；
概述

- You can find the summary of the movie on this website.
  你可以在這個網站上找到這部電影的簡述。

  延伸學習 a brief summary of... 某事的簡短摘要
  in summary 總而言之

09 minutes

[ˋmɪnɪts]
(n) 會議記錄

- Can you take the meeting minutes?
  你可以做會議記錄嗎？

  延伸學習 take minutes 做會議記錄

10 clarify

[ˋklærəˏfaɪ]
(v) 澄清

相關詞
clarity (n) 清晰；清楚
clarification (n) 闡明

- Sorry but I don't quite follow you. Please, could you clarify what you mean by "go big or go home"?
  不好意思，但我聽不太懂。請問可以説明一下你説的「go big or go home」是什麼意思嗎？

- Ah, I see. Thanks for clarifying.
  阿，我了解了。感謝説明。

  延伸學習 ask for clarifications 請求闡述。

 測驗

▶ 是非題

_____ 1. To proceed means to move forward or to continue to do something.

_____ 2. If a movie says it will be continued, you're likely to see a sequel in the future.

_____ 3. People usually enjoy being interrupted.

_____ 4. To disrupt means to prevent something from continuing.

_____ 5. A session refers to a period of time for certain activities.

_____ 6. To postpone an event means to adjust the schedule and advance the date.

_____ 7. If the meeting is cancelled, you no longer need to attend it.

_____ 8. To summarize means to include every detail of something.

_____ 9. To take minutes means to keep track of time.

_____ 10. You clarify something by making it easier to understand.

▶ 填空題

1. The typhoon totally _____ our plans of traveling around the country.

2. We need to _____ with the project since we are already behind schedule.

3. Employees are required to attend a training _____ in order to understand how the business runs.

4. The couple decided to _____ the wedding after the big fight.

5. She _____ to dance despite her knee injury.

6. Due to some technical issues, the online forum needs to be _____ . Please rejoin later.

7. Please _____ the main idea of the book and write a brief report.

8. He _____ her speech because he was too eager to share his thoughts.

9. Please _____ the second point on your proposal because it is a little confusing.

10. It is very important to take _____ so that you know what topics have been covered during the meeting.

(Answer)

是非題：

1. O　　2. O　　3. X　　4. O　　5. O　　6. X　　7. O　　8. X　　9. X　　10. O

填空題：

1. disrupted　　2. proceed　　3. session　　4. cancel

5. continues / continued　　6. postponed　　7. summarize　　8. interrupted

9. clarify　　10. minutes

填空題翻譯：

1. 這颱風徹底打亂了我們在這國家的旅行計畫。

2. 我們必須要繼續進行專案因為我們已經落後了。

3. 為了瞭解公司如何運作，員工需要參加一個訓練課程。

4. 在大吵一架之後這對情侶決定取消婚禮。

5. 儘管膝蓋受傷她仍然繼續跳舞。

6. 由於一些技術上的問題，線上討論要延後。請稍候再參加。

7. 請摘要這本書並且寫一個簡短的報告。

8. 他打斷了她的演講因為他急著要分享他的想法。

9. 請闡述你提案中的第二項，因為它有點令人困惑。

10. 作會議記錄很重要，因為這樣你才知道會議中涵蓋了哪些主題。

Unit 34 公關
PR

Track
034

relations	publicity	represent
representative	spokesperson	statement
state	establish	exclusive
rumor	maximize	minimize

01 relations

[rɪˋleʃənz]

(n) [U] 公共關係

- She works in public relations.
  她在公關公司／部門工作。

- The candidate hired a public relations company to help <u>improve / promote</u> his image.
  候選人聘請了公關公司來幫助他提升他的形象。

  延伸學習 public relations (PR) 公共關係

02 publicity

[pʌbˋlɪsətɪ]

(n) 關注；宣傳

- The girl received wide publicity for her YouTube video.
  這個女孩的 YouTube 影片廣受關注。

- Her actions attracted both positive and negative publicity.
  她的舉動引起了正面和負面的關注。

03 represent

[ˌrɛprɪˋzɛnt]

(v) 代表

- Steve Jobs represented Apple.
  史蒂夫・賈伯斯（Steve Jobs）代表蘋果。

- In Chinese culture, pigs represent laziness.
  在中國文化中，豬代表懶惰。

04 representative

[rɛprɪˋzɛntətɪv]

(n) 代表人

- You can talk to me. I'm their representative.
  妳可以跟我說。我是他們的代表人。

- The global corporation has representatives running business in many countries.
  這家全球企業在許多國家都有代表人負責營運。

05 spokesperson

[ˋspoksˌpɝsn]

(n) 發言人

- She is the spokesperson of the government.
  她是政府發言人。

- She speaks on behalf of the government.
  她代表政府發言。

06 statement

[ˋstetmənt]

(n) 聲明；陳述

- The politician made a public statement to silence the rumors.
  這位政治人物發表公開聲明以消除謠言。

  延伸學習 a financial / public / written / false statement
  財務證明／公開聲明／書面聲明／虛假陳述
  make a statement 陳述、發表聲明

07 state

[stet]

(v) 陳述；聲明；說明

相關詞
overstate (v) 誇大、
understate (v)
避重就輕

- The singer repeatedly stated that he did nothing wrong.
  這歌手重複聲明他沒有做錯事。

補充說明

over, under 可以結合許多單字形成新的單字,但是它們都保有原單字的意思,所以非常好理解!

例如:

state (v) 陳述:overstate (v) 過度陳述 → 誇大
　　　　　　understate (v) 陳述過少 → 避重就輕、understated (adj) 避重就輕的

age (n) 年齡:overage (adj) 超過年齡的、underage (adj) 未達規定年齡的

joy (n) 開心:overjoyed (adj) 極度開心

burden (n) 負擔:overburden (v) 使過度負擔

rate (n) (v) 評估、價格:overrate (v) 評價過高、overrated (adj) 評價過高的
　　　　　　　　　　　underrate (v) 評價過低、underrated (adj) 評價過低的

estimate (v) 估計:overestimate (v) 高估、underestimate (v) 低估

08 establish

[ə`stæblɪʃ]

(v) 建立

相似詞
constitute (v) 組成、
construct (v) 建立、
compose (v) 組成

- The firm was established in 1995.
  這間公司是在 1995 年建立的。

- How do you establish strong relationships with clients?
  您如何與客戶建立牢固的關係?

09 exclusive

[ɪk`sklusɪv]

(adj) 獨有的

- Those who work in public relations often get exclusive tickets to various activities.
  從事公共關係工作的人通常會獲得各種活動的獨家門票。

- This is an exclusive party. Only VIP members are invited.
  這是一個私人派對,只有 VIP 會員受邀參加。

10 rumor [ˋrumɚ] (n) 謠言	• **Rumor** has it that he is having an affair. 據說他有婚外情。 延伸學習 rumor has it that... 據説 spread / silence / quash rumors 散播／消除／剷除謠言
11 maximize [ˋmæksəˌmaɪz] (v) 最大化	• We would help you **maximize** your advantages. 我們會幫你把優勢最大化。
12 minimize [ˋmɪnəˌmaɪz] (v) 最小化	• One of the responsibilities of a PR agency is to **minimize** its clients' weaknesses. 公關公司的其中一個責任就是幫助客戶將缺點最小化。

 測驗

▶ 是非題

_____ 1. Public relations is the activity of keeping a good relationship with the public.

_____ 2. You can easily attract publicity by commuting to work.

_____ 3. Bees represent diligence in both English and Chinese.

_____ 4. The person who is speaking is called the spokesperson.

_____ 5. A statement is always in written form.

_____ 6. An emperor could establish an empire.

_____ 7. An exclusive ticket is a very special ticket.

_____ 8. Rumors can be trusted.

_____ 9. If you maximize your credit card, you'll make more money.

_____ 10. To minimize is to make something smaller.

▶ 填空題

1. From the celebrity's frequent updates on social media, many people consider that he enjoys _____.

2. The suspect _____ that he was innocent when the police caught him.

3. In this book, I will teach you 5 ways to increase your productivity and _____ your capabilities.

4. This is an _____ event. Only those who are on the guest list can enter.

5. The government hopes to _____ the damage brought by the earthquake by providing refugees with temporary shelters.

6. Comments made by some netizens online cannot _____ what the whole nation thinks.

7. The Roman Empire was _____ by Augustus Caesar.

8. We don't know whether the rumor is true or not since it has not been confirmed by the _____.

9. The Internet is a place where _____ can be spread very fast.

10. Many celebrities donate to charities so as to boost _____.

Answer

是非題：

1. O   2. X   3. O   4. X   5. X   6. O   7. O   8. X   9. X   10. O

填空題：

1. publicity   2. stated   3. maximize   4. exclusive   5. minimize

6. represent   7. established   8. spokesperson   9. rumors

10. public relations / publicity

填空題翻譯：

1. 從那位名人頻繁更新社群媒體來看，很多人覺得他喜歡受到關注。

2. 嫌疑犯在警察抓到他的時候聲稱他是無辜的。

3. 在這本書裡我會教你 5 個增加你的生產力還有將你的能力最大化的方法。

4. 這是獨家的活動，只有來賓列表中的人可以進入。

5. 藉由提供受災戶暫時的避難所，政府希望將地震帶來的傷害最小化。

6. 網路鄉民的評論不能代表整個國家的想法。

7. 羅馬帝國是由凱薩大帝建立的。

8. 因為發言人還沒有確認，我們不知道謠言是真是假。

9. 網路是一個謠言可以被快速傳播的地方。

10. 許多名人為了增進公共關係捐錢給慈善機構。

國際會議
International Conference

Track
035

attend	attendee	convention
council	committee	present
presentation	chairperson	event
destination	note	notice
notification	etiquette	

01 **attend**

[ə`tɛnd]

(v) 出席

- We are going to attend an international conference.
  我們要去參加一個國際會議。

02 **attendee**

[ə`tɛndi]

(n) 出席者

- More than 200 attendees are expected to participate in the event!
  預計有超過 200 個出席者將參加那個活動！

03 **convention**

[kən`vɛnʃən]

(n) 大會

- The international conference will be held in the convention center.
  那個國際會議會辦在國際會議中心。

  延伸學習 a convention center 會議中心
  Taipei International Convention Center
  臺北國際會議中心

04 **council**

[`kaʊnsl̩]

(n) 議會

- The monthly meetings of the local council are live-streamed on the Internet.
  地方議會每個月的會議都有在線上直播。

  延伸學習 the Security Council in the United Nations
  聯合國安理會

05 **committee**

[kə`mɪtɪ]

(n) 委員會

- She is a member of the Olympic committee.
  = She is on the Olympic committee.
  她是奧運委員會的一員。

  延伸學習 a committee meeting 委員會議

06 **present**

[prɪ`zent]

(v) 呈現；表達

[`prɛznt]

(adj) 現在

(n) 禮物；現在

- Yesterday is history, tomorrow is a mystery, but today is a gift. That is why it is called the present.
  昨天是歷史，明天是個謎，但今天是個禮物。這是為什麼它叫做 present（禮物／現在）。

  延伸學習 to present sth. 呈現、報告某物／某事
  (I am) present. 我在（點名的時候說的）

07 presentation

[ˌprizɛnˋteʃən]

(n) 報告

- Students are required to give a presentation at the end of the semester for this course.
  在學期結束的時候這門課程的學生需要上臺報告。

延伸學習 to give a presentation 報告

08 chairperson

[ˋtʃɛrˌpɝsn]

(n) 主席

相似詞
chairman (n) 主席

- The chairperson will monitor the meeting.
  主席會主持會議。

- I (would like to) yield my time to the chairperson.
  我把發言時間讓給主席（使用）。

09 event

[ɪˋvɛnt]

(n) 事件

- Where is the event located?
  What's the location of the event?
  活動在哪裡？

延伸學習 event location 活動地點

10 destination

[ˌdɛstəˋneʃən]

(n) 目的地

- The destination of our conference was Vancouver.
  我們會議的目的地在溫哥華。

11 note

[not]

(v) (n) 注意；筆記；
字條

- Please note that the elevator will be out of service from 7 a.m. to 8 p.m..
  請注意電梯從早上 7 點到晚上 8 點沒有運作。

- Please take notes in class.
  上課請做筆記。

- I've left a note on your desk. Didn't you see it?
  我在你桌上留了字條。你沒有看到嗎？

延伸學習 Please note that... 請注意

12 notice

[`notɪs]

(n) (v) 通知；注意到

補充
aware (adj) 注意到；意識到

- Did you see the notice on the bulletin board?
  你有看到公告欄上面的通知嗎？

- Did you notice that she seemed down today?
  你有注意到他今天看起來心情不好嗎？
  Yes, I'm well aware of it.
  我有清楚察覺到。

13 notification

[ˌnotəfə`keʃən]

(n) 通知

- I received a notification, telling me the conference was postponed.
  我收到一個通知說會議延期了。

14 etiquette

[`ɛtɪkɛt]

(n) 禮儀

- You should be aware of international etiquette when attending a conference abroad.
  在國外參加會議的時候應該要注意國際禮儀。

  延伸學習 international etiquette 國際禮儀

 測驗

▶ 是非題

_____ 1. If you attend a conference, you are the attender.

_____ 2. A convention center usually refers to a place where people hold large meetings.

_____ 3. Members of the city council represent the city and make certain decisions.

_____ 4. A committee can be a part of a council.

_____ 5. You can present a report, and you can represent a person.

_____ 6. A chairperson is someone who manufactures chairs.

_____ 7. A location refers to a place or a position.

_____ 8. A destination is the first stop of your journey.

_____ 9. You notice something when it catches your attention.

_____ 10. Shaking hands is considered an international etiquette.

▶ 填空題

1. Please _____ that the deadline of the report is this Friday. Make sure you submit it on time.

2. I'm so excited to _____ my best friend's wedding.

3. I hope we will discuss the political issues more thoroughly in the _____.

4. He will give a _____ about e-commerce on Monday.

5. The _____ has invited many celebrities to her party.

6. After a long flight, they finally arrived at their _____.

7. This event was funded by the town _____.

8. We need to conform to international _____ when attending a large convention.

9. Please text me and let me know where the event is _____.

10. Sandra is a member of the finance _____ and is responsible for providing oversight for financial organizations.

Answer

是非題：

1. X   2. O   3. O   4. O   5. O   6. X   7. O   8. X   9. O   10. O

填空題：

1. note   2. attend   3. convention   4. presentation   5. chairperson
6. destination   7. council   8. etiquette   9. located   10. committee

填空題翻譯：

1. 請注意繳交報告的期限是星期五，請準時繳交。
2. 我很興奮要參加我最好的朋友的婚禮。
3. 我希望在會議中我們會更深入討論政治議題。
4. 星期一他會做一個關於電子商務的報告。
5. 主席邀請了許多名人參加他的派對。
6. 長途飛行之後他們終於抵達了目的地。
7. 這活動是由城鎮管委會贊助的。
8. 參加大型會議的時候我們必須要遵守國際禮儀。
9. 請傳簡訊告訴我活動的地點在哪裡。
10. Sandra 是財政委員會的成員，她負責監督財務機構。

Unit 36

出差
Business Trip

Track 036

abroad	aboard	itinerary
luggage	transport	commute
commuter	vessel	cruise
vehicle	credit	adapt
adapter	tour	

01 abroad

[ə`brɔd]

(adv) 在國外、到國外

- She is planning to take the TOEFL exam because she wants to study abroad in the future.
  她在計畫考托福因為她未來想要出國唸書。

延伸學習 travel / study abroad 出國旅遊／出國唸書

02 aboard

[ə`bord]

(adv) 上（船、飛機、火車）；在（船、飛機、火車）上

- All aboard?
  都上船／飛機／火車了嗎？

- All passengers aboard needed to pay for the performance.
  船上所有人看表演皆需付費。

延伸學習 Get on board. 上船／飛機／火車
聘用新員工或是讓某人加入可以說：
bring someone on board

補充說明

broad (adj) 寬、abroad (adv) 到國外、board (v) 上（船、火車或飛機）、aboard (adv) 上（船、火車或飛機）broaden (v) 使……寬廣
All aboard? Let's board the plane and travel abroad to broaden (v) our horizons!
都上飛機了嗎？讓我們一起搭飛機旅行到國外拓展我們的視野吧！

03 itinerary

[aɪ`tɪnəˌrɛrɪ]

(n) 旅遊行程

相似詞
schedule (n) 行程、
agenda (n) 議程

- The travel agent will plan an itinerary for us.
  旅行社會幫我們規劃旅遊行程。

- What is the next stop on our itinerary?
  我們旅遊行程的下一站是哪裡？

04 luggage

[`lʌgɪdʒ]

(n) [U] 行李

相似詞
baggage (n) [U] 行李

- Make sure that your luggage is not oversized or overweight before you check it in.
  在托運行李前先確定行李沒有過大或是超重。

- Our luggage was damaged in transit.
  我們的行李在運輸途中損壞了。

延伸學習 pack your luggage / baggage 收拾行李
check in 報到

05 transport

[`træns͵pɔrt]

(n) [U] 運輸；交通工具

- What means of transport do you use to get to work?
  你使用什麼交通工具去上班？

  延伸學習 public transportation 大眾運輸工具
  means of transportation / transport 運輸工具

06 commute

[kə`mjut]

(v) (n) 通勤

- How do you commute to work?
  你如何上下班？

- I study English during my one-hour commute.
  我在一小時的通勤時間中學習英語。

07 commuter

[kə`mjutɚ]

(n) 通勤者

- Commuters are required to wear masks when taking public transportation / transport.
  通勤者搭乘大眾運輸工具的時候必須戴口罩。

08 vessel

[`vɛsl]

(n) 船；血管

- Several cargo vessels left the port.
  幾艘貨船離開了港口。

  延伸學習 blood vessels 血管

09 cruise

[kruz]

(n) (v) 郵輪；旅遊航行

- Have you ever taken a cruise vacation?
  你有參加過郵輪旅行嗎？

  延伸學習 cruise around the city 環遊城市

10 vehicle

[`viɪkl]

(n) 車輛

- Cars and motorcycles are both vehicles.
  車子和摩托車都是車輛。

11 credit

[`krɛdɪt]

(n) 信譽

相關詞
credit card 信用卡
debit card 金融卡

- You can pay with a credit card or a debit card.
  你可以用信用卡或是金融卡支付。

- You can pay by cash or by credit card.
  你可以用現金或信用卡付款。

12 adapt [ə`dæpt] (v) 適應；調整；改編	• He finds it difficult to adapt to a new environment. 他覺得很難適應新環境。 • The best-selling novel will soon be adapted into a film. 最暢銷的小說很快就會被改編成電影。 • The movie is adapted from a popular novel. 這電影是由暢銷小說改編的。
13 adapter [ə`dæptə] (n) 轉接器	• Don't forget to bring your charger and adapter when traveling abroad. 出國旅遊的時候不要忘記帶你的充電器和轉接器。
14 tour [tʊr] (n) 旅遊；觀光	• We provide multiple guided tours in the museum. 我們在博物館中提供許多導覽。 • I'll give you a tour of the city. 我帶你逛一逛這個城市。 延伸學習 go on / embark on / set off on a tour 出發去旅遊 a tour guide 導遊 a guided tour 導覽

 測驗

▶ 是非題

_____ 1. If you study in another country, you study aboard.

_____ 2. An itinerary is the plan or schedule of a journey.

_____ 3. The plural forms of luggage and baggage are still luggage and baggage.

_____ 4. Trains are a form of transportation.

_____ 5. Commute is another word for travel.

_____ 6. A vessel is a means of transportation like an airplane.

_____ 7. A vehicle can transport people or goods.

_____ 8. If you purchase something on credit, you pay the full amount right away.

_____ 9. To adapt can mean to become more familiar to a new environment.

_____ 10. You can go to a tour by visiting different places.

▶ 填空題

1. Please take the _____ with you at all times so you know which attraction we are visiting next.

2. The truck towed away several _____ that had parked illegally on the road earlier.

3. This restaurant does not take _____ , so please prepare enough cash.

4. Congratulations, you are hired! Please let me know when you will be able to be _____

5. When we arrived at the hotel, a man came to take our _____ .

6. We enjoy going on a package _____ because everything is well - planned.

7. I don't have a car so I always take public _____ to work.

8. There are tens of thousands of _____ taking the train every single day.

9. You need an _____ when you travel to another country in order to charge your cell phone and other electronic devices.

10. A fishing _____ is at the port and will unload its cargo soon.

Answer

是非題：

1. X   2. O   3. O   4. O   5. X   6. O   7. O   8. X   9. O   10. X

填空題：

1. itinerary   2. vehicles   3. credit cards   4. on board   5. luggage / baggage

6. tour   7. transportation   8. commuters   9. adapter   10. vessel

填空題翻譯：

1. 請隨身攜帶旅遊行程，你才知道我們接下來要看哪一個景點。

2. 稍早卡車把路上幾部違停車輛拖走了。

3. 這間餐廳不接受信用卡，所以請準備足夠的現金。

4. 恭喜你錄取了！請讓我們知道你什麼時候可以來上班。

5. 我們抵達飯店的時候有人來拿我們的行李。

6. 我們喜歡參加旅行團，因為全部事情都已經規劃好了。

7. 我沒有車所以我總是搭大眾運輸工具去工作。

8. 每天都有幾萬個通勤者搭火車上下班。

9. 為了幫你的手機和其他電子用品充電，出國的時候你需要帶轉接器。

10. 港口有一艘漁船，它即將要卸貨。

機場
Airport

Track **037**

flight	shuttle
public	arrival
arrive	entrance
enter	conveyor
baggage	upgrade
fragile	boarding

01 flight

[flaɪt]

(n) 班機;航班

- When is your flight leaving?
  你的航班什麼時候離開?

02 shuttle

[`ʃʌtl]

(n) 接駁車

- The shuttle bus will take you to the airport.
  接駁車會帶你到機場。

- The airport offers free shuttle buses between terminals.
  在不同航廈之間機場有提供免費接駁車。

03 public

[`pʌblɪk]

(n) 公眾

補充
public area (n)
公共區域

- Please lower your voice in public (areas).
  在公共區域請降低音量。

- This is a public area. Please keep your voice down.
  這裡是公共區域。請降低音量。

04 arrival

[ə`raɪvl]

(n) 抵達

- We are waiting for your arrival.
  我們在等待你的到來。

- We are waiting for you at the arrival gate.
  我們在等候的閘門等你。

05 arrive

[ə`raɪv]

(v) 到達

- After 10 hours on the plane, I've finally arrived at Taoyuan International Airport.
  在搭了 10 小時的飛機之後,我終於抵達桃園國際機場。

06 entrance

[`ɛntrəns]

(n) 入口

相反詞
exit (n) (v) 出口;離開

- Where is the entrance of the building?
  這棟建築的入口在哪裡?

- The check-in counter is next to the entrance.
  報到臺在入口旁邊。

07 **enter**

[ˋɛntɚ]

(v) 進入；輸入

- How can I enter the library?
  我要如何進去圖書館？
- Enter your name right here.
  在這裡輸入你的名字。

08 **conveyor**

[kənˋveɚ]

(n) 運輸工具

補充
conveyor belt 傳輸帶

- My suitcase is over there on the conveyor belt.
  我的行李在傳輸帶上。

09 **baggage**

[ˋbæɡɪdʒ]

(n) 行李

相似詞
carousel (n) 圓盤傳送帶
補充
baggage claim
行李領取區

- You can claim / retrieve your luggage at the baggage claim / carousel.
  你可以在行李領取區提領行李。

10 **upgrade**

[ˋʌpˋɡred]

(v) 升級

- I would like to upgrade from economy class to business class.
  我想要從經濟艙升等到商務艙。
- You can upgrade to business class by following a few simple procedures.
  遵循這幾個簡單的步驟你就可以升等到商務艙。
- Your system should be upgraded.
  你的系統應該要升級了。

11 fragile

['frædʒəl]
(adj) 脆弱的

相似詞
delicate (adj) 脆弱；精緻的

- There are several fragile items in my luggage. Please handle it carefully.
  我的行李裡面有幾個易碎物品，請小心處理。

- The baby is very <u>fragile / delicate</u>; she may get hurt easily, so you need to hold her gently.
  小嬰兒很脆弱；他很容易受傷所以請溫柔地抱他。

12 boarding

['bordɪŋ]
(n) 登機

相關詞
departure (time, gate)
(n) 離開

- You'll need your boarding pass to board the plane.
  你必須要有登機證才能登機。

- You can find information about the boarding time and the boarding gate on your boarding pass.
  你可以在登機證上面看到登機時間和登機門的資訊。

延伸學習 boarding <u>pass / time / gate</u> 登機證／時間／門

▶ 是非題

_____ 1. You can book a restaurant, and you can book a flight as well.

_____ 2. A shuttle usually travels between two places regularly.

_____ 3. You can do anything you want in a public area because it is shared by all people.

_____ 4. To arrive means to depart.

_____ 5. The antonym for the word entrance is exit.

_____ 6. A conveyor belt is used for transporting objects such as suitcases or packages.

_____ 7. The baggage claim area is where baggage are inspected by X-ray.

_____ 8. You can upgrade your hotel room from a deluxe room to a standard room.

_____ 9. If something is fragile, it breaks easily.

_____ 10. A boarding pass is a ticket you need in order to attend boarding school.

▶ 填空題

1. The park is a _____ , so please behave yourself while having fun.

2. Please bring your _____ and passport to the gate 30 minutes before the plane takes off.

3. My _____ is departing in 3 hours, so I'll have to take the bus to the air port right now or I won't be able to make it in time.

4. The singer's fans are all waiting for his _____ at the airport.

5. I don't see my suitcase at the _____! I'm worried that it's lost!

6. Your cellphone will be _____ with the new software automatically.

7. I'll take the _____ from Taipei Main Station to the mall.

8. I'm waiting for my suitcase to appear on the _____ .

9. She just went through a heartbreak and is very _____ right now.

10. The door with a pink door knob is the bookstore's _____ .

Answer

是非題：

1. O   2. O   3. X   4. X   5. O   6. O   7. X   8. X   9. O   10. X

填空題：

1. public area   2. boarding pass 3. flight   4. arrival   5. baggage claim

6. upgraded   7. shuttle   8. conveyor belt 9. fragile   10. entrance

填空題翻譯：

1. 公園是公共場所，所以在玩的時候還是要注意你的行為。

2. 請在飛機起飛 30 分鐘前帶你的登機證和護照到登機門。

3. 再 3 小時我的航班就要起飛了，所以我要趕快搭公車到機場，否則我沒辦法準時抵達。

4. 那位歌手的粉絲都在機場等待他的到來。

5. 我沒有在行李領取區看到我的行李箱，我擔心它不見了！

6. 你的手機系統會自動升級。

7. 我會搭從臺北車站到百貨公司的接駁車。

8. 我在等我的行李出現在傳輸帶上。

9. 她剛分手，所以現在心理非常脆弱。

10. 那個有粉紅色門把的門是書店的入口。

Unit 38

海關
Customs

Track 038

agent   agency
customs   inspect
forbid   restrict
constraint   liquid
belongings   passenger
seat belt   confiscate

01 agent
['edʒənt]
(n) 代理人;代辦員

- The travel agent can customize tours for you.
這旅行代辦員可以幫你客製化行程。

  延伸學習 travel agent 旅行代辦員

02 agency
['edʒənsı]
(n) 代理機構

- This travel agency offers great package tours!
這旅行社提供很棒的套裝行程!

03 customs
['kʌstəmz]
(n) 海關

- The officer asked me several questions when I went through customs.
當我通關的時候海關人員問了幾個問題。

  延伸學習 go through customs 通過海關

04 inspect
[ın`spɛkt]
(v) 檢查

相似詞
examine (V) 檢查

- When you go through customs, your carry-on items would be inspected / examined / screened.
當你通過海關的時候,你的隨身行李會被檢查。

05 forbid
[fə`bıd]
(v) 禁止

不規則三態
forbid, forbade, forbidden

- To prevent inflight danger, many common items are forbidden / prohibited / not allowed to take on board.
為了預防飛行途中發生危險,許多常見的物品在飛機上都是禁止攜帶的。

06 restrict
[rı`strıkt]
(v) 限制

相似詞
restriction (n) 限制

- Many common items are restricted by the Ministry of Transportation and Communications.
許多常見物品被交通部管制。

07 constraint

[kən`strent]

(n) 限制

- To stay safe and healthy, we should strictly abide by the <u>restrictions / constraints</u>.
  為了保持安全與健康，我們應嚴格遵守規定。

08 liquid

[`lɪkwɪd]

(n) [C or U] 液體

- There are restrictions on liquids that can be brought on board.
  帶上飛機的液態物品有限制。

- Most countries have restrictions on the types and quantity of liquid you may carry in your hand baggage through security at an airport.
  每個國家對於在機場安檢的時候，於手提行李內可以攜帶的液體種類及數量皆有限制。。

09 belongings

[bə`lɔŋɪŋz]

(n) 財產；攜帶物品

- Don't' forget your <u>personal belongings</u> when you leave.
  離開的時候不要忘了你的私人物品。

  (延伸學習) personal belongings 私人物品

10 passenger

[`pæsndʒɚ]

(n) 乘客

- This is the final boarding call for passengers Cindy and Jenny Sung booked on flight 123C to Taipei. Please proceed to gate 6G immediately.
  這是給乘客 Cindy 和 Jenny Sung 搭乘航班 123C 往臺北最後的登機通知。請立刻前往 6G 閘門。

11 seat belt

[sitbɛlt]

(n) 安全帶

- The plane is about to take off. Please <u>fasten your seat belt</u>.
  飛機即將起飛，請繫上安全帶。

- Ladies and gentlemen, we will be experiencing some turbulence shortly. Please be seated and keep <u>your seat belt fastened</u>.
  各位先生女士，我們即將通過亂流。請坐穩並繫好安全帶。

  (延伸學習) fasten seatbelt 繫上安全帶

12 **confiscate**

['kɑnfɪsˌket]

(v) 沒收

• Restricted items, such as liquids, will be confiscated on board.

被限制的物品，例如液態物品，在飛機上會被沒收。

 測驗

▶ 是非題

_____ 1. While an agent is an organization, an agency is a person.

_____ 2. The customs is the place where products are customized.

_____ 3. A synonym for the word inspect is examine.

_____ 4. If something is forbidded, it is not allowed.

_____ 5. To restrict something is to set limits on something.

_____ 6. A liquid is a solid substance.

_____ 7. Personal belongings are the things that a person possesses.

_____ 8. A cargo plane also carries passengers.

_____ 9. You can fasten your seatbelt as well as fasten a door.

_____ 10. If your personal belongings are confiscated, they are taken away from you.

▶ 填空題

1. Smoking is strictly _____ in this area. Please take your cigarettes somewhere else.

2. Our _____ will help to arrange flight tickets and hotel rooms.

3. Since _____ are not allowed on planes, Joanne decides to pack her toner in her luggage.

4. These packages will be checked by _____.

5. The train is usually full of _____ in the morning.

6. The research team is _____ the effects of this medicine and will publish a report about it soon.

7. There are speed _____ in this town so be sure not to drive too fast.

8. Please make sure you bring all of your _____ before you leave the hotel because we will check out today.

9. Please _____ your seat belt before the flight takes off.

10. His phone was _____ and now he's not able to contact his family.

Answer

是非題：

1. X   2. X   3. O   4. X（應為 forbidden）   5. O   6. X   7. O   8. X

9. O   10. O

填空題：

1. prohibited / forbidden   2. travel agent   3. liquids   4. customs

5. passengers   6. inspecting   7. restrictions   8. personal belongings

9. fasten   10. confiscated

填空題翻譯：

1. 這裡禁止吸菸。請把你的香菸帶到別的地方。

2. 我們的旅遊代辦人員會協助安排機票和飯店。

3. 因為飛機上禁止帶液態物品，Joanne 決定把化妝水放到行李箱內。

4. 這些包裹會被海關檢查。

5. 早上的火車總是充滿乘客。

6. 研究團隊在檢查藥物的效果，他們很快就會公布相關的報告。

7. 這個城鎮有車速限制，所以不要開太快。

8. 因為我們今天要離開飯店，在離開前請確定你帶了所有的私人物品。

9. 在飛機起飛之前請繫好安全帶。

10. 他的手機被沒收了，現在他沒辦法聯絡他的家人。

飛機上
On the Plane

seat   change
approach   tray
order   complimentary
premium   beverage
fare   broadcast
lavatory

01 seat

[sit]

(n) 座位

- I would like to book an <u>aisle seat</u> if possible.
  如果可能的話我想要訂靠近走道的座位。

- Excuse me <u>sir / ma'am</u>, you're in my seat.
  先生／女士，不好意思，這是我的位子。

- All passengers should remain seated (adj) when the plane takes off.
  當飛機起飛的時候所有乘客都應保持坐著。

延伸學習 aisle seat 走道座位
window seat 靠窗的座位
middle seat 中間的座位

02 change

[tʃendʒ]

(v) 改變；更改

- I would like to sit with my husband, would you mind <u>changing / switching / swapping seats</u> with me?
  我想跟我先生坐在一起，您介意跟我換座位嗎？

延伸學習 change / switch / swap seats 換座位

03 approach

[ə`protʃ]

(v) (n) 接近；方法

相似詞
way (n) 方法、
method (n) 方法

- The flight attendant approached the passenger and asked her what she would like to drink.
  空服員接近乘客並詢問她想喝什麼。

- The teacher adopted many approaches to teach her students.
  那位老師採用了許多方法來指導她的學生。

延伸學習 try / adopt / develop a(n) new / alternative / novel approach to... 嘗試／採用／發展新的／不同的方法以……（做某事）

04 tray

[tre]

(n) 盤子，托盤

- Please put down your tray table for the meal.
  請將餐桌放下來放餐點。

- Please stow / put up your tray table and straighten your seat during takeoff and landing.
  在起飛和降落的時候請把餐桌收起來並豎直椅背。

延伸學習 tray table 飛機上的桌子

05 order

['ɔrdɚ]

(v) 點菜

- Don't take too long to <u>place an order</u> when the flight attendant asks you what you want to drink.

→ Don't take too long to order (v).

當空服員問你要喝什麼的時候請不要花太久時間點餐。

延伸學習 place an order 點餐、下訂單

06 complimentary

[ˌkɑmpləˋmɛntərɪ]

(adj) 免費的；贈送的

- Complimentary drinks on flights usually include coffee, tea, coke, sprite, and apple juice.

機上的免費飲料通常包含咖啡、茶、可樂、雪碧和蘋果汁。

延伸學習 complimentary drinks 免費飲料

07 premium

[ˋprimɪəm]

(adj) 高級

(n) 額外補貼

- Red wine is a premium drink that requires an <u>additional / extra</u> fee.

紅酒是需要額外付費的高級飲料。

延伸學習 premium options 高級（付費）選項

premium drinks 高級（付費）飲料

08 beverage

[ˋbɛvərɪdʒ]

(n) 飲料

相似詞
drink (n) 飲料

- What beverage would you like to drink?

你想喝什麼飲料？

- Cold beverages include ginger ale, sparkling water, and cranberry juice.

冷飲包含薑汁汽水、氣泡水和蔓越莓汁。

延伸學習 alcoholic beverages 酒精飲料

09 fare

[fɛr]

(n) 車資

相關詞
ticket (n) 票
相似詞
price (n) 價格

- You can search for low fares on the application.

你可以在這 APP 上尋找便宜車資。

延伸學習 bus fare, train fare 公車、火車的車資

10 broadcast

[`brɔd͵kæst]

(n) (v) 播報

- The captain broadcasted an announcement.
  機長播報了一個公告。

- The captain requested the cabin crew to be seated in the broadcast.
  在播報中機長要求機組人員回到座位上。

11 lavatory

[`lævə͵torɪ]

(n) 盥洗室

相似詞

toilet (n) 廁所、
restroom (n) 洗手間

- The lavatory is <u>vacant / occupied</u>.
  盥洗室是空的／有人。

▶ 是非題

_____ 1. An aisle is the space between rows of seats or shelves.

_____ 2. You can switch the lights on, so you can also swap the lights on.

_____ 3. If something approaches you, it is getting closer to you.

_____ 4. You can put food and drinks on a tray.

_____ 5. To place an order means to decide where you want to go.

_____ 6. Complimentary drinks only include soft drinks such as coke and juice.

_____ 7. If something is premium, it usually has a higher quality.

_____ 8. The fare is the price of a train or bus ticket.

_____ 9. If you want others to keep a secret for you, you can ask them not to broadcast it.

_____ 10. You can conduct chemical experiments in a lavatory.

▶ 填空題

1. I became more and more nervous as the date of the exam _____.

2. Please don't put your feet on the _____ since it is for food and drinks.

3. I enjoy refreshing _____ such as sparkling water and iced tea.

4. Liz _____ phone numbers with a guy she met at the bar.

5. I won't be able to go to the game but I'm looking forward to the live _____.

6. Jess booked his flight yesterday and he requested for the _____ seat.

7. I called our supplier and _____ an order for the necessary materials.

8. Those bottles of vodkas and whiskies on the shelf are _____ drinks. They require an additional fee.

9. These are _____ drinks, so you don't have to pay for them.

10. The train _____ becomes more expensive during the holiday season.

[Answer]

是非題：

1. O   2. X   3. O   4. O   5. X   6. X   7. O   8. O   9. O   10. X

填空題：

1. approached   2. tray table   3. beverages   4. swapped   5. broadcast
6. aisle   7. placed   8. premium   9. complimentary   10. fare

填空題翻譯：

1. 當考試日期接近，我變得越來越緊張。

2. 請不要把腳放到餐桌上，因為它是用來放食物和飲料的。

3. 我喜歡像是氣泡水和冰紅茶這種清爽的飲料。

4. Liz 和一個她在酒吧遇到的男生交換電話號碼。

5. 我無法去看比賽，但我很期待看現場直播。

6. Jess 昨天訂了機票並且要求要坐走道位。

7. 我打給供應商並且下訂了一些必要材料。

8. 櫃上的伏特加和威士忌是高級（付費）飲料。他們需要額外付費。

9. 這些是免費飲料，你不需要付費。

10. 火車車資隨著假期變得越來越貴。

Unit 40

機場與新冠肺炎
Airport & Coronavirus

Track
040

quarantine	screening
announce	fee
waive	residual
refund	refundable
apply	regulation
limit	limited

01 quarantine

[ˋkwɔrənˌtin]

(n) (v) 隔離

相似詞
isolate (v) 隔離、
isolation (n) 隔離

• Under Taiwan's immigration quarantine regulations, all inbound passengers are required to undertake a 14-day home quarantine, regardless of nationality.
根據臺灣出入境檢疫法規，無論國籍，所有入境旅客均必須進行 14 天居家隔離。

延伸學習 airport quarantine inspection 機場隔離檢驗

02 screening

[ˋskrinɪŋz]

(n) 檢驗

相關詞
scanning (n) 掃描、
examination (n) 檢查、
inspection (n) 檢驗

• The airport screening procedures aim to prevent dangers from happening.
機場檢查程序的目的是為了防止危險發生。

延伸學習 passport / medical screening 護照、醫療檢查

03 announce

[əˋnaʊns]

(v) 公告；宣布

相關詞
announcement (n) 公告

• The captain announced that there will be turbulence later.
機長宣布待會會有亂流。

04 fee

[fi]

(n) 服務費；費用

• Due to the coronavirus, passengers are permitted to book new flights without a change fee.
因為冠狀病毒，我們允許旅客訂新航班而無需支付更改費。

延伸學習 change fee 更改費用

05 waive

[wev]

(v) 放棄

• All change fees are waived for tickets issued on or before March 2nd.
3 月 2 日或之前簽發的機票將免收所有變更費。

• If you think you are eligible to waive a course, you can apply for it.
如果你認為你有免修資格，你可以去申請。

延伸學習 waive a course 免修課程

06 residual

[rɪˋzɪdʒʊəl]
(adj) 剩餘的

- If the customer books a new flight that is priced lower, the customer may change it for free but no <u>residual value</u> will be given.
如果客戶預訂了價格更低的新航班,則客戶可以免費更改,但不會得到剩餘的錢。

延伸學習 residual value 剩餘的錢、剩餘價值

07 refund

[ˋriˌfʌnd]
(n) 退款

- I found a defect in the product, so I returned it and <u>asked for a refund</u>.
我發現產品有缺陷,所以我退貨並要求退款。

延伸學習 <u>ask for / demand</u> a refund 要求退費

08 refundable

[rɪˋfʌndəbl̩]
(adj) 可退還的

- The ticket fares are non-refundable.
車資是不退還的。

延伸學習 non-refundable 不可退的

09 apply

[əˋplaɪ]
(v) 適用於

- The principle may be applied to various situations.
這原則適用於各種情況。

- The no-change-fees policy applies to all kinds of tickets.
無變更手續費的規定適用於所有類型的機票。

10 regulation

[ˌrɛgjəˋleʃən]
(n) 規定

相似詞
rule 規定、**law** 法律、
order 指令

- At critical times like this, it's important that we abide by all the regulations.
在這樣的危急時刻,遵守所有的規定很重要。

延伸學習 follow / abide by regulations / restrictions 遵守規定
regulations and rules 規章與條例
security / safety regulations 安全／保安條例
import / export restrictions 進出口限制

11 limit

[ˈlɪmɪt]

(n) (v) 限制；極限

相關詞
ceiling (n) 天花板（也可指工作上的限制）、
border (n) 邊界、
extreme (n) 極端

- The sky's the limit.
  沒有極限。

- Don't limit your challenges; challenge your limits.
  不要為你的挑戰設限；挑戰你的極限。

- You shouldn't exceed the <u>speed limit</u>, or else you will be fined.
  妳不應超速否則會被罰鍰。

  延伸學習 speed limit 速限

12 limited

[ˈlɪmɪtɪd]

(adj) 有限的

- Children here <u>have limited access to</u> education.
  這裡的兒童受教育的機會有限。

  延伸 學習 have limited access to...

 測驗

▶ 是非題

_____ 1. A person or an animal can be put in quarantine.

_____ 2. A person can be screened to know whether he / she has a disease or not.

_____ 3. If you announce something, you say it under your breath.

_____ 4. Change fees refer to the price differences of a product due to inflation or deflation.

_____ 5. You can waive at someone as a friendly gesture.

_____ 6. Residual value is the worth of something after it's been used for an period of time.

_____ 7. If a product is refundable, you can apply for compensation when there's a defect in the product.

_____ 8. You can apply for a job as well as apply for a lipstick.

_____ 9. A regulation is an official rule.

_____ 10. You can limit something by controlling its amount.

▶ 填空題

1. Pam has started doing regular _____ to check her health since she turned 70.

2. If I pass the test, I will be able to _____ this semester's English course.

3. Travelers are required to spend 14 days in _____ during the pandemic.

4. She realized the dress she bought didn't fit and would like to demand a _____.

5. Your rules don't _____ to me. I make my own rules.

6. There will be an amount of _____ if you want to change your ticket.

7. I'm taking a day off tomorrow and will have _____ access to emails. Please contact my colleague for assistance.

8. Factories need to abide by the safety _____ while manufacturing the goods.

9. The judges _____ the champion after the fierce competition.

10. An expert will help me to evaluate the _____ value of my car.

Answer

是非題：

1. ○   2. ○   3. X   4. X   5. X   6. ○   7. X   8. X   9. ○   10. ○

填空題：

1. screenings   2. waive   3. quarantine   4. refund   5. apply

6. change fees   7. limited   8. regulations   9. announced   10. residual

填空題翻譯：

1. 自從 Pam 70 歲之後，她有定期做健康檢查。

2. 如果我通過測驗，我就能免修這學期的英文課。

3. 在防疫期間旅客需要隔離 14 天。

4. 她發現她買的洋裝不合身所以要求退費。

5. 你的規則不適用在我身上，我制定自己的規則。

6. 如果你想要改機票會有機票更改費用。

7. 我明天休假所以會很少使用電子郵件，需要幫助請聯絡我的同事。

8. 在製造商品的時候，工廠需要遵守安全規定。

9. 在激烈的比賽過後評審公布了優勝者。

10. 專家會幫我衡量我的車子的剩餘價值。

商品通關
Moving Goods Through Customs

Track
041

document	documentary	temporary
permanently	related	relate
relative	relevant	personnel
adopt	border	extend
copy		

01 document

[`dɑkjəmənt]

(n) 文件

- Traders should provide electronic documents.
  貿易商應提供電子文件。

02 documentary

[,dɑkjə`mɛntərɪ]

(n) 紀錄片

- The documentary is based on a true event.
  這紀錄片是基於真實的事件。

03 temporary

[`tɛmpə,rɛrɪ]

(adj) 暫時的

- To help stop the spread of coronavirus (COVID-19), the government has temporarily changed customs border procedures including transit and export .
  為了幫助阻止冠狀病毒（COVID-19）的傳播，政府已臨時更改了海關邊境程序，包括過境和出口。

- Temporary restrictions have been adopted by the government to prevent the spread of the disease.
  政府已採取臨時限制措施以防止疾病的傳播。

04 permanently

[`pɝ-mənəntlɪ]

(adv) 永久的

- In the Disney movie, the Little Mermaid, the evil witch Ursula told Ariel that if the prince kisses her before the sun sets on the third day, she will remain human, permanently.
  在迪士尼電影《小美人魚》中，邪惡的女巫烏蘇拉和艾莉兒說，如果王子在第三天的日落之前親吻她，她就能永遠當人類。

05 related

[rɪ`letɪd]

(adj) 相關的

相似詞

associate (v) with
相關

- Other related policies are listed below.
  其他的相關法規如下。

- They are distantly related.
  → They are distant relatives.
  他們是遠親。

- Are you two related? You look alike!
  你們兩個是親戚嗎？長得好像喔！

  延伸學習 be related to someone 跟某人有親屬關係

06 relate

[rɪ`let]

(v) 有關

- I can relate myself to those who have serious acne problems.
  我可以理解那些有嚴重痘痘問題的人。

- I can relate to their problems.
  我可以理解他們的問題。

  延伸學習 relate to someone / something 與……有關
  relate to someone
  和某人感同身受，能理解他的感受

07 relative

[`rɛlətɪv]

(adj) 相對的；親戚

- I've been working here for a year, but I'm still a relative newcomer to this company.
  我在這邊工作一年了，但相較起來我還算這間公司的新人。

- Molly is my cousin, so she is a relative of mine.
  Molly 是我的表妹，所以她是我的親戚。

- I've invited all of my relatives to my wedding.
  我已經邀請所有親戚來參加我的婚禮。

  延伸學習 relatively high / low / old 相對高／低／舊（老）

08 relevant

[`rɛləvənt]

(adj) 相關的

相反詞
irrelevant (adj) 不相關

- Relevant steps / measures are taken to ensure safety.
  為了確保安全需要採取相關措施。

- Is it relevant to our discussion?
  這跟我們討論的內容有關嗎？

09 personnel

[ˌpɝsn`ɛl]

(n) 人員

- All relevant personnel should leave.
  所有相關人員都必須離開。

10 adopt

[ə`dɑpt]

(v) 採取；領養

- Since the current method isn't effective, I think we should adopt a different approach.
  因為目前的方法沒有效果，我覺得我們應該採取不同的做法。

  延伸學習 to adopt a measure / method 採取措施、方法
  to adopt a child 領養小孩

11 border

[`bɔrdɚ]

(n) 邊界

- The EU has opened its borders to 15 countries.
  歐盟對 15 個國家開啟了邊界。

  延伸學習 cross a border 跨越邊界

12 extend

[ɪk`stɛnd]

(v) 延伸；延長

- We are working hard to extend public awareness of the dangers of the virus.
  我們正在努力提高公眾對病毒危害的認識。

- India has been locked down for nearly a month, and Prime Minister, Narendra Modi, has recently extended it for one more month.
  印度已經被封鎖了近一個月，印度總理納倫德拉‧莫迪（Narendra Modi）最近將其延長了一個月。

  延伸學習 extend your arms / legs 延展手臂／腿
  　　　　　extend one's membership 延續會員

13 copy

[`kɑpɪ]

(n) 副本；複製品

相反詞
soft copy 電子檔

- Please submit a hard copy of the document.
  請提交文件的紙本。

- I'll need a copy of that file.
  我需要該文件的副本。

  延伸學習 hard copy 紙本

 測驗

▶ 是非題

_____ 1. A documentary is fictional.

_____ 2. If something is temporary, it does not last for a long time.

_____ 3. The word everlasting is an antonym for the word permanent.

_____ 4. Jason and Mick are cousins, so Jason relates to Mick.

_____ 5. If something is relatively good / bad, it is being compared with other similar things.

_____ 6. If two things are not related to each other at all, we can say that they are largely irrelevant.

_____ 7. Your address is your personnel information.

_____ 8. To adopt a child is to give birth to one.

_____ 9. A border is a line that separates two countries.

_____ 10. Lengthen is a synonym for the word extend.

▶ 填空題

1. The pain caused by the wound was only _____. It started to heal after I applied some ointment.

2. Please only discuss issues that are _____ to the topic of this meeting.

3. Most people prefer watching a fictional movie to a _____.

4. The new policies in the company will have a huge impact on the _____.

5. Kate plans to _____ her visa and get a job as soon as possible.

6. I can totally _____ to Jack's experience because the same thing happened to me before.

7. People tend to try to kick old habits and _____ new ones at the beginning of a year.

8. Eating too much junk food can damage your health _____.

9. For assignment, please submit a _____ for the professor to grade it.

10. To learn more information about the event, please refer to the _____ flyer.

Answer

是非題：

1. X   2. O   3. X   4. X   5. O   6. O   7. O   8. X   9. O   10. O

填空題：

1. temporary   2. relevant / relative   3. documentary   4. personnel   5. extend

6. relate   7. adopt   8. permanently   9. hard copy

10. relevant

填空題翻譯：

1. 傷口造成的疼痛是暫時的，在我塗上藥之後就開始復原了。

2. 請只討論跟這次會議相關的話題。

3. 比起紀錄片，大部分的人更喜歡看虛構的電影。

4. 公司最新的規定對全體人員都會有很大的影響。

5. Kate 計畫延長她的簽證並且盡快找到工作。

6. 我對他的經驗完全感同身受，因為我以前也發生過相同的事情。

7. 新的一年的開始，人們都想要拋棄舊的習慣並且建立新的習慣。

8. 吃太多垃圾食物會永久傷害你的健康。

9. 今天的作業請大家繳交紙本讓教授批改。

10. 想要了解關於這個活動更多的資訊請見相關的傳單。

醫療衛生一
Medicine & Hygiene 1

medical	hygiene	sanitary
sanitize	sanitation	dispose
pharmacist	presription	diagnose
diagnosis	vaccine	vaccinate
treatment	treat	cure

01 medical

[ˋmɛdɪkl̩]

(adj) 醫學的

相似詞
medicine (n) 藥；醫學

- 20 percent of the patients had to receive advanced medical care.
百分之 20 的病患須要接受進一步的治療。

延伸學習 medical school / care / center / treatment
醫學院／醫療照顧／醫療中心／醫療

02 hygiene

[ˋhaɪdʒin]

(n) 衛生

相關詞
clean (adj) 乾淨的、
hygienic (adj) 衛生的

- It's not hygienic / sanitary to dine without washing your hands first.
吃東西前沒有洗手不衛生。

延伸學習 personal hygiene 個人衛生

03 sanitary

[ˋsænəˌtɛrɪ]

(adj) 衛生的

- The sanitary conditions here are terrible / poor.
這裡的衛生狀況很差。

04 sanitize

[ˋsænəˌtaɪz]

(v) 消毒

- Please use hand sanitizer to sanitize your hands.
請用消毒洗手液幫你的雙手消毒。

05 sanitation

[ˌsænəˋteʃən]

(n) 消毒

- In the absence of sanitation and hygiene, they are forced to rely on antibiotics.
在缺乏衛生條件下，他們被迫依賴抗生素。

06 dispose

[dɪˋspoz]

(v) 丟掉；拋棄

用法
dispose +of
相關詞
disposable (adj) 拋棄式、
disposal (n) 清除；處理；拋棄

- Please dispose of the trash as soon as possible.
請盡快把垃圾丟掉。

07 pharmacist

['fɑrməsɪst]

(n) 藥師

相關詞
pharmacy (n)
藥局；藥學

- Pharmacists prescribe medicine(s) for patients.
  藥師為病患開藥。

08 prescription

[prɪ'skrɪpʃən]

(n) 處方籤

相關詞
prescribe (v) 開藥

- The doctor gave me a prescription after the diagnosis.
  在診斷過後醫生給我處方籤。

09 diagnose

['daɪəgnoz]

(v) 診斷

用法
diagnose + with

- He was <u>diagnosed with</u> cancer.
  他被診斷有癌症。

10 diagnosis

[ˌdaɪəg'nosɪs]

(n) 診斷

- The doctor made an initial diagnosis. A specialist will carry out further examinations later.
  醫生做了初步的診斷。專家將會做進一步的檢查。

- The plural form of diagnosis is diagnoses.
  diagnosis 的複數型態是 diagnoses。

11 vaccine

['væksin]

(n) 疫苗

- Scientists are trying to develop vaccines for the novel disease.
  科學家們正在嘗試開發針對這種新型疾病的疫苗。

12 vaccinate

['væksn͵et]

(v) 接種疫苗

- Pets should be vaccinated before they are taken home.
  寵物在被帶回家之前要先接種疫苗。

13 treatment

[`tritmənt]

(n) 治療;對待

- Doctors are searching for effective treatment to treat the injured.
  醫生在找有效的治療方式來治療傷患。

- I don't deserve such treatment.
  我不應得到這樣的待遇。

延伸學習 receive treatment 接受治療
effective treatment 有效的治療

14 treat

[trit]

(v) 治療;招待;對待

- My parents treated us fairly.
  我的父母公平對待我們。

- My treat! Let me treat you to dinner / a movie.
  我請客!讓我請你吃晚餐／看電影。

- Let me buy you a drink!
  讓我請你喝飲料!

15 cure

[kjʊr]

(n) (v) 治癒;治療藥物

用法
cure someone of
something

- He is miraculously cured!
  他奇蹟似地被治癒的!

- There is currently no cure for cancer.
  目前沒有能夠治癒癌症的方式／藥物。

- We are still looking for ways to cure cancer.
  我們仍在尋找治癒癌症的方法。

- The dog cured him of his depression.
  那隻狗治好了他的憂鬱症。

▶ 是非題

_____ 1. When you're sick, you should eat medicine.

_____ 2. Hygiene refers to the condition or the practices taken in order to keep a person or the environment clean.

_____ 3. Germs will thrive under good sanitary condition.

_____ 4. To dispose the trash means to throw away the trash.

_____ 5. You are able to find some ointment in a pharmacy.

_____ 6. A prescription includes the details instructed by a doctor.

_____ 7. The plural form of diagnosis is diagnosises.

_____ 8. A vaccine is used to prevent people from getting a certain disease.

_____ 9. Patients go to the hospital to receive treatment.

_____ 10. Pain killers can cure people for headaches.

▶ 填空題

1. It's important to brush your teeth daily to maintain good oral _____.

2. Those toothpicks are _____; just throw them away when you finish using them.

3. I'm going to the _____ to buy some medicine for my stomach ache.

4. The _____ of the disease has finally been developed and will be released to the public soon.

5. The baseball player needed special _____ for his injuries. .

6. Currently there is no direct _____ for many mental illnesses.

7. Clean water and _____ are fundamental to a civilized society.

8. Ever since she became ill, she had to receive _____ treatment regularly.

9. She was _____ with diabetes and had to strictly control her diet.

10. The doctor _____ some pills for her and told her to have enough rest.

Answer

是非題：

1. X　　2. O　　3. X　　4. X　　5. O　　6. O　　7. X（應為 diagnoses）　　8. O

9. O　　10. X（用法應為 cure of）

填空題：

1. hygiene　　2. disposable　　3. pharmacy　　4. vaccine　　5. treatment

6. cure　　7. sanitation　　8. medical　　9. diagnosed　　10. prescribed

填空題翻譯：

1. 每天刷牙對維持口腔衛生很重要。

2. 這牙籤是拋棄式的。用完直接丟掉就好了。

3. 我要去藥局買肚子痛的藥。

4. 這疾病的疫苗終於開發出來了，即將要問世。

5. 這位棒球員的傷需要特別的治療。

6. 目前許多精神疾病沒有直接的治療方式。

7. 乾淨的水和衛生對一個文明社會來說是很基本的。

8. 自從她生病之後，她需要定期接受治療。

9. 她被診斷有糖尿病，所以需要嚴格控制飲食。

10. 醫生開了一些藥給她並且叫她充分休息。

醫療衛生二
Medicine & Hygiene 2

Track
043

dental	spread
infect	infectious
contagious	sterilize
disease	surface
symptom	surgery
operate	

01 dental

[`dɛnt!]

(adj) 牙齒的

- The health care insurance includes dental care.
  這健康保險包含牙齒照護。

  延伸學習 dental care / hygiene 牙齒保健／口腔衛生

02 spread

[sprɛd]

(v) 散播

不規則三態
spread spread

- The pandemic has been spread to the whole world.
  大流行（疾病）已經傳播到全世界了。

  延伸學習 spread rumors / the word 散播謠言／傳播這件事

03 infect

[ɪn`fɛkt]

(v) 感染

相反詞
disinfect (v) 消毒、
disinfectant (n) 消毒劑

- He is infected by / with the disease.
  他被疾病感染了。

04 infectious

[ɪn`fɛkʃəs]

(adj) 傳染力強的

相關詞
infection (n) 感染

- The disease spreads easily; in other words, it is very infectious.
  這疾病很容易傳播；換句話說，它傳染力很強。

05 contagious

[kən`tedʒəs]

(adj) 感染力強的

- The flu is highly contagious! Make sure to wear a mask.
  這個流感很容易傳染！請一定要戴口罩。

  延伸學習 a contagious smile / laugh / feeling
  有感染力的微笑／笑聲／感覺

06 sterilize

[`stɛrəˌlaɪz]

(v) 消毒

相關詞
bleach (n) 漂白水

- A surgeon's equipment must be sterilized before use.
  外科醫師的器具在使用之前一定要先消毒。

07 disease

[dɪ`ziz]

(n) 疾病

相似詞
illness (n) 疾病、
ailment (n) 疾病

- Based on his symptoms, it is likely that he has contracted the disease.
  根據他的症狀，他很有可能已經得到這疾病了。

08 surface

[`sɝfɪs]

(n) (v) 表面；浮現

相關詞
external (adj) 外部的
相反詞
internal (adj) 內部的

- It is said that the virus can live on surfaces for more than 2 days.
  據說這病毒可以在物體表面存活超過 2 天。

- New problems have surfaced.
  新的問題浮現了。

09 symptom

[`sɪmptəm]

(n) 症狀

相似詞
syndrome (n) 症候群

- The surgeon successfully identified and treated the symptoms of pancreatic cancer.
  這外科醫師成功找到胰臟癌的症狀並且治療它。

  延伸學習 display / exhibit / show / have symptoms 顯現症狀
  develop symptoms 形成症狀

10 surgery

[`sɝdʒərɪ]

(n) 手術

相似詞
operation (n) 手術

- After undergoing the plastic surgery, the patient was told to pick up the prescription at the counter.
  在接受整形手術之後，病患被告知在櫃檯拿處方籤。

  延伸學習 major / minor / successful / extensive surgery
  重大的／小的／成功的／大範圍的手術
  perform / undergo surgery 進行／接受手術

11 operate

[`ɑpəˌret]

(v) 運作

相關詞
operation (n)
手術；營運

- I don't know how the (education) system (in this country) operates.
  我不知道這國家的教育制度如何運作。

 測驗

▶ 是非題

_____ 1. You should make an appointment with a dentist before you get a dental check-up.

_____ 2. The disease has spread means it has stopped.

_____ 3. When someone has been infected by a disease, it means he / she has contracted the disease.

_____ 4. A contagious disease is also infectious.

_____ 5. We can easily sterilize things by washing them with clean water.

_____ 6. You may feel ill without getting a disease.

_____ 7. The surface of something is the interior of something.

_____ 8. Symptoms of the flu include headaches, fever, sore throat, fatigue and so on.

_____ 9. A surgery is usually performed by a teacher.

_____ 10. A CEO should know how to operate a business.

▶ 填空

1. The patient is scheduled to undergo a / an _____ this afternoon.

2. He wants to know if we can _____ skin with UV radiation.

3. Using _____ floss every day keeps your teeth clean.

4. Short-term memory loss is usually the first _____ of Alzheimer's.

5. Everything seemed fine on the _____, but we know that, deep down, something is wrong.

6. The firm runs the biggest chili peppers _____ in the world.

7. We should prevent the disease from _____ by wearing masks.

8. Scientists are working together to combat the _____.

9. You will turn into a zombie if you are _____ by that strange virus.

10. The baby's _____ smile brightened up her parents' day.

是非題：

1. O　　2. X　　3. O　　4. O　　5. X　　6. O　　7. X　　8. O　　9. X　　10. O

填空題：

1. surgery / operation　　2. sterilize　　3. dental　　4. symptom　　5. surface

6. operation　　7. spreading　　8. disease　　9. infected

10. contagious

填空題翻譯：

1. 病患今天下午有安排要進行手術。

2. 他想要知道我們能不能用紫外線輻射來消毒皮膚。

3. 每天使用牙線可以保持牙齒乾淨。

4. 短期失憶通常是阿茲海默症的第一個症狀。

5. 表面上一切看起來都沒事，但我們知道有些事情不對勁。

6. 這公司經營全世界最大的辣椒事業。

7. 我們應該戴口罩以避免疾病擴散。

8. 科學家正在合作對抗這疾病。

9. 如果被這奇怪的病毒感染，你會變成殭屍。

10. 小嬰兒負有感染力的微笑點亮了他的父母的一天。

Unit 44

重要／不重要；大／小
Significant / insignificant

Track
044

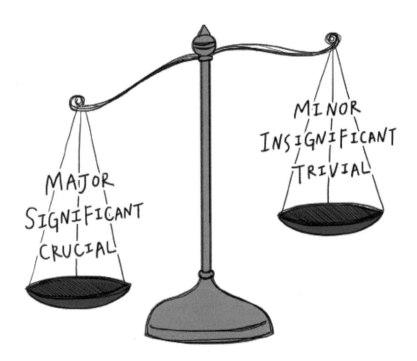

crucial	significant	essential
vital	fundamental	major
majority	minor	minority
primary	central	trivial
tremendous		

01 crucial

[ˋkruʃəl]

(adj) 重要的；關鍵的

用法
crucial + to

- The CEO's opinion is crucial to us.
  執行長的意見對我們來說很重要。
- Those essential elements are crucial to the ecosystem.
  這些基本要素對生態系統至關重要。

延伸學習 crucial moment / part / point
重要的時刻／部分／事項

02 significant

[sɪgˋnɪfəkənt]

(adj) 重要的；顯著的

相反詞
insignificant (adj)
不重要的

用法
significant to

- I don't see significant changes in the new version of the product.
  我沒有在新版本的產品中看到顯著的改變。

延伸學習 significant difference / change / impact / side effects
顯著的不同／改變／影響／副作用

03 essential

[ɪˋsɛnʃəl]

(adj) 重要的

- Physical education, just like math or English, is an essential part of education.
  體育，就像數學或英文，是教育裡面很重要的一部分。

延伸學習 essential part / component / element
重要的部分／重要組成部分／基本要素

04 vital

[ˋvaɪtl]

(adj) 重要的

- My sister plays a vital role in my life.
  我的妹妹在我的生命中扮演重要角色。

延伸學習 vital part / information / role
重要部分／資訊／角色

05 fundamental

[ˌfʌndəˋmɛntl]

(adj) 根本的

- We need to make fundamental changes to our education systems.
  我們的教育應該要有根本的改變。

06 major

[`medʒə]

(adj) 主要的；重要的
(v) 主修

- Cindy majors in English.
  Cindy 主修英文。

- It's a major problem that we must tackle.
  那是一個我們必須要處理的大問題。

  延伸學習 major role / problem / part 主要角色／問題／部分
  major in a subject 主修某科系

07 majority

[mə`dʒɔrətɪ]

(n) 多數

- The majority of people in the world don't know what Tourette syndrome is.
  世界上大部分的人不知道妥瑞氏症是什麼。

08 minor

[`maɪnə]

(adj) 次要；不重要的
(v) 輔修

- She minors in Education.
  她輔修教育。

- He only made minor changes to the painting. You can't really tell the difference.
  他對這幅畫只有做了些微的更改，看不太出來有什麼變化。

  延伸學習 minor difference / change / issue
  細微差異／小改變／小問題
  minor in English 輔修英文

09 minority

[maɪ`nɔrətɪ]

(n) 少數

- The charity focuses on helping the minority.
  這慈善機構專注於幫助弱勢族群。

10 primary

[`praɪˌmɛrɪ]

(adj) 主要的；初階的

相關詞
prime (adj) 首要的、
premium (adj) 高級的

- Keeping people safe is our primary concern.
  確保人身安全是我們的首要考量。

  延伸學習 primary focus / concern / source of income
  主要的重點／首要關注的問題／主要薪水來源

11 **central**	• The evidence is <u>central to</u> the case.
['sɛntrəl]	這證據對案件很重要。
(adj) 核心的；重要的	延伸學習 Central Asia 中亞
用法	
central + to	

12 **trivial**	• Why would you get angry at something so trivial?
['trɪvɪəl]	為什麼你要對這麼小的事情動怒？
(adj) 瑣碎的	延伸學習 trivial <u>matters / things</u> 不重要的事、瑣事

13 **tremendous**	• We spend a tremendous amount of time on this project.
[trɪ'mɛndəs]	我們在這個專案花費了大量的時間。
(adj) 巨大的	延伸學習 tremendous <u>impact / pressure / amount</u>
相似詞	巨大的影響／壓力／份量
massive (adj)、	
mammoth (adj)、	
gigantic (adj) 巨大的	

 測驗

▶ 是非題

_____ 1. At certain situations, critical shares similar meanings with crucial.

_____ 2. A significant person is ordinary.

_____ 3. Luxuries can be afforded by everyone.

_____ 4. A vital role is someone or something that's extremely important.

_____ 5. Basic is a synonym for the word fundamental.

_____ 6. You can major on a subject.

_____ 7. The minority is usually the smaller group of people in a society.

_____ 8. A primary school is an elementary school.

_____ 9. A trivial issue is usually quite complex.

_____ 10. You can make tremendous changes by taking small steps.

▶ 填空題

1. The rent of an apartment is usually higher if it's at a _____ location.

2. Good eating habits are _____ to your health.

3. Eating and sitting too much are the _____ causes of obesity.

4. The decision is very _____ and will likely affect all employees.

5. We need to make sure the _____ structure of this building is stable enough.

6. It's just a _____ injury; don't worry about it.

7. The _____ goal for the sales department is to sell good products to customers.

8. The Internet has made _____ changes to people's lives.

9. I can't believe that tiny machines can make such a _____ noise.

10. Water is _____ to all living creatures.

Answer

是非題：

1. O   2. X   3. X   4. O   5. O   6. X（應為 major in）   7. O   8. O

9. X   10. O

填空題：

1. central / prime 2. vital   3. major   4. crucial   5. fundamental

6. minor   7. primary   8. significant 9. tremendous   10. essential

填空題翻譯：

1. 在核心地段的房租通常比較貴。

2. 好的飲食習慣對你的健康至關重要。

3. 飲食過量以及經常坐著是導致過重的主要原因。

4. 這個決定很重要而且有可能會影響全體員工。

5. 我們要確保這棟建築的基本結構是夠穩的。

6. 這只是個小傷，不用擔心。

7. 業務部的主要目標是把好產品賣給顧客。

8. 網路對人們的生活造成了重大改變。

9. 我不敢相信小小的機器可以製造這麼大的噪音。

10. 水對所有生物都是不可缺少的。

銀行業務
Banking

currency	convert
deposit	withdraw
figure	account
digital	branch
asset	valuable
complementary	complement

01 currency

[ˋkɝ·ənsɪ]

(n) 貨幣

- It's simple to exchange foreign currency online.
  在線上換國外貨幣很容易。

02 convert

[kənˋvɝt]

(v) 轉換

- You can convert YouTube videos to mp3 files on many websites.
  在很多網站你都可以把 YouTube 影片轉換為 mp3 檔。

  延伸學習 convert TWD to USD 把臺幣轉換為美金
  convert a Word file to a PDF file
  將 Word 檔轉換為 PDF 檔

03 deposit

[dɪˋpɑzɪt]

(n) (v) 存；存款

- To open an account, you should at least deposit a thousand dollars.
  如果要開戶，你至少要存 1000 元。

- A one-thousand-dollar deposit is required to open an account.
  你需要存 1000 元才能開戶。

  延伸學習 deposit money in the bank 將錢存入銀行

04 withdraw

[wɪðˋdrɔ]

(v) 提取；取出

- You are not allowed to withdraw too much money from an account at once.
  不能一次從銀行帳戶中提出太多錢。

  延伸學習 withdraw money from a bank 提款

05 figure

[ˋfɪgjɚ]

(n) (v) 數字；身材；
認為

相關詞
digit (n) 數字

- He lost his six-figure income.
  他失去了他 6 位數的薪水。

- She wants to lose weight because she doesn't like her figure.
  她想減肥因為她不喜歡自己的身材。

- I just can't figure out why she left.
  我想不通她為什麼要離開。

  延伸學習 a six-figure salary / income 6 位數的薪水

06 account

[əˈkaʊnt]

(n) 帳戶；訴説

相關詞
password (n) 密碼、
PIN (number)
個人識別碼

- The witness gave the police a detailed account of the accident.
  目擊者給警察關於意外詳細的説明。

延伸學習 open a bank account 開銀行帳戶

07 digital

[ˈdɪdʒɪtl̩]

(adj) 數位的

- Our digital banking services include paying bills and transferring funds online.
  我們的數位銀行服務提供付款和線上轉帳。

- You can pay bills and transfer funds digitally.
  你可以以數位付款和轉帳。

08 branch

[bræntʃ]

(n) 分部；分店

- You can open an account at one of our 60 branches.
  你可以在我們 60 個分部當中開戶。

09 asset

[ˈæsɛt]

(n) 資產

相似詞
property (n) 資產

- The company went bankrupt, so their assets were put up for sale.
  公司破產了，所以他們的資產被拍賣了。

- The little mermaid has a valuable asset - her voice.
  小美人魚有個很有價值的資產—她的聲音。

10 valuable

[ˈvæljʊəbl̩]

(n) 貴重物品
(adj) 有價值的

相關詞
personal belongings
個人物品

- This is valuable information.
  這是很有價值的資訊。

- You can store your valuables in a safe deposit box in a bank.
  你可以把貴重物品放在銀行裡面的保險櫃。

11 complementary

[ˌkɑmplə`mɛntərɪ]

(adj) 補充的

注意
不要和 **complimentary**
（免費附贈的）搞混

• To open an account, applicants should provide one of the following complementary ID documents.
要開設帳戶，申請人應提供以下相關身分證件。

---

12 complement

[`kɑmpləmənt]

(v) 補足

• Some people look for someone who is similar to them while others seek a partner who can complement them with their differences.
找對象的時候有些人找跟自己個性相似的，有些人找互補的。

• The pudding and caramel complement each other perfectly.
布丁和焦糖搭配在一起非常完美。

 測驗

▶ 是非題

_____ 1. Currency is the noun for currently.

_____ 2. Transform is a synonym for convert.

_____ 3. You can deposit in a stock market.

_____ 4. To withdraw money from a bank means to take money out.

_____ 5. To figure out means to find out.

_____ 6. A person may only have one account.

_____ 7. Digital learning is the most traditional way to learn.

_____ 8. A branch is located in the headquarters.

_____ 9. A useful skill can be one's valuable asset.

_____ 10. Complementary is a synonym for similar.

▶ 填空題

1. The government spent an estimated _____ of 100 million dollars on this project.

2. Thank you for your _____ advice. I really learned a lot.

3. Japanese _____ is relatively low now, so you can consider buying some for your future trip to Japan.

4. Smartphones have replaced _____ cameras for many people.

5. I'm running out of cash so I'll go to the bank and _____ some money later.

6. I'd like to make a _____ into my savings account.

7. I share a Netflix _____ with my sister.

8. I am thrilled that my favorite bakery has opened a new _____ close to my office!

9. Please _____ your Word document into a PDF file.

10. The wealthy man has _____ in both domestic and overseas regions.

Answer

是非題：

1. X　　2. O　　3. X（應為 invest）　　4. O　　5. O　　6. X　　7. X　　8. X

9. O　　10. X

填空題：

1. figure　　　2. valuable　　　3. currency　　　4. digital　　　5. withdraw

6. deposit　　　7. account　　　8. branch　　　9. convert　　　10. asset

填空題翻譯：

1. 政府花了將近一億元在這個專案上。

2. 謝謝你寶貴的建議，我真的學到很多。

3. 日幣現在相對便宜，你可以考慮先買一些，將來去日本旅遊可以用。

4. 對任何人來說，智慧型手機取代了數位相機。

5. 我的現金快用完了，所以我等一下要去銀行提款。

6. 我要存錢到我的儲蓄戶頭。

7. 我跟妹妹共用 Netflix 帳號。

8. 我很開心我最喜歡的麵包店在我的公司附近開了分店！

9. 請把 WORD 檔案轉為 PDF 檔。

10. 那富裕的男人在國內和海外都有資產。

Unit 46 投資
Investment

Track 046

invest	investment	market
estate	interest	rate
scale	fluctuate	analysis
analyze	portfolio	gain
estimate		

01 invest
[ɪn`vɛst]
(v) 投資

相關詞
investor (n) 投資人

- It's risky to invest in stock markets.
  投資股票市場有風險。

- You can invest in yourself by learning a new skill.
  你可以藉由學習新技能投資自己。

02 investment
[ɪn`vɛstmənt]
(n) 投資

- Since we have lost so much money in our last investment, maybe we should consider another strategy.
  因為我們上次的投資損失很多，或許我們應考慮別的策略。

03 market
[`mɑrkɪt]
(n) 市場

- She made a fortune by investing in the stock market.
  她投資股票市場賺很多錢。

  延伸學習 stock market 股票市場
  　　　　 bond market 債券市場

04 estate
[ɪs`tet]
(n) 地產；財產

相關詞
realtor (n) 房仲

- Real estate is considered a good investment by some people.
  某些人視房地產為很好的投資。

- Desperate for money, he started selling off real estate.
  他因急需用錢而開始賣房產。

  延伸學習 real estate 房地產

05 interest
[`ɪntərɪst]
(n) 利息

- The interest rate is low recently, so it might be a good time to get a loan / borrow money from the bank.
  最近利率很低，所以現在可能是跟銀行貸款的好時機。

- My parents helped us buy an apartment by offering us an interest-free loan.
  我的父母免利息借我們錢幫我們買房。

06 rate

[ret]
(n) 速度；比率
(v) 評比

- At this rate, we won't be able to get our work done before Friday.
  依照這個速度，我們星期五之前沒辦法完成工作。

- Unfortunately, the unemployment rate has risen due to the virus.
  很不幸的，因為這病毒，失業率增加了。

- This Michelin restaurant is really overrated.
  這家米其林餐廳得到的評價真的過高了。

- This movie is actually very good! I think it's underrated.
  這部電影其實還不錯！我覺得它得到的評價過低。

延伸學習 to rate a restaurant / a movie / a hotel
評比餐廳／電影／飯店

07 scale

[skel]
(n) 規模；量尺；秤
用法
on a ...scale

- On a scale of 1 to 10, how would you rate this movie?
  1-10 分你會如何評價這部電影？

- The typhoon caused destruction on a massive scale.
  颱風導致了大規模的破壞。

延伸學習 a weight scale 體重機

08 fluctuate

[`flʌktʃʊˌet]
(v) 浮動

- Currency fluctuates all the time.
  貨幣一直在波動。

- The unpredictable woman's mood fluctuates from time to time.
  這位難以捉摸的女人的情緒會不時地浮動。

09 analysis

[ə`næləsɪs]
(n) 分析

- The expert's analysis and comments on the subject is truly thought-provoking.
  專家對此主題的分析和評論會誘發人們思考。

10 analyze

[`æn!ˌaɪz]
(v) 分析

相關詞
analyst (n) 分析師

- A corporate analyst should analyze the data of a company.
  公司分析師應分析公司的數據。

259

11 portfolio [port`foli͵o] (n) 投資組合;作品集	• You need more works in your portfolio. 你的作品集需要更多作品。 **延伸學習** investment portfolio 投資組合
12 gain [gen] (n) (v) 得到;獲得	• No pain, no gain. 一分耕耘,一分收穫。 **延伸學習** gain or loss (of investment) 得到或失去(投資) gain weight / reputation / knowledge 增重/獲得名聲/獲得知識
13 estimate [`ɛstə͵met] (n) (v) 估計 **相關詞** **estimated (adj)** 估計的	• It is estimated that oil prices will drop in the near future. 據估計油價在未來會下跌。 • The realtor estimated the value of the house at 12 million dollars. 房地產經紀人估計這所房子的價值為 1200 萬元。 • We only need an estimate of the number of the passengers. 我們只需要知道乘客大概有幾人。

 測驗

▶ 是非題

_____ 1. You will definitely make profit if you invest in the stock market.

_____ 2. Anything valuable is called real estate.

_____ 3. An interest-free loan means you don't need to pay additional fees.

_____ 4. You can rate an application after using it.

_____ 5. A fish has scales.

_____ 6. When one's weight fluctuates, it means he / her is healthy.

_____ 7. Analyze is a synonym for learn.

_____ 8. A portfolio is a collection of one's work.

_____ 9. "No pain, no gain." means you won't get anything without working for it.

_____ 10. The estimated number is the exact number.

▶ 填空題

1. The entrepreneur is looking for people to _____ in his business.

2. His heart _____ increased when he was riding the rollercoaster.

3. Please measure the ingredients with a _____ before you combine them.

4. An _____ of two hundred people will participate in the activity.

5. You'll need an impressive _____ to apply for the prestigious art school.

6. We will _____ the results for future improvements.

7. Since _____ rates are low now, it's probably a good time to invest in real estate.

8. I don't know what to wear recently because the temperature _____ frequently.

9. Many investors aim to _____ passive income from investments in the

_____.

Answer

是非題：

1. X   2. X   3. O   4. O   5. O   6. X   7. X   8. O   9. O   10. X

填空題：

1. invest   2. rate   3. scale   4. estimate   5. portfolio

6. analyze   7. interest   8. fluctuates   9. gain, stock market

填空題翻譯：

1. 創業家在找人投資他的事業。

2. 當他在搭雲霄飛車的時候，他心跳的速度增加了。

3. 在你把食材混和之前請用秤先測量過。

4. 大約 200 人會參加這個活動。

5. 你需要很厲害的作品集才能進那間有名的藝術學校。

6. 我們會分析結果以讓未來更加進步。

7. 現在利率很低，可能是投資房地產的好時機。

8. 我最近都不知道要穿什麼，因為氣溫起起伏伏。

9. 許多投資人希望藉由投資股票獲得被動收入。

公司併購
Merger

Track
047

merge	column
row	broker
method	means
combine	shareholder
stakeholder	stake
conglomerate	

01 merge

[mɝdʒ]

(v) 合併；融合

相似詞
combine (v) 結合、
fuse (v) 結合、
absorb (v) 吸收
相反詞
separate (vt) 分割

- Day slowly merged into night.
  白天慢慢轉變成黑夜了。

- The board of directors are considering merging the two companies.
  董事會在考慮將兩個公司合併。

02 column

[`kɑləm]

(n) 專欄；欄

- How do I merge two columns in Word?
  如何在 Word 裡面把兩個欄位合併？

- Carrie Bradshaw is a columnist who writes a weekly column called "Sex and the City."
  Carrie Bradshaw 是寫「慾望城市」這個每週專欄的專欄作家。

延伸學習 表格的格子稱為 cell

03 row

[raʊ]

(n) 列

- I would like the students in the second row to answer question 2.
  我想請第二列的同學回答第二題。

- I want to sit in the front row so that I can see clearer.
  我想要坐前排才能看得更清楚。

- She won the competition three years in a row.
  她連續三年都在比賽中勝出。

04 broker

[`brokɚ]

(n) 仲介；經紀人

- When you spot an opportunity to buy someone's business, sell yours, or merge with another business, it's advisable to consult a broker or an advisor.
  當您發現購買某人的事業、出售您的業務或與另一業務合併的機會時，建議諮詢經紀人或顧問。

- All brokers are agents, but not all agents are brokers.
  所有經紀人都是代理商，但並非所有代理商都是經紀人。

05 method

[ˋmɛθəd]

(n) 方法

相似詞
means、way (n) 方法、
measure (n) 措施

• If the same problems happen every time, why not try a different method?
如果每次都發生一樣的問題，何不嘗試不一樣的方法？

06 means

[minz]

(n) 手段；方式

相似詞
approach (n) 方法

• Exams are a means of assessing a student's ability.
測驗是評量學生能力的一種方法。

延伸學習 means of transportation / communication
交通方式／溝通方式
by means of... 藉由……的方式
by no means / by all means 絕對不能／可以

07 combine

[kəmˋbaɪn]

(v) 結合

• Let's combine our ideas.
我們把想法結合在一起吧。

• Next, combine all ingredients.
接下來，把所有食材混和在一起。

08 shareholder

[ˋʃɛr͵holdɚ]

(n) 股東

• Shareholders have the right to vote on proposed mergers.
股東有權對擬議的合併進行表決。

09 stakeholder

[ˋstek͵holdɚ]

(n) 利益關係人

• Shareholders are always stakeholders in a corporation, but stakeholders are not always shareholders.
股東一定是利益關係人，但利益關係人不一定是股東。

• Stakeholders can be employees, customers, or suppliers.
利益關係人可以是員工、顧客或是供應商。

10 stake

[stek]

(n) 賭注、木樁

- What's at stake?
  最關鍵的是什麼？

- There were three lives at stake.
  有三個人命在旦夕。

- The stakes are high in the election.
  選舉中的賭注很高。

- He holds a 30 percent stake in the firm.
  他持有該公司 30%的股份。

- The only way to kill a vampire is to drive a wooden
  stake through a vampire's heart.
  殺死吸血鬼的唯一方法是用木樁穿過吸血鬼的心臟。

11 conglomerate

[kən`glɑmərɪt]

(n) 大集團

- The conglomerate was composed of several
  combined companies formed by mergers.
  這間企業集團是透過併購幾間合併公司組成的。

 測驗

▶ 是非題

_____ 1. Combine is a synonym for merge.

_____ 2. Columns are horizontal.

_____ 3. Rows are vertical.

_____ 4. A broker is similar to an agent.

_____ 5. A method is a way of doing something.

_____ 6. "By all means" is another way to say "of course."

_____ 7. We can combine ingredients by cleaning them.

_____ 8. A shareholder is always a member of the board of directors.

_____ 9. A high-stake activity is usually risky.

_____ 10. It is very rare to find a conglomerate.

▶ 填空題

1. Without her car, she has no _____ of transportation.
2. We've decided to consult an experienced _____ before we sell our company.
3. The great speaker _____ serious issues with a sense of humor in his speech.
4. Many readers are most interested in the gossip _____ in newspapers.
5. Alphabet Inc. is an American multinational _____, which is the parent company of Google and several former Google subsidiaries.
6. Some students prefer to sit in the last _____ of the classroom.
7. The wolf _____ into the forest and disappeared.
8. Cindy has a special _____ for memorizing verbs.
9. Now that the scandal came to light, the politician's job is at _____.
10. She is a 50 percent _____ in the company, so her opinions matter to the board.

Answer

是非題：

1. O　　2. X（應為 vertical）　　3. X（應為 horizontal）　　4. O　　5. O　　6. O

7. X　　8. X　　9. O　　10. X

填空題：

1. means　　2. broker　　3. combined　　4. column　　5. conglomerate

6. row　　7. merged　　8. method　　9. stake　　10. shareholder

填空題翻譯：

1. 沒了車子她失去了交通工具。

2. 我們在賣公司之前決定先諮詢一位有經驗的經紀人。

3. 那位很棒的講者在演講中將嚴肅議題和幽默感結合。

4. 許多讀者對報紙中的八卦專欄最感興趣。

5. Alphabet Inc. 是美國一間多國大集團，它是 Google 以及許多前 Google 子公司的母公司。

6. 有些學生比較喜歡坐在教室的後排。

7. 那隻野狼融入了森林之後消失了。

8. Cindy 用一個特別的方式記動詞。

9. 在醜聞被揭露之後，那位政治人物的工作危在旦夕。

10. 她是公司持有 50% 股份的股東，所以她的意見對董事會很重要。

Unit 48

製造業
Manufacturing

plant   component
automated   pattern
shift   sample
recall   assemble
warehouse   rack
cut

01 plant

[plænt]

(n) 廠

- Whether a nuclear power plant should be built is a question.
  是否應該建造核電廠是個問題。

  延伸學習 power plant 電廠
  nuclear power plant 核能發電廠

02 component

[kəm`ponənt]

(n) 元件；零件

- Entertainment is an indispensable component in our lives.
  娛樂是我們生活中不可或缺的組成部分。

- One key component of success is giving yourself a deadline.
  成功的一個關鍵因素是給自己一個截止日期。

  延伸學習 computer / electrical / automobile components
  電腦／電子／汽車零件

03 automated

[`ɔtometɪd]

(adj) 自動的

- It is said that automated vehicles will roam the streets in the near future.
  據說自動車在不久的將來就會在街上奔馳。

  延伸學習 automated vehicles → self-driving cars 自動車
  automated systems 自動化系統

補充說明

automated vs automatic：

auto 這個字首的意思是 "self"「自己」的意思，例如：autopilot（飛機的自動駕駛儀）、automatic（自動的）、automated（使……自動化的）。
automatic 跟 automated 差別在於自動化的程度，automatic 較低階，例如：automatic doors（自動門）；而 automated 是較高級的自動化系統，例如：automated vehicles（自動駕駛車）。

04 pattern

[`pætɚn]

(n) 圖案；模式

- I love the pattern of your bag!
  我喜歡妳包包的圖案！

- As our climate continues to change, animals modify their routes and behavior patterns accordingly.
  隨著氣候變遷，動物會跟著改變他們的路線跟行為模式。

05 shift

[ʃɪft]

(n) (v) 輪班

- He shifted from the night shift to the day shift.
  他從夜班換到日班。

延伸學習 day / night shift 日班／夜班

06 sample

[`sæmpl]

(n) (v) 樣本；試用／試吃

- You can sample food samples at Costco.
  在好市多可以試吃食物。

- Here is a sample for you to sample.
  這裡有個樣本給妳試用。

07 recall

[rɪ`kɔl]

(v) 記得；回想；召回

- I don't recall saying that.
  我不記得我有說那些話。

- After finding a major defect, the company recalled all of the products.
  在發現了重大缺陷後，公司召回了所有產品。

08 assemble

[ə`sɛmbl]

(v) 組裝；集合

相關詞
assembly (n)
集會；集合

- In the broadcast, the dean told us to assemble in the assembly hall.
  在廣播中，主任叫我們在禮堂集合。

延伸學習 assemble furniture / data / evidence / a team
組裝家具／資料／證據／團隊

09 warehouse

[`wɛr͵haʊs]

(n) 倉庫

- We store our stock in a warehouse.
  我們把庫存收在倉庫。

- Most of our merchandise is stocked in the warehouse.
  我們大部分的商品都儲存在倉庫。

10 rack

[ræk]

(n) 架子

- Hang your clothes on a rack.
  把衣服吊在架上。

- Stack the files on a rack over there.
  將文件堆放在那裡的架子上。

11 cut

[kʌt]

(v) 切;割;削減;縮短

• In order not to exceed the budget, it is advisable to cut back on our expenses.

為了不超出預算,建議要減少支出。

延伸學習 cut back on sugar 減少吃糖

 測驗

▶ 是非題

_____ 1. A plant is another way to say a retail store.

_____ 2. Element is a synonym of component.

_____ 3. An automated vehicle cannot drive on its own.

_____ 4. A pattern is a kind of repeated design.

_____ 5. Someone who wants to stay healthy should cut back on water.

_____ 6. If you shift all your attention to one thing, that means you are now focusing on it.

_____ 7. You can sample food at some supermarkets.

_____ 8. To recall someone means to call the person again.

_____ 9. To assemble something means to put something together.

_____ 10. People usually store valuable things in warehouses.

▶ 填空題

1. A factory can also be called a _____.

2. Do you _____ the time when we were young?

3. The _____ on her dress attracted my eye because they were bright and colorful.

4. To stay healthy, you had better _____ deep-fried food.

5. He sleeps in the morning because he is working the night _____.

6. I couldn't _____ the device because a part was missing.

7. I was given a free shampoo _____ when I was shopping in the department store.

8. We store some of our old furniture in the _____.

9. Clothes look better when they are hung on a _____.

10. Trust is an essential _____ of a good relationship.

Answer

是非題：

1. X　　2. O　　3. X　　4. O　　5. X　　6. O　　7. O　　8. X　　9. O　　10. X

填空題：

1. plant　　　2. recall　　　3. patterns　　　4. cut back on　　5. shift

6. assemble　　7. sample　　　8. warehouse　　9. rack　　　　10. component

填空題翻譯：

1. 工廠（factory）也可以稱為工廠（plant）。

2. 你還記得我們年輕的時候嗎？

3. 她洋裝上的圖案吸引了我的目光，因為那些圖案明亮又多彩。

4. 為了維持健康，你最好少吃炸的。

5. 他白天睡覺因為他上夜班。

6. 我無法組裝這設備因為有一部分不見了。

7. 在百貨公司逛街的時候有人給我一個洗髮精的試用包。

8. 我們把一些舊家具存放在倉庫。

9. 衣服掛在架子上比較好看。

10. 信任是一段好的感情的必備要素。

旅遊
Travel

Track
049

brochure	serve
service	tourist
guide	feature
picturesque	historical
landmark	gourmet
excursion	

01 brochure

[broˋʃʊr]
(n)（旅遊）小冊子

相關詞
booklet 小冊子、
pamphlet 小冊子、
flyer 傳單、
poster 海報

- The job description says that the responsibilities include giving out brochures.
  工作說明中有說工作內容包含發手冊。

- Monsieur, please take a brochure!
  先生，拿個手冊吧！

- A brochure?! I'm not so sure.
  手冊？！我不想要耶。

02 serve

[sɝv]
(v) 服務

- "Your majesty, it is my honor to serve you," said the servant. "I am always at your service."
  「陛下，服務您是我的榮幸。」僕人說。「我會一直服務您。」

03 service

[ˋsɝvɪs]
(n) 服務

- The service here is wonderful, so I've decided to tip more.
  這裡的服務真好，所以我決定要給更多小費。

04 tourist

[ˋtʊrɪst]
(n) 遊客

相關詞
tour (v) (n) 旅遊

- There are many tourist <u>attractions / spots</u> waiting for us to visit!
  這裡有很多旅遊景點等著我們去參觀！

05 guide

[gaɪd]
(n) (v) 帶領；指南；
導遊

相關詞
guideline (n) 指導方針

- Guide dogs are trained to guide their owners. They help their owners find the way.
  導盲犬被訓練用來帶領他們的主人，他們會幫主人找路。

- Since you are a local, you can be our tour guide!
  既然你是當地人，你可以當我們的導遊！

  延伸學習 look for travel guides on the Internet
  在網路上找旅遊指南

06 feature

[ˈfitʃɚ]
(v) 以……為特色

- The concert features songs that called for inspiration and empathy.
  演唱會以激勵人心的歌曲當作特色。

- The parade features flamboyant clothing.
  這遊行以誇張的服飾當作特色。

07 picturesque

[ˌpɪktʃəˈrɛsk]
(adj) 如詩如畫的

- Wow! The scenery is just like a picture. It is picturesque!
  這裡的風景就像圖畫一樣。它美得如詩如畫！

08 historical

[hɪsˈtɔrɪkḷ]
(adj) 歷史的

- This historical city is rich in culture.
  這古老的城市富有文化。

補充說明

historical (adj)　VS　historic (adj)
historical 是指「有歷史的」、「古老的」，例如 historical novels 以古代為背景的小說；historic 是指「具歷史意義的」，例如 historic sites 歷史地標 historic buildings 具歷史意義的建築。historic events 跟 historical events 文法都正確，但意思不同，historical events 是古代的事件、historic events 是指古代具有意義、有代表性的事件。

09 landmark

[ˈlændˌmɑrk]
(n) 地標

- Taipei 101 is a <u>famous / significant</u> landmark.
  臺北 101 是有名的／重要的地標。

10 gourmet

[ˈgʊrme]
(adj) 美味的
(n) 美食家

相關詞
delicacies (n) 美味食物

- I heard that they serve gourmet meals here.
  我聽說這裡提供美味的餐點。

- Although he considers himself a gourmet, we think he is merely a picky eater.
  雖然他認為自己是美食家，但我們覺得他只是個挑食的人。

11 excursion

[ɪk`skɝʒən]

(n) 短程旅遊；遠足

相關詞
journey (n) 旅行、
expedition (n) 旅程

• We will have an excursion to HsinChu on the weekend.

我們週末會去新竹遠足。

延伸學習 to go on an excursion / a journey / an expedition

去短程旅遊／去旅行／去長程旅遊

 測驗

▶ 是非題

_____ 1. A brochure is similar to a dictionary.

_____ 2. If you provide someone service, you're in his/her service.

_____ 3. A tourist is someone who guides people to see the attractions of a place.

_____ 4. When you guide someone, you lead the way.

_____ 5. To feature someone in a song is to include the person as a important part.

_____ 6. If a place is picturesque, it looks fake and strange.

_____ 7. A recently-built shopping center can be a historical building.

_____ 8. A landmark can be a building, a tree, or even a stone.

_____ 9. A gourmet meal has very high quality.

_____ 10. An excursion is usually a long journey.

▶ 填空題

1. The class is going on an _____ tomorrow so the students are very excited.

2. This room is for staff only; _____ are not allowed to enter.

3. The _____ scenery of the mountains took my breath away!

4. The _____ coffee is the best I've ever had!

5. Many patrons of that restaurant love it not only for its excellent food but also for its superb _____.

6. The museum _____ modern art.

7. The Eiffel Tower is one of the most famous _____ in the world.

8. I want to visit all of the attraction spots listed in the _____.

9. People in the past used compasses（羅盤）to help them _____ the way.

10. Tainan is one of the oldest cities in Taiwan, so you can find many _____ buildings there.

Answer

是非題：

1. X　　2. X（應為 at）　　3. X　　4. O　　5. O　　6. X　　7. X　　8. O　　9. O

10. X

填空題：

1. excursion　　2. tourists　　3. picturesque　　4. gourmet　　5. service

6. features　　7. landmarks　　8. brochure　　9. guide　　10. historical

填空題翻譯：

1. 這個班級明天要去遠足，所以同學都非常興奮。

2. 這個房間只有員工可以進入；旅客不能進入。

3. 如詩如畫的山景讓我驚豔！

4. 這美味的咖啡是我喝過最好喝的！

5. 這間餐廳許多常客不只喜歡它優秀的餐點也喜歡它優良的服務。

6. 這博物館以現代藝術為特色。

7. 艾菲爾鐵塔是全世界最著名的地標之一。

8. 我想要參觀手冊裡面列出的所有旅遊景點。

9. 以前的人使用羅盤幫助他們指引方向。

10. 臺南是臺灣一個古老的城市，所以你可以在那邊找到許多古老的建築。

Unit 50

住宿
Accomodation, Housing

Track
050

relocate   accommodation   accomodate

contain   rent   lease

rural   remote   urban

apartment   isolate   resident

reside   appliance

01 relocate

[ri`loket]

(v) 搬遷

相似詞
move (v) 搬

- She is moving because her company is going to relocate to another city.
  她要搬家因為她的公司要搬遷到另一個城市。

02 accommodation

[ə͵kɑmə`deʃən]

(n) 住宿

- Accommodation and transportation are the two most important factors in traveling.
  住宿和交通是旅遊中最重要的兩個要素。

03 accommodate

[ə`kɑmə͵det]

(v) 容納；裝載；配合

- The room accommodates up to 6 people.
  這房間可以容納 6 個人。

- The lawyer adjusted his schedule to accommodate his client.
  律師為了配合客戶調整了自己的行程。

04 contain

[kən`ten]

(v) 包含；控制

- Soybean milk contains protein.
  豆漿含有蛋白質。

- She couldn't contain her emotions and burst out crying.
  她沒辦法控制情緒地哭了出來。

- Italy struggles to contain the coronavirus.
  義大利努力遏制冠狀病毒。

05 rent

[rɛnt]

(v) 租

- I'm planning to rent an apartment near campus. Are there any apartments for rent?
  我正計畫在學校附近租公寓。這裡有公寓出租嗎？

06 lease

[lis]

(v) 租

- The tenant broke the lease agreement by moving out early.
  房客因提前搬出而違反了租賃協議。

延伸學習 lease an apartment / a car 租公寓／租車

278

07 rural

[ˋrʊrəl]

(adj) 鄉村的

- I prefer living in rural areas instead of crowded cities.
  比起擁擠的城市我比較喜歡住在鄉下地方。

08 remote

[rɪˋmot]

(adj) 遙遠的

- The beautiful restaurant is <u>situated / located</u> in a remote town.
  這美麗的餐廳坐落於遙遠的城鎮。

- Where is the remote control? I can't find it anywhere.
  遙控器在哪裡？我找不到它。

09 urban

[ˋɝbən]

(adj) 都市的

相關詞
suburban (adj) 郊區

- As a city dweller, I'm used to the convenient lifestyle in urban areas.
  作為城市居民，我習慣了城市中便利的生活方式。

- The environment is polluted due to urban development.
  由於城市發展，環境受到污染。

補充說明

urban legend 直接翻譯為「都市傳說」，但中文的都市傳說通常指一些鬼故事，而英文的 urban legend 是指無稽之談，又稱為 urban myth。

10 apartment

[əˋpɑrtmənt]

(n) 公寓

相似詞
condo (n) 公寓、
flat (n) 公寓（英式說法）

- If you were a billionaire, would you like to live in a stand-alone house, an apartment, a penthouse, or a mansion?
  如果你是億萬富翁，你會想住獨棟房子、公寓、頂樓公寓，還是豪宅？

11 isolate

[ˋaɪsḷ͵et]

(v) 孤立；隔離

相似詞
quarantine (n) (v) 隔離

- The naughty boy was isolated by his classmates because he kept saying rude things to them.
  那個調皮的男孩被同學孤立，因為他一直對同學們說無禮的話。

- The Grump chose to live in an isolated area to stay away from everyone.
  為了遠離所有人，The Grump（grump 意思是脾氣暴躁的，他是美國知名童書作家 Dr. Suess 的一個角色）選擇住在一個偏僻的地方。

12 resident

['rɛzədənt]

(n) 居民；住戶

- To protect public health and safety, the governor of Maryland ordered that no resident should leave their home unless it is for an essential job or for an essential reason such as obtaining food or medicine, seeking urgent medical attention, or for other necessary purposes.

  為了保護公共健康和安全，馬里蘭州州長命令居民不得離開家，除非是為了重要工作或出於為了獲取食物或藥品，尋求緊急醫療護理或出於其他必要目的之類的重要原因。

13 reside

[rɪ`zaɪd]

(v) 居住

- Those who reside in Maryland should abide by the order or they might face penalties.

  住馬里蘭州的人要遵守規定不然將有可能面對懲處。

14 appliance

[ə`plaɪəns]

(n) 家電

相關詞
furniture (n) [U] 家具

- Nowadays, even kitchen appliances are available for rent!

  現在就連廚房用品都可以用租的！

延伸學習 household / electronic appliances 家電

 測驗

▶ 是非題

_____ 1. I can relocate a cup onto another table.

_____ 2. If someone is looking for accommodation, he / she is looking for someone to stay with.

_____ 3. Contain is a synonym for accommodate.

_____ 4. You can lease an apartment.

_____ 5. Most people work in rural areas.

_____ 6. Urban areas are usually more crowded.

_____ 7. An apartment is called a flat in British English.

_____ 8. A patient who is tested positive for the Covid-19 virus should be isolated for a period of time.

_____ 9. A resident is someone who has made a reservation.

_____ 10. A washing machine is a household appliance.

▶ 填空題

1. I prefer _____ areas to the countryside.

2. The rude boy was _____ by his classmates.

3. This chocolate bar _____ peanuts.

4. I'm looking for an _____ that's close to campus.

5. Although I live on the second floor, as a _____ of this building, I believe I have the right to use the elevator.

6. Instead of buying a car, I want to _____ one first.

7. The restaurant had to _____ because the landlord raised the rent.

8. Most of the household _____ she bought were imported from Japan.

9. Instead of working in the city, the doctor chose to serve in a _____ community.

10. Luke's garage is too small to _____ his boat.

Answer

是非題：

1. X　　2. X　　3. O　　4. O　　5. X　　6. O　　7. O　　8. O　　9. X　　10. O

填空題：

1. urban　　　　2. isolated　　　　3. contains　　　　4. apartment　　　　5. resident

6. lease / rent　　7. relocate　　　8. appliances　　9. rural　　　　10. accommodate

填空題翻譯：

1. 比起鄉村我更喜歡都市。

2. 那個無理的男孩被同學們孤立。

3. 這條巧克力磚含有花生。

4. 我在找學校附近的公寓。

5. 雖然我住二樓，身為這棟房子的住戶，我覺得我有權利使用電梯。

6. 比起買車，我反而想先用租的。

7. 那間餐廳要搬遷因為房東調漲了店租。

8. 她買的家電大部分是日本進口的。

9. 那醫生沒有選擇在城市工作，反而在鄉下的社區服務。

10. Luke 的車庫太小了以至於放不下他的船。

購物
Shopping

annual	anniversay
catalog	discount
prompt	necessary
necessity	retail
trend	bargain

01 annual

[`ænjʊəl]
(adj) 年度的

相關詞
annually (adv) 每年、
yearly (adj) (adv) 每年的

- The annual budget for each division is planned at the beginning of the year.
  年初會計畫每個部門的年度預算。

  延伸學習 annual budget / income / report / conference / event 年預算／年收入／一年的報告／一年一度的會議／每年的活動

02 anniversary

[ˌænə`vɝ-sərɪ]
(n) 紀念日

- My parents are celebrating their 30th anniversary this year.
  今年我父母歡慶結婚 30 週年。

03 catalogue

[`kætəlɔg]
(n) 型錄

- I found this beautiful dress in the catalogue.
  我在型錄裡面找到這件美麗的洋裝。

04 discount

[`dɪskaʊnt]
(n) 折扣

- You can get a discount with a coupon.
  你可以用折價券拿到折扣。

- Do you offer discounts? May I have a discount?
  這個有折扣嗎？可以給我一點折扣嗎？

  延伸學習 discount / a discounted (adj) price 優惠價

05 prompt

[prɑmpt]
(n) (v) 提示；促使

- A: Where can I find the answer?
  在哪裡可以找到答案？
- B: Just follow the prompts.
  跟著提示就可以了。

- The catalogue prompted me to buy a pair of new shoes.
  這型錄促使我買了一雙新鞋。

06 necessary

[`nɛsəˌsɛrɪ]
(adj) 必要的

- Is it really necessary to buy so many cosmetics?
  真的有必要買這麼多化妝品嗎？

07 necessity

[nə`sɛsətɪ]

(n) 必須

- Of course! These are just basic necessities for a girl.
  當然！這些只是女生的基本必需品。

- Food and water are basic necessities of life.
  食物和水是生命的基本必需品。

08 retail

[`ritel]

(n) 零售

相關詞
retailer (n) 零售商

- You can now find the product in retail stores.
  你可以在零售店找到這個產品。

  延伸學習 retail price / outlet 零售價／零售店

09 trend

[trɛnd]

(n) 趨勢

- It seems to be a trend to wear thick-soled sneakers.
  厚底球鞋似乎是個流行。

10 bargain

[`bɑrgɪn]

(v) (n) 討價還價；便宜貨

相關詞
haggle (v) 討價還價

- What a bargain!
  真划算！

  延伸學習 bargain over prices 討價還價

 測驗

▶ 是非題

_____ 1. An annual meeting happens once a year.

_____ 2. An anniversary happens every quarter.

_____ 3. You can find a wide range of products in a supermarket's catalogue.

_____ 4. A discounted price is a lower price.

_____ 5. Prompt is a synonym of cue.

_____ 6. Necessary is an antonym of must.

_____ 7. A convenience store is an example of a retail store.

_____ 8. A trend is always predictable.

_____ 9. Something expensive is called a bargain.

_____ 10. You might get a discount if you haggle.

▶ 填空題

1. For many people, smartphones have become a _____ that they cannot live without.

2. Install the software system by following the _____.

3. The man was in big trouble because he forgot his wedding _____.

4. The _____ price of the bag is two thousand dollars, but I can give you a _____.

5. I can't believe you bought the house at such a low price! It's a real _____!

6. The dress looked better in the _____.

7. It is common to _____ over prices in traditional markets.

8. Our family goes on a(n) _____ vacation every year.

9. It is the latest _____ to wear ripped jeans (jeans with holes).

是非題：

1. O　2. X　3. O　4. O　5. O　6. X　7. O　8. X　9. X　10. O

填空題：

1. necessity　2. prompts　3. anniversary　4. retail, discount　5. bargain

6. catalogue　7. haggle　8. annual　9. trend

填空題翻譯：

1. 對許多人來說，智慧型手機已經成為他們不能沒有的必需品。

2. 跟著提示安裝軟體。

3. 那個男人有麻煩了，因為他忘了自己的結婚紀念日。

4. 這包包的零售價是兩千元，但我可以給你打個折。

5. 我不敢相信你用這麼低的價格買到這房子！真是划算！

6. 這件洋裝在型錄裡比較好看。

7. 在傳統市場討價還價很常見。

8. 我們家庭每年都固定會去旅遊。

9. 穿有破洞的牛仔褲是最新潮流。

Unit 52

餐廳用餐
Dining at a Restuarant

Track
052

reservation	reserve	reserved
permit	permission	allow
tip	bill	treat
unwritten	reasonable	appetizer
refreshment	refresh	refreshing
remind	utensil	

01 reservation

[ˌrɛzɚˋveʃən]

(n) 預約

- I'd like to make a dinner reservation for two.
  我要預約晚餐兩位。

02 reserve

[rɪˋzɝv]

(v) 預約；保留

相似詞
book (v) 預定、
preserve (v) 保留、
conserve (v) 保育

- I'll reserve a seat for you.
  我會幫你保留位子。

- The table is reserved.
  這桌有人預訂了。

- All rights reserved.
  版權所有。

03 reserved

[rɪˋzɝvd]

(adj) 保守；內向

- She doesn't talk much. In fact, she's quite reserved.
  她的話不多。事實上，她滿內向的。

- The emperor is described as cautious, reserved, and sometimes, aloof.
  這皇帝被形容為小心謹慎、拘謹保守，還有偶爾冷漠。

04 permit

[pɚˋmɪt]

(n) 許可證
(v) 許可

相似詞
allow (v) 允許

- Smoking is not permitted in the restaurant.
  餐廳裡面禁止吸菸。

- You will need a permit to park here.
  在這裡停車需要許可證。

延伸學習 a work permit 工作證

05 permission

[pɚˋmɪʃən]

(n) 許可

- You will need your parent or guardian's permission to go on the field trip.
  你需要家長或是監護人的同意才能參加遠足。

06 allow

[ə`laʊ]

(v) 允許

相似詞
grant (v) 同意
相反詞
deny (v)、refuse (v)、
reject (v) 拒絕

- You are not allowed to smoke here.
  這裡不允許抽菸。

- Harry is not allowed to go to Hogsmeade without his guardian's permission.
  沒有監護人的同意，哈利不能去活米村。

補充說明

禁菸區可以稱作：a non-smoking area or a smoke-free area
ex: This is a non-smoking area. 這裡是禁菸區。

07 tip

[tɪp]

(n) 小費

- There is a tipping culture in the United States. You should tip the <u>waitress / waiter</u> who serves you at restaurants. The tip, depending on the service you receive, ranges from 15 to 20 percent of the total meal cost.
  美國有小費文化。在餐廳你需要給服務你的女／男服務員小費。根據你得到的服務，小費落在總餐費的百分之 15 到 20 之範圍。

08 bill

[bɪl]

(n) 帳單

- Let me get the bill / check. / It's my treat!
  讓我來買單吧！我請客！

- Let's split the bill. / Separate check, please.
  我們分開付。

09 treat

[trit]
(n) 招待
(v) 對待；治療

- It's been a real treat talking to you.
  跟你講話真開心。

- She divorced her ex-husband because he treated her poorly.
  因為她前夫對她不好，她跟他離婚了。

- The doctor will treat the patient later.
  醫生等一下會治療病患。

延伸學習 trick or treat
不給糖（treat 招待）就搗蛋（trick 惡作劇）

10 unwritten

[ʌn`rɪtn]
(adj) 沒記錄的；
不成文的

- Tipping is one of the unwritten / unspoken rules in the United States.
  在美國，付小費是不成文的規定。

延伸學習 unwritten rules 不成文規定

11 reasonable

[`riznəbl]
(adj) 合理的

- The food here is delicious, and the prices are reasonable.
  這裡的食物很好吃，價格也合理。

- They offer products at very reasonable prices.
  他們提供的商品價格都合理。

- That's not a reasonable explanation.
  那理由不合理。

12 appetizer

[`æpə͵taɪzɚ]
(n) 開胃菜

相關詞
entree (n) 主菜

- Would you like any appetizers?
  要來點開胃菜嗎？

- Which appetizer would you like to order?
  你要點哪道開胃菜？

13 refreshment

[rɪ`frɛʃmənt]

(n) 小點心；輕食

相關詞
dessert (n) 甜點

- I'm not hungry, so I'd just have some light refreshments.
  我不餓，所以我吃點輕食就好。

- Refreshments will be served during the break.
  休息的時候會提供輕食。

14 refresh

[rɪ`frɛʃ]

(v) 刷新；使……恢復
精神；使……涼爽

相關詞
rejuvenate (v)
使恢復活力

- Let me refresh your memory.
  讓我提醒你一下。

- I hope a cup of iced tea will refresh you.
  希望一杯冰紅可以讓你覺得涼爽。

延伸學習 refresh the page 重新整理網頁

15 refreshing

[rɪ`frɛʃɪŋ]

(adj) 清涼的；
耳目一新的

- A bottle of cold beer is very refreshing.
  一瓶啤酒很清爽。

- It is a refreshing change to see a politician speaking so honestly.
  看到如此誠實的政治人物，令人耳目一新。

16 remind

[rɪ`maɪnd]

(v) 提醒

- Let me remind you of what you said last week.
  讓我來提醒你，上週你說了什麼。

- Please remind me to make a reservation tomorrow.
  請提醒我明天要訂位。

- Do remind me about the event because I'm very forgetful.
  請務必提醒我這個活動，因為我很健忘。

17 utensil

[ju`tɛnsl]

(n) 廚房器具

相關詞
tableware (n) 餐具

- Not knowing how to use kitchen utensils, the little mermaid uses a fork to comb her hair.
  不知道如何使用廚房器具，小美人魚用叉子梳頭髮。

▶ 是非題

_____ 1. We can reserve a table in advance.

_____ 2. Permit is a synonym of prohibit.

_____ 3. Eating is allowed in most libraries.

_____ 4. We can pay the bill with credit cards.

_____ 5. We usually treat a person when we are angry with him / her.

_____ 6. A reasonable price is too expensive.

_____ 7. Appetizers are served before the main course.

_____ 8. Green tea is a kind of refreshment.

_____ 9. A song can remind you of a place.

_____ 10. We normally use utensils to clean the floor.

▶ 填空題

1. I cannot make phone calls now because I haven't paid the _____.

2. She has such a small appetite that she was full after having the _____.

3. The supervisor _____ his colleagues and subordinates with kindness and respect.

4. You can't use the conference room whenever you want. You have to make a _____ online first.

5. Do you think what he said was an excuse or a _____ explanation?

6. The minty gum was very _____. I'm wide awake now!

7. The children are taught to wash their _____ after having lunch.

8. I would like to _____ you that the report is due next week.

9. I'm sorry but you cannot enter the building without a _____.

10. Due to the restraining order, the man is not _____ to visit his ex-wife.

Answer

是非題：

1. O   2. X   3. X   4. O   5. X   6. X   7. O   8. O   9. O   10. X

填空題：

1. bill   2. appetizer   3. treated   4. reservation   5. reasonable

6. refreshing   7. utensils   8. remind   9. permit

10. allowed / permitted

填空題翻譯：

1. 我沒辦法打電話因為我還沒付電話費。

2. 她的食量如此小以至於吃完開胃菜她就飽了。

3. 這位主管對他的同事和下屬既和善又尊重。

4. 你不能隨時使用會議室。需要先在線上預約。

5. 你覺得她說的是藉口還是一個合理的解釋？

6. 那薄荷味的口香糖很清涼。我整個清醒了！

7. 孩子們被教導在吃飯過後洗餐具。

8. 我要提醒大家下週要交報告。

9. 不好意思，但沒有許可證不可以進入這棟大樓。

10. 因為限制令，這個男人不能見他的前妻。

交通
Transportation

tenant	renovate
renovation	direction
register	registration
adjacent	feature
accessible	route
distance	plumber

01 tenant

[ˋtɛnənt]

(n) 租客

相似詞
renter (n) 租戶
相反詞
landlord (n) 房東

- You become a tenant after you rent a house.
  在租房子之後你就變成租客了。

- The landlord treats her tenants like family.
  這位房東把租客當作家人般對待。

02 renovate

[ˋrɛnəˏvet]

(v) 翻新；整修

- After living in our house for more than 30 years, I would like to renovate it.
  住了 30 年後，我想要翻新我們家。

03 renovation

[ˏrɛnəˋveʃən]

(n) 翻新；整修

- The building is under renovation.
  這棟建築在整修當中。

04 direction

[dəˋrɛkʃən]

(n) 方向

- I have no sense of direction.
  我沒有方向感。

- Can you give me the directions to your house?
  可以告訴我你家怎麼走嗎？

  延伸學習 a sense of direction 方向感

05 register

[ˋrɛdʒɪstɚ]

(v) 註冊；登記

- I would like to register for the class.
  我想要註冊這門課。

- You will receive a discount if you register online.
  如果妳在線上註冊的話會有折扣。

- The house is registered under my name.
  房子登記在我的名下。

06 registration

[ˏrɛdʒɪˋstreʃən]

(n) 註冊；登記

- I might need to see your driver's license and
- registration number of the car.
  請出示駕照及汽車登記號碼。

07 adjacent

[ə`dʒesənt]

(adj) 鄰近的；相鄰

- My house is adjacent to the train station.
  我家緊鄰著火車站。

  延伸學習 adjacent buildings / rooms / areas
  相鄰的建築／房間／地區

---

08 feature

[fitʃɚ]

(v) (n) 以……為特色；特色

- The park features a huge playground.
  這公園以巨大的遊樂場為特色。

- One of the features of the park is a huge playground.
  這公園其中一個特色是巨大的遊樂場。

  延伸學習 title of a song ft. (features) a singer
  歌名 ft. 歌手＝與某位歌手串場／合作演出

---

09 accessible

[æk`sɛsəbl]

(adj) 可接近；可得到的

- My house is accessible by train.
  搭火車可以到達我家。

- They have accessible facilities for people who are physically disabled.
  他們為殘障人士提供無障礙設施。

  延伸學習 accessible housing 無障礙建築

---

10 route

[rut]

(n) 路線

- It seems like we have taken the wrong route.
  我們好像走錯路了。

---

11 distance

[`dɪstəns]

(n) 距離

- Our house is within walking distance (of the subway station).
  我們家（距離捷運站）走路可以到。

- Social distancing, also called physical distancing, is a measure taken to prevent the spread of a contagious disease by maintaining a physical distance between people.
  社會距離，也稱為身體距離，是通過保持人與人之間的距離來防止傳染性疾病傳播的措施。

12 plumber

[ˈplʌmɚ]

(n) 水電工

- We called a plumber to fix the toilet.
  我們叫水電工來修馬桶。

 測驗

▶ 是非題

_____ 1. A tenant is also called a renter.

_____ 2. To renovate a house, you'll have to tear the house down.

_____ 3. We can use Google maps to look for directions.

_____ 4. It's better to make a registration before you go to a restaurant.

_____ 5. When two things are adjacent, they are very far away from each other.

_____ 6. A feature is something special about something.

_____ 7. An accessible place is somewhere easy to reach.

_____ 8. A route is delicious to eat.

_____ 9. We can calculate the distance between places.

_____ 10. A plumber is good at building furniture.

▶ 填空題

1. The couple broke up because they couldn't maintain a long _____ relationship.

2. A good _____ always pays the rent on time.

3. If you want to take the online course, you should _____ one month in advance.

4. The faucet won't stop leaking. We'll need a _____ to repair it.

5. One of the special _____ of the new phone is its three camera lenses.

6. Free education is _____ to everyone in this country.

7. I've seen this tree three times! I think we've taken the wrong _____.

8. The earthquake seriously damaged the building, so we need to _____ it.

9. A: Can you show me the _____ to the conference room?

10. B: Sure! Go straight ahead and turn right over there. It's _____ to the auditorium.

[Answer]

是非題：

1. O　　2. X　　3. O　　4. X　　5. X　　6. O　　7. O　　8. X　　9. O　　10. X

填空題：

1. distance　　2. tenant　　3. register　　4. plumber　　5. features

6. accessible　　7. route　　8. renovate　　9. direction　　10. adjacent

填空題翻譯：

1. 那對情侶分手了，因為他們無法維持遠距離戀愛。

2. 一個好的租客總是準時交房租。

3. 如果你想要上線上課程，你需要提前一個月註冊。

4. 水龍頭不停地漏水。我們要找水電工來修理。

5. 這新手機的其中一個特色是其三個相機鏡頭。

6. 這國家的每個人都可以得到免費的教育。

7. 我已經看到這棵樹三次了！我覺得我們走錯路了。

8. 地震嚴重損壞了這棟建築，所以我們需要重新整修。

9. A：可以告訴我會議室怎麼走嗎？

10. B：當然！直走之後在那邊右轉。它在視聽室隔壁。

Unit 54

娛樂
Entertainment

Track 054

entertainment	recreation
amusement	amuse
amused	exhibit
demonstrate	display
statue	masterpiece
restore	

01 entertainment

[ˌɛntɚˈtenmənt]

(n) 娛樂

- What do you do for entertainment?
  你休閒娛樂都做什麼？

- I listen to music and read novels for entertainment.
  我把聽音樂和讀小説當作休閒活動。

02 recreation

[ˌrɛkrɪˈeʃən]

(n) 休閒

補充
recreational (adj)
休閒的

- My dad's favorite recreation is watching TV.
  我爸爸最喜歡的休閒活動是看電視。

- Recreational facilities at the hotel include a swimming pool, sauna, and gym.
  這間飯店的休閒設施包含游泳池、三溫暖和健身房。

延伸學習 a recreation center 休閒中心

03 amusement

[əˈmjuzmənt]

(n) 娛樂；消遣

- DisneyLand and Universal Studios are amazing amusement parks!
  迪士尼樂園和環球影城是令人驚艷的遊樂園！

延伸學習 amusement park 遊樂園

04 amuse

[əˈmjuz]

(v) 逗樂

- The funny story amused me.
  這好笑的故事把我逗樂了。

05 amused

[əˈmjuzd]

(adj) 被逗樂的

補充
amusing
有趣的；好玩的

- I am amused by the amusing story.
  我被那好笑的故事逗樂了。

06 exhibit

[ɪgˈzɪbɪt]

(v) 展示

- They are exhibiting modern art at the exhibition.
  展覽館在展示現代藝術。

- Barney plans to hold an exhibition for his suits.
  Barney 計畫為他的西裝舉辦展覽。

07 demonstrate

[`dɛmən‚stret]

(v) 示範

- The instructor will demonstrate how to repair the device manually.
  指導員會示範如何手動修理設備。

08 display

[dɪ`sple]

(v) 展示

- Many paintings are displayed in the gallery.
  藝廊裡展示了許多畫作。

09 statue

[`stætʃʊ]

(n) 雕像

- I took a photo with the Statue of Liberty when I visited New York.
  我在紐約旅遊的時候跟自由女神合照。

10 masterpiece

[`mæstɚ‚pis]

(n) 傑作

- The Statue of Liberty is definitely a masterpiece.
  自由女神絕對是個傑作。

- Taroko Gorge is nature's masterpiece.
  太魯閣是大自然的傑作。

11 restore

[rɪ`stor]

(v) 恢復

- We better visit the city after they have restored order.
  我們最好在這城市恢復秩序後再去旅遊。

- Power has been restored after a temporary blackout.
  在短暫停電之後電力已經恢復了。

延伸學習 restore one's health 恢復健康

 測驗

▶ 是非題

_____ 1. Watching movies is a kind of entertainment.

_____ 2. Recreation is another word for entertainment.

_____ 3. DisneyLand is an amusement park.

_____ 4. If something is amusing, it is serious.

_____ 5. Display is a synonym for exhibit.

_____ 6. To demonstrate means to show.

_____ 7. A statue is made of air.

_____ 8. A masterpiece is a signature of a master.

_____ 9. It's possible to restore one's hearing with surgery.

▶ 填空題

1. This is not just a great piece of work, but a _____.

2. The baby's funny reaction _____ his mom.

3. Video games might appear as _____; however, they may also be a means of developing insight or intellectual growth.

4. The teacher _____ how to recycle properly.

5. Harry Potter _____ peace in the wizarding world by bringing down Voldemort.

6. Many new books are _____ in the library.

7. The _____ looked so vivid that I thought it was a real person.

8. The _____ center offers a wide range of facilities, including indoor pools, weight rooms, basketball courts, dance studios, art studios, game rooms, and libraries.

9. The Terracotta Army（兵馬俑）_____ was one of the best _____ I've ever seen.

10. The mother watched her son's performance with great _____.

Answer

是非題:

1. ○   2. X   3. ○   4. X   5. ○   6. ○   7. X   8. X   9. ○

填空題:

1. masterpiece   2. amused   3. entertainment   4. demonstrated   5. restores / restored

6. displayed / exhibited   7. statue   8. recreation

9. Exhibition, exhibitions   10. amusement

填空題翻譯:

1. 這不止是很棒的作品,而是個傑作。

2. 寶寶好笑的反應把他媽媽逗樂了。

3. 線上遊戲可能像是娛樂,然而它們也可能是發展洞察力或知識成長的一種媒介。

4. 老師示範如何正確做資源回收。

5. 哈利波特在打敗佛地魔之後讓魔法世界恢復和平。

6. 圖書館展示許多新書。

7. 那雕像看起來如此栩栩如生以至於我以為它是真人。

8. 休閒中心包含很多設施,包含室內泳池、重訓室、籃球場、舞蹈教室、藝術室、遊戲室和圖書館。

9. 兵馬俑展是我看過最好看的展覽。

10. 媽媽愉悅地看著兒子的表演。

政治
Politics

politics	politicize
political	percentage
percent	poll
survey	prompt
strategy	bureau
bureaucratic	vote

01 politics

[ˋpɑlətɪks]

(n) 政治

相關詞
politician (n) 政治家

- He majors in politics.
他主修政治。

- My dad loves to talk about politics.
我爸喜歡講政治。

02 politicize

[pəˋlɪtəˌsaɪz]

(v) 將……政治化

- The chief of WHO said "Please don't politicize this virus."
世界衛生組織的首席說：「請不要將病毒政治化。」

03 political

[pəˋlɪtɪkl]

(adj) 政治的

- The public may not be able to tell on the surface, but it is in fact a political issue.
大眾從表面可能看不出來，但是它實際上是一個政治議題。

04 percentage

[pəˋsɛntɪdʒ]

(n) 百分比

- A candidate can be nominated if he / she is supported by a specified percentage of registered voters.
如果被一定比例有註冊的投票者支持，他／她就可以被提名為選人。

延伸學習 a small / large percentage of... 很小／大的百分比

05 percent

[pəˋsɛnt]

(adv) 百分比

- Sixty percent of the people who took the survey agreed to donate to charity.
填寫問卷中有百分之六十的人同意捐款給慈善機構。

- The department store is having a huge sale! Most products are 70 percent off!
百貨公司大特價！大部分的商品都 3 折！

06 poll

[pol]

(n) 調查

- The poll shows that few people genuinely care about global warming.
調查顯示極少人真的關心全球暖化。

延伸學習 election / opinion polls 選舉／意見調查

07 survey

[sɚˋve]

(n) 問卷;調查

(v) 調查;檢查

- According to the survey, 80 percent of the respondents find Mandarin a difficult language.
  根據（問卷）調查，百分之八十的受訪者覺得中文是個困難的語言。

- The inspector surveyed our luggage carefully.
  檢查員仔細審查我們的行李。

- 80 percent of the people surveyed admitted that they have downloaded music illegally.
  問卷調查中百分之八十的人承認他們曾經違法下載音樂。

（延伸學習）conduct / do / carry out a survey 實施調查

08 prompt

[prɑmpt]

(v) 促使

- The urge to read English novels prompted me to study English.
  讀英文小說的渴望促使我學習英文。

- I don't know what prompted him to do something so terrifying.
  我不知道什麼事情促使他做這麼可怕的事。

- His comments prompted angry responses from netizens.
  他的評論促使網路鄉民生氣地回覆。

（延伸學習）prompt sb. to do sth. 促使某人做某事

09 strategy

[ˋstrætədʒɪ]

(n) 策略

相似詞

approach (n) 方法、method (n) 方法;辦法

- To win this game, we need to come up with a new strategy.
  為了贏得這場比賽，我們需要想新的策略。

（延伸學習）marketing / military / political strategy
行銷／軍事／政治策略

10 bureau

[ˋbjʊro]

(n) 局

- The weather bureau says that it will rain tomorrow.
  氣象局說明天會下雨。

11 bureaucratic

[ˌbjʊrəˋkrætɪk]

(adj) 官僚的

- In the movie "Julie and Julia," Julie says that she is not a "heartless bureaucratic goon."

在《美味關係》這部電影當中，Julie 說她不是一個無情的官僚笨蛋。

延伸學習 bureaucratic and political 又官僚又政治的
bureaucratic ways of thinking 官僚的想法

12 vote

[vot]

(n) (v) 投票；選票

- Don't forget to vote for your ideal candidate!

別忘了投給你的理想候選人！

- Remember to cast your vote!

記得去投票！

延伸學習 cast a vote 投票

 測驗

▶ 是非題

_____ 1. Politics is a subject that students study in elementary school.

_____ 2. A politician is always honest.

_____ 3. Sixty percent off means the original price times 0.6.

_____ 4. We can use surveys to find out people's opinions.

_____ 5. Polls are often conducted during elections.

_____ 6. Prompt is a synonym for force.

_____ 7. A strategy is something that you can gain from experience.

_____ 8. Bureaucratic is usually a positive adjective.

_____ 9. There are many bureaus in the government.

_____ 10. Everyone on earth has the right to vote.

▶ 填空題

1. After learning how wonderful it is to learn English, Cindy was _____ to study English every day.

2. After learning English for a while, Cindy has come up with her own learning _____.

3. I hope the government can simplify their _____ procedures. They always take a long time to get a simple task done.

4. Taiwanese citizens that have reached the age of 18 have the right to _____ in referendums.

5. We should elect public servants instead of _____.

6. The media carried out a _____ to find out which candidate had more supporters.

7. According to the weather _____, torrential rain would occur this afternoon.

8. We are just learning English. Please don't _____ everything! Not everything is about politics.

9. Please take a moment to fill out the _____.

10. Surprisingly, female workers constitute a large _____ of the labour force.

Answer

是非題：

1. X   2. X   3. X（應為 0.4）   4. O   5. O   6. X   7. O   8. X   9. O

10. X

填空題：

1. prompted   2. strategies   3. bureaucratic   4. vote   5. politicians

6. poll / survey   7. bureau   8. politicize   9. survey   10. percentage

填空題翻譯：

1. 在了解學英文有多好之後，Cindy 被激發想要每天讀英文。

2. 在學習英文一段時間後，Cindy 發現了自己的學習策略。

3. 我希望政府可以把官僚程序簡單化。他們總是花很長時間完成簡單的事情。

4. 滿 18 歲的臺灣公民有權利參與公投。

5. 我們應該要選出公僕而不是政治人物。

6. 媒體開始調查哪一個候選人有更多支持者。

7. 根據氣象局，今天下午會有大雨。

8. 我們只是在學英文。請不要將所有事情政治化！不是所有事情都跟政治有關。

9. 請花一點時間填寫問卷。

10. 令人驚訝的是，女性員工占了勞動力很大的一部分。

Unit 56

政治延伸
Related to Politics

constitute   compose
construction   complicated
complicate   comprehend
intensive   intense
record   reputation

01 constitute

[`kɑnstə͵tjut]

(v) 組成

相關詞
constitution 憲法；組成

- In Taiwan, people between 25 to 54 years old constitute 46 percent of the population.
  在臺灣，25-54 歲的人占了人口的百分之 46。

02 compose

[kəm`poz]

(v) 組成

補充
be composed (adj) + of

- Women compose 48 percent of the population.
  女性占了人口的 48%。

  延伸學習 compose music / a poem 寫歌／寫詩

03 construction

[kən`strʌkʃən]

(n) 建造

相關詞
construct (v) 建構

- The building is under construction.
  這建築在建造中。

04 complicated

[`kɑmplə͵ketɪd]

(adj) 複雜的

相關詞
complex (n) 綜合大樓
(adj) 複雜的

- Me: Are you in a relationship? Friend: It's complicated.
  我：你們在交往嗎？朋友：一言難盡。

05 complicate

[`kɑmplə͵ket]

(v) 使……複雜

- Her appearance complicated the matter even more!
  她的出現讓事情更複雜了！

06 comprehend

[ˌkɑmprɪˈhɛnd]

(v) 理解

相關詞
comprehensive (adj)
理解的

- Hard as I try, I couldn't comprehend the complex text.

儘管我很努力，我還是無法理解這複雜的文章。

07 intensive

[ɪnˈtɛnsɪv]

(adj) 密集的

相關詞
extensive (adj) 延伸的

- I took an intensive course to improve my English ability in a short amount of time.

我上了密集課程，在短時間內提升英文能力。

08 intense

[ɪnˈtɛns]

(adj) 緊張的

- They had an intense / a heated debate.

他們有一場激烈的辯論。

09 record

[ˈrɛkɚd]

(n) 記錄

[rɪˈkɔrd]

(v) 記錄

相關詞
track record 成績紀錄

- To open an account, you must have a good credit record.

你必須要有好的信用記錄才能開戶。

- He is only 10. He doesn't have a record.

他才 10 歲。他沒有（犯罪）記錄。

- You are not allowed to record movies in a movie theater.

在電影院看電影不能錄影。

補充說明

電影中常聽到 "for the record" 意思是「公開來説」、「鄭重聲明」，不過這是口語的用法，文章中會看到的是 "on the record"；另外「私下説」是 "off the record"。

10 reputation

[ˌrɛpjəˈteʃən]

(n) 名聲

- The scandal ruined / destroyed his reputation.
  醜聞毀了他的名聲。

- My reputation couldn't be worse.
  我的名聲不能更糟了。

延伸學習 establish / build / earn one's reputation
建立／贏得名聲

▶ 是非題

_____ 1. Constitute is an antonym for destroy.

_____ 2. One year is composed of four seasons.

_____ 3. Human beings are constructed by monkeys.

_____ 4. A small house can be called a complex.

_____ 5. A complicated question is hard to understand.

_____ 6. Comprehend is a synonym for understand.

_____ 7. An intensive course usually lasts for several years.

_____ 8. To keep a record means to keep a diary.

_____ 9. You can record your daily life by taking pictures.

_____ 10. A reputation is something that babies love.

▶ 填空題

1. Women and children _____ the majority of the world's refugees.

2. Wait for me to get my phone! I want to _____ this special moment.

3. The math problem was so _____ that not even the math teacher knew how to solve it.

4. His _____ was ruined when the scandal came to light.

5. Perhaps you don't _____ the severity of the condition.

6. I don't want to _____ the situation, but I believe I have the right to say something.

7. The story is _____ of three parts.

8. Do you keep a _____ of your expenses?

→ Do you _____ your expenses?

9. The patient is now in _____ care. We don't know if he will make it.

10. His house is _____ from reusable materials.

(Answer)

是非題：

1. O   2. O   3. X   4. X   5. O   6. O   7. X   8. X   9. O   10. X

填空題：

1. constitute / compose   2. record   3. complex / complicated   4. reputation

5. comprehend   6. complicate   7. composed

8. record (n) / recode (v)   9. intensive   10. constructed

填空題翻譯：

1. 女人和小孩組成全世界大部分的難民。

2. 等我拿手機！我想要記錄這特別的一刻。

3. 這道數學題如此難，以至於數學老師都不會解。

4. 當醜聞被揭發後，他的名聲也毀了。

5. 或許你不了解情況的嚴重性。

6. 我不想要讓情況變複雜，但我覺得我有權說話。

7. 這故事是由三個部分組成的。

8. 你會記錄你的花費嗎？

9. 病患在加護病房。我們不知道他會不會活下來。

10. 他家是用可回收材料建造的。

教育
Education

civil	enroll
course	program
pursue	persevere
persist	typical
flexible	ignorance

01 civil

[`sɪvl]

(adj) 文明的

相關詞
civilian (n) 平名百姓
civilization (n) 文明

- We live in a civil society.
  我們住在文明社會。
- Although we were angry, we remained civil to each other.
  雖然我們很生氣,但我們仍禮尚往來。

02 enroll

[ɪn`rol]

(v) 註冊;錄取

- I will enroll in an intensive course to improve my English.
  為了加強英文,我會註冊一堂密集課程。

03 course

[kors]

(n) 課程

- There are many free online courses for us to learn anything on the Internet.
  線上有很多免費課程可以讓我們學任何東西。

04 program

[`progræm]

(v) (n) 寫程式;程式節目課程

相關詞
programmer (n)
程式工程師、
programming (n)
寫程式

- The computer is programmed to finish the tasks automatically.
  這電腦已被編程為會自動完成任務。
- The Ellen Show is one of my favorite TV programs.
  The Ellen Show 是我最喜歡的電視節目之一。

  延伸學習 a computer program 電腦程式
  enroll in a program 參加／註冊課程

05 pursue

[pɚ`su]

(v) 追求

相關詞
pursuit (n) 追求

- She left the company to pursue a career as an entrepreneur.
  她離開公司追求創業職涯。

  延伸學習 pursue education / knowledge / dreams
  追求教育／知識／夢想

06 persevere

[ˌpɝsə`vɪr]

(v) 堅持不懈

相關詞
perseverance (n)
毅力

- People who persevere try over and over again to reach their goals.
堅持不懈的人不斷嘗試以實現自己的目標。

- I believe that perseverance is one of the elements of success / keys to success.
我相信毅力是成功的其中一個關鍵因素。

07 persist

[pə`sɪst]

(v) 堅持

用法
persist with + N
persist in doing sth.

- Those who persist (in doing what they love) are more likely to succeed.
這些堅持（做自己喜歡的事情）的人更有機會成功。

- You should consult a doctor if the symptoms persist.
如果症狀持續你應該向醫生諮詢。

08 typical

[`tɪpɪkl]

(adj) 典型的

- The genius looks just like any typical high school student.
那天才看起來就像任何一個普通的高中生。

- It was just a typical day when the incident happened.
事件發生的時候只是很普通的一天。

- Stinky tofu is a typical Taiwanese street food.
臭豆腐是典型的臺灣小吃。

09 flexible

[`flɛksəbl]

(adj) 有彈性的；靈活的

相關詞
flexibility (n) 彈性

- I have a flexible schedule.
我的行程很彈性。

- When you face adversaries, stay flexible and adjust to the situation.
當你遇到困難，請保持彈性並且視情況調整。

- Stretch your body every day so that you can be more flexible.
每天伸展身體才能變得更柔軟。

延伸學習 a flexible mattress 一張有柔軟的床墊

10 ignorance

[ˈɪgnərəns]

(n) 無知

相關詞
ignorant (adj) 無知的

• Stop talking! Your ignorance is showing.
不要再說話了！你已顯露了你的無知。

 測驗

▶ 是非題

_____ 1. Hitting someone with a baseball bat is a civil behavior.

_____ 2. To enroll in a course means to join it.

_____ 3. An online class can also be called an online course.

_____ 4. A program is a kind of game.

_____ 5. You can pursue someone you love.

_____ 6. To persevere means to continue doing something.

_____ 7. It can be annoying when someone persists in bothering you.

_____ 8. A typical primary school student lives in a cupboard under the stairs.

_____ 9. A flexible schedule is a schedule that cannot be changed.

_____ 10. An ignorant person might be scammed easily.

▶ 填空題

1. I'm thinking of joining an online _____ to improve my English.

2. Don't be afraid to _____ your dreams.

3. Although Mia's family is struggling financially, she _____ with her studies.

4. People who refuse to admit their _____ even when they actually have no idea about what they are doing are very annoying.

5. We should respect each other in a _____ society.

317

6. Before Spiderman was bitten by a spider, he was just a _____ student.

7. The mother is finding a preschool to _____ her child.

8. If you practice yoga on a regular basis, your body will gradually become more _____.

9. The engineer wrote a _____ to help the company reduce their workload.

10. When Cindy faces obstacles, she always chooses to _____ instead of giving in.

Answer

是非題：

1. X　　2. O　　3. O　　4. X　　5. O　　6. O　　7. O　　8. X　　9. X　　10. O

填空題：

1. course　　　2. pursue　　　3. persisted　　　4. ignorance　　　5. civil

6. typical　　　7. enroll　　　8. flexible　　　9. program　　　10. persevere

填空題翻譯：

1. 我在考慮加入線上課程以增進我的英文能力。

2. 不要害怕追尋自己的夢想。

3. 雖然 Mia 的家庭有財務困難，她仍堅持繼續就學。

4. 不知道自己在做什麼卻拒絕承認自己的無知的人很惹人厭。

5. 在文明社會中我們應互相尊重。

6. 在蜘蛛人被蜘蛛咬之前，他只是個一般的學生。

7. 那位媽媽在找幼稚園幫她的小孩註冊。

8. 如果你定期做瑜珈，你的身體會漸漸變得柔軟。

9. 那工程師寫了一套幫助公司減少工作量的程式。

10. 當 Cindy 遇到困難，她都選擇堅持下去，而不是放棄。

Unit 58

閱讀
Reading

Track 058

- preface
- premises
- cover
- burden
- marginalize
- edition
- premise
- journalist
- layout
- margin
- edit

01 preface

[ˈprɛfɪs]

(n) (v) 前言；序

- In the preface, the author dedicated this book to his daughter.
  在前言中，作者將這本書獻給他女兒。

- Let me preface this by saying thank you to all of my loyal viewers.
  讓我在影片開始之前，跟所有忠實的觀眾說聲謝謝。

02 premise

[ˈprɛmɪs]

(n) 前提

- We should develop a strategy based on the premise that global warming might continue to worsen.
  基於全球暖化可能會惡化的前提，我們應該發展新的策略。

  延伸學習 based on the premise that... 基於……的前提之下

03 premises

[ˈprɛmɪsɪz]

(n)（某機構的）房屋連同地基；廠區

- Smoking is prohibited on school premises.
  校區內禁止吸菸。

04 journalist

[ˈdʒɝnəlɪst]

(n) 新聞工作者；新聞記者；報紙撰稿人

- A reporter is a kind of journalist.
  新聞記者是新聞工作者的一種。

- Reporters, columnists, and anchors are all journalists.
  記者、專欄作家，和主播都是新聞工作者。

05 cover

[ˈkʌvɚ]

(n) (v) 封面；覆蓋；涵蓋

- Don't judge a book by its cover.
  人不可貌相。（不要從書封來評斷一本書）

- In our course, we will cover a wide range of topics.
  在我們的課程當中，我們會涵蓋很多主題。

- She covered her legs with a blanket.
  她用毯子蓋住雙腿。

- I'm counting on my best friend to cover for me.
  我期待我最好的朋友罩我。

06 layout

[`le͵aʊt]
(n) 布局;設計

- I like the layout of this book because it's clear and well-organized.
  我喜歡這本書的設計,因為它清楚又整齊。

- The interior designer showed the homeowner the layout of the house.
  室內設計師給屋主看房子的設計。

延伸學習 layout of a magazine cover / book / building / room
雜誌封面設計/書的設計/建築的布局/房間的布局

07 burden

[`bɝdn]
(n) (v) 負擔

用法
burden (v) sb. with sth.
使……負擔

- Due to my poor eyesight, reading has become a burden for me.
  因為我眼睛不好,閱讀變成了負擔。

- I don't want to burden you with my work.
  我不想要讓我的工作變成你的負擔。

延伸學習 shoulder / carry burden 扛起負擔
be / become a burden to someone 變成某人的負擔

08 margin

[`mɑrdʒɪn]
(n) 邊緣

- I like to take notes in the margins of a textbook rather than using a notebook.
  我喜歡在課本的邊緣做筆記而不是用筆記本。

- He won the election by a narrow margin.
  這次選舉他險勝。

- They lived in isolation on the margin of society.
  他們在社會邊緣孤立地生活。

09 marginalize

[`mɑrdʒɪnl͵aɪz]
(v) 邊緣化

- We are marginalized because of political reasons.
  我們因為政治原因被邊緣化。

補充說明
邊緣人的英文是 an outcast(被排斥的人)或是 an outsider(局外人)。

10 edit [ˋɛdɪt] (v) 修改 [相關詞] **editor (n)** 編輯	• Make sure to edit your written assignment before you submit it. 提交作業前，請務必先檢視修改過。
11 edition [ɪˋdɪʃən] (n) 版本	• This is the new / latest / paperback edition of the book. 這是這本書的新／最新版本／平裝本。

 測驗

▶ 是非題

_____ 1. You can usually find the preface before the first chapter of a book.

_____ 2. Another word for premises is buildings.

_____ 3. A journalist performs operations on patients.

_____ 4. People wear masks to cover their noses and mouths.

_____ 5. You can design the layout of your room.

_____ 6. A burden is something that you deeply adore.

_____ 7. The margin of something means the edge of something.

_____ 8. Most people like to be marginalized.

_____ 9. Correcting spelling mistakes is a way of editing.

_____ 10. A boy who looks exactly like his father can be described as a smaller edition of his father.

▶ 填空題

1. The student likes to doodle in the _____ of her textbooks.

2. The robber _____ his face with a mask when he robbed the bank.

3. Many students rely on their teachers to _____ their essays for them.

4. The interior designer is working on the _____ of the house.

5. Afraid of being _____, she strove to fit in.

6. I will _____ my speech with a poem.

7. The paperback _____ of a novel is usually cheaper than the hardback version.

8. Before we start the debate, I want to make sure that you all agree with the _____ that men and women are equal.

9. The sick boy left his family because he didn't want to be a _____ to them.

10. The _____ travels all around the world to report international news.

Answer

是非題：

1. ○   2. ○   3. X（應為 surgeon）   4. ○   5. ○   6. X   7. ○   8. X

9. ○   10. ○

填空題：

1. margins   2. covered   3. edit   4. layout   5. marginalized

6. preface   7. edition   8. premise   9. burden   10. journalist

填空題翻譯：

1. 這學生喜歡在她課本的邊緣塗鴉。

2. 強盜搶銀行的時候用面罩遮住了臉。

3. 很多學生依賴老師幫他們修改作文。

4. 室內設計師正在幫房子設計格局。

5. 害怕被邊緣化，她努力融入。

6. 我會用一首詩幫我的演講開場。

7. 小說的平裝版通常比精裝版便宜。

8. 在辯論開始之前，我想要確認你們都同意男女平等這個前提。

9. 那位生病的男孩離開了家人，因為他不想成為他們的負擔。

10. 這位記者環遊世界報導國際新聞。

全球經濟
Global Economy

brand	soar
surge	accelerate
increase	decrease
reduce	debt
inform	informative

01 **brand**

[brænd]

(n) 品牌

- Apple is one of the most valuable global brands.
  蘋果是最有價值的國際品牌之一。

  延伸學習 a brand name product 名牌商品
  name brand clothes 名牌衣服
  又稱為 designer clothes

02 **soar**

[sor]

(v) 翱翔；高飛；高升

- The stocks of self-driving vehicles are soaring.
  自動車的股價正在上漲。

- In the musical "High School Musical," there's a song called "Breaking Free." The lyrics include a sentence that starts with "Soaring, flying!" It's a very beautiful song.
  在音樂劇「歌舞青春」裡面，有一首歌叫做「Breaking Free.」裡面有句歌詞是「翱翔！飛翔！」它是一首很美的歌曲。

03 **surge**

[sɝdʒ]

(n) (v) 激增

- The number of patients diagnosed with the disease has surged in the past few days.
  在過去幾天中，被診斷出患有這種疾病的患者數量激增。

- Amazon said it would hire 100,000 workers to handle an expected surge in demand for home delivery of household goods.
  亞馬遜表示，將僱用 10 萬名工人，以應對家庭用品上門配送的預期增長。

04 **accelerate**

[æk`sɛlə,ret]

(v) 加速

相似詞
speed up (v) 加速、
hurry (v) 加快

- Time is running out; you better accelerate!
  時間不夠了，你最好加速！

325

05 increase

[ɪn`kris]
(v) 增加

[`ɪnkris]
(n) 增加

If you want to improve your English proficiency, you probably should increase the amount of time you spend on studying English.
如果你想要加強英文能力，你可能應該增加你讀英文的時間。

• There is an increase in unemployment rate.
失業率增加了。

06 decrease

[dɪ`kris]
(v) 減少

[`dikris]
(n) 減少

相似詞
reduce (v) 減少

• The government's new policy aims to decrease the negative effects caused by the recession.
政府新政策的目標是減少經濟衰退帶來的負面影響。

• There's a sharp decrease in foreign visitors.
外國觀光客急劇減少。

07 reduce

[rɪ`djus]
(v) 減少

• We should reduce and recycle waste / garbage.
我們應該減少並且回收垃圾。

延伸學習 reuse, reduce, and recycle
重複使用、減少、並且回收

08 debt

[dɛt]
(n) 負債

• He is deep in debt, so he is working very hard to pay off his debts.
他負了很多債，所以他要努力工作還債。

09 inform

[ɪn`fɔrm]
(v) 通知

• We would like to inform you that it's time for you to pay the bills.
我們要通知你繳費時間到了。

• We are sorry to inform you that your credit card has been maxed out.
我們很遺憾的通知你信用卡已經刷超出額度（刷爆）了。

10 **informative**

[ɪnˋfɔrmətɪv]
(adj) 情報的；提供資訊的

- Wikipedia is a very informative website. You can find a lot of information there.
維基百科是資訊豐富的網站。你可以在上面找到很多資訊。

 測驗

▶ 是非題

_____ 1. You can open a bank account at a brand of a bank.

_____ 2. An airplane starts to soar when it is about to reach its destination.

_____ 3. A surge is an increase.

_____ 4. To accelerate means to slow down.

_____ 5. To increase means to add.

_____ 6. The unemployment rate has decreased during the coronavirus outbreak.

_____ 7. You can reduce waste by recycling properly.

_____ 8. If someone is in debt, it means that person owes someone something.

_____ 9. Information is equal to knowledge.

_____ 10. A dictionary is informative.

▶ 填空題

1. If you want to lose weight, you should _____ the amount of dessert you consume every day.

2. After a few tries, the bird is now _____ happily in the sky.

3. The elevator has been shut down due to the emergency repair. We will keep you _____ of the progress.

4. Due to low fertility rate, the percentage of the elderly has _____.

5. The man works double shifts in order to pay off his _____.

6. The driver _____ to overtake other vehicles.

7. If you want to learn about management, you should check out this website. You'll find it very _____.

8. Learning about the good news, she felt a _____ of joy.

9. We hope to _____ air pollution by taking public transportation.

10. The wealthy man wears nothing but name _____ clothes

Unit 60

2020
2020

Track 060

unprecedented	launch
concern	pandemic
epidemic	adversity
hurdle	overcome
fortitude	solidarity

01 unprecedented

[ʌnˋprɛsəˌdɛntɪd]

(adj) 前所未有的

- The word "unprecedented" has been trending in 2020 because many things are happening for the first time.

  在 2020 年，「前所未有」這個字非常流行，因為很多事情第一次發生。

02 launch

[lɔntʃ]

(v) 發射；發起

- Governments have launched new assessments to test the disease.

  政府已經啟動了新的評估以測試這種疾病。

  延伸學習 launch a rocket / program 發射火箭／發起活動

03 concern

[kənˋsɝn]

(n) (v) 關心

- There are growing concerns about people's mental health.

  人們越來越擔心心理健康。

- My parents are concerned about my well-being.

  我的父母關心我的幸福。

04 pandemic

[pænˋdɛmɪk]

(n) 大流行病

- The pandemic has a great impact on the global economy.

  大流行病對全球經濟產生重大影響。

05 epidemic

[ˌɛpɪˋdɛmɪk]

(n) 流行病

- The epidemic has burdened hospitals greatly.

  流行病使醫院負擔沉重。

06 adversity

[ədˋvɝsətɪ]

(n) 困難

- In the face of adversity, we should remain strong.

  面對逆境，我們應保持堅強。

  延伸學習 in adversity 在逆境中

07 hurdle

[ˋhɝdl̩]

(n) 困難

相似詞
challenge (n) 挑戰、
difficulty (n) 困難、
obstacle (n) 障礙、
barrier (n) 障礙

• Let's collaborate and overcome the hurdle together.
讓我們共同合作，共同克服障礙。

08 overcome

[ˏovɚˋkʌm]

(v) 克服

• I believe that we will overcome all the obstacles as long as we keep persevering.
我相信只要我們堅持不懈，我們將克服所有障礙。

延伸學習 overcome difficulties / obstacles / hurdles / challenges / adversities / barriers
克服困難／障礙／障礙／挑戰／難關／障礙

09 fortitude

[ˋfɔrtəˏtjud]

(n) 毅力

相關詞
courage (n) 勇氣、
perseverance (n) 毅力

• We need strength and fortitude in this very difficult time.
在這個非常艱難的時期，我們需要力量和毅力。

10 solidarity

[ˏsɑləˋdærətɪ]

(n) 團結

相似詞
unity (n) 團結、
unite (v) 團結
相反詞
solitude (n) 獨處

• In a time of isolation, we choose solidarity.
在孤立的時候，我們選擇團結。

▶ 是非題

_____ 1. An unprecedented event is an event that has never happened before.

_____ 2. You can launch a rocket but you cannot launch a program.

_____ 3. If someone is concerned about it, it means he / she is worried about it.

_____ 4. A pandemic is another word for epidemic.

_____ 5. An epidemic is a disease that spreads rapidly.

_____ 6. Jenny is in adversity when she is eating her favorite food.

_____ 7. A hurdle is another word for stepping stone.

_____ 8. The boy has overcome his fear of spiders. It means that he is not afraid of spiders anymore.

_____ 9. A person with fortitude is more likely to overcome difficulties.

_____ 10. Solidarity is a synonym of solitude.

▶ 填空題

1. The seasonal _____ flu causes many people in the region to fall ill every year.

2. She didn't succeed overnight; in fact, she overcame many _____.

3. To combat the _____, we must work in _____.

4. Environmental destruction has risen on an _____ scale.

5. She showed great _____ when she suffered the loss of her daughter.

6. You look so tired lately. What's wrong? I'm _____ about you.

7. The company is planning to _____ their new product next month.

8. Successful people do not give up in _____.

9. I managed to _____ my stage fright after months of practice.

(Answer)

是非題：

1. O   2. X   3. O   4. X   5. O   6. X   7. X   8. O   9. O   10. X

填空題：

1. epidemic   2. hurdles   3. pandemic / solidarity   4. unprecedented

5. fortitude   6. concerned   7. launch   8. adversity   9. overcome

填空題翻譯：

1. 季節性流感導致這個地區每年很多人生病。

2. 她不是在一夜之間成功的，事實上她克服了許多困難。

3. 為了對抗大流行我們應該團結合作

4. 環境破壞已經以前所未有的規模上升。

5. 當她失去女兒時，她表現出極大的堅毅。

6. 你最近看起來好累。怎麼了？我很擔心你。

7. 公司計劃在下個月推出他們的新產品。

8. 成功的人不會在面對困難的時候放棄。

9. 在幾個月的練習過後，我成功克服了舞臺恐懼症。

語研力 E040

Cindy情境式必考多益單字滿分筆記

60個主題，緊扣多益考試方向，超有感情境式學習單字，帶你攻占多益滿分。

作　　　者	宋品瑩 Cindy
顧　　　問	曾文旭
統　　　籌	陳逸祺
編輯總監	耿文國
主　　　編	陳蕙芳
校稿人員	李念茨
插圖設計	王奕鈞
內文排版	吳若瑄
封面設計	吳若瑄
法律顧問	北辰著作權事務所

初　　　版	2020年09月
初版五刷	2022年02月
出　　　版	凱信企業集團—凱信企業管理顧問有限公司
電　　　話	（02）2773-6566
傳　　　真	（02）2778-1033
地　　　址	106 台北市大安區忠孝東路四段218之4號12樓
印　　　製	世和印製企業有限公司
信　　　箱	kaihsinbooks@gmail.com

定　　　價	新台幣360元 / 港幣120元
產品內容	1書

總 經 銷	采舍國際有限公司
地　　　址	235 新北市中和區中山路二段366巷10號3樓
電　　　話	（02）8245-8786
傳　　　真	（02）8245-8718

國家圖書館出版品預行編目資料

Cindy情境式必考多益單字滿分筆記 / 宋品瑩著.
-- 初版. -- 臺北市：凱信企管顧問, 2020.09
　面；　公分
ISBN 978-986-98690-8-9(平裝)

1.多益測驗 2.詞彙

805.1895　　　　　　　　　　109010292

凱信集團

用對的方法充實自己，
讓人生變得更美好！

凱信集團

用對的方法充實自己，
讓人生變得更美好！